THE HIGHLANDER'S SWORD

Amanda Forester

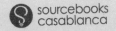
sourcebooks
casablanca

Published by Sourcebooks Casablanca, an imprint of Sourcebooks,
Inc.
P.O. Box 4410, Naperville, Illinois 60567-4410
(630) 961-3900
FAX: (630) 961-2168
www.sourcebooks.com

Printed and bound in the United States of America
QW 10 9 8 7 6 5 4 3 2 1

Prologue

Gascony, France, 1346

IF THEY CAUGHT HIM, HE WOULD HANG. OR PERHAPS, he mused with the detached calm born of shock, he would be eviscerated first, then hung. Best not to find out. Sir Padyn MacLaren ran through a throng of shocked ladies-in-waiting to the tower stairs before his fiancée screamed in fury. Or rather his ex-fiancée, since the lovely Countess Marguerite had just made it clear she intended to marry Gerard de Marsan. The same de Marsan who had tried to slit MacLaren's throat and now lay on the floor—dead.

Soldiers from the floor below rushed up the stairs to their lady's aid. MacLaren wiped the blood from his eyes. The slash down his face was bleeding something fierce, but he gave it no mind. He needed to get past the guards, or his bloodied face would be the least of his troubles.

"Hurry!" MacLaren said to the first man up the stairs. "Gerard de Marsan has attacked the countess. To her, quick! I will fetch the surgeon." The guards ran past him, and he dashed out the inner gate before the alarm sounded and soldiers poured from their barracks. MacLaren raced toward the outer gate, but the portcullis crashed down before him. Turning toward the stone staircase that led to the wall walk, he ran to a young guard who looked at him, unsure.

"Who attacks us?" MacLaren asked the young man, who stammered in response.

"Go ask your captain. I'll keep watch." MacLaren ran past the guard up the stairs to the battlement. Without stopping to think or break his stride, he ran through the battlements over the embrasure and into the air. For a moment he was suspended in time, free without the ground beneath him, then he plunged down the sheer drop to the moat below. The shock of cold water and muck robbed him of breath, and he struggled to the other side. MacLaren scrambled up the embankment and crawled into the brush, bolts flying toward him from the castle walls. Rushing through the thicket to the road, he pulled a surprised merchant from his horse and rode for cover.

MacLaren raced from Montois castle without looking back. Along the road, a dusty figure of a knight rode toward him. MacLaren drew his sword and charged. The knight reined in and threw up his visor. It was Chaumont, his second in command.

"Marguerite has betrayed us to the English," Chaumont called.

"She told me that herself," growled MacLaren, pointing to his cut face. "We need to get to camp and warn the men, or they will all be put to the sword."

Chaumont nodded. "I got word of her betrayal

shortly after you rode for Montois and commanded the men to pull back to Agen."

"Ye've done well." MacLaren exhaled.

"Indeed I have. Nice of you to notice."

The thundering riders approaching cut short their conversation. They abandoned the road in favor of an overland route through dense forested terrain in which they hoped to lose the pursuing soldiers. They traveled many hours into the night, until they finally felt safe enough to stop by the shores of a small black lake.

"You need tending, my friend," said Chaumont.

"Have ye a needle?" MacLaren asked grimly.

MacLaren stood without flinching while Chaumont stitched the gash on his face. MacLaren focused on the dark water before him, unbidden memories of the day's events washing over him. He had faced the English to protect Marguerite before they could reach her castle at Montois. The hard-fought victory had been won, but his closest kin had been lost.

"Patrick died for nothing." MacLaren's voice shook as he struggled with the words. "What an utter fool I was, trusting that deceitful wench. I should be dead on that field, not him." MacLaren clenched his jaw, holding back emotion. "There is nothing left for me here. 'Tis time I take my men and go back where I belong."

"What is it like, this land of your birth?" asked Chaumont, finishing his work.

MacLaren closed his eyes, remembering. "Balquidder. 'Tis a wild place, full of wind and rain. It can be a hard life at times, but I'm never more alive than when I'm in the Highlands." He turned to the young French knight. "Your friendship is the only thing I will regret to leave behind."

Chaumont looked at him intently. "Take me with you."

"Your place is here."

Chaumont shook his head. "If you had not given me a chance, I would still be some rich man's squire, polishing his armor and servicing his wife. I have served you in times of war, and I will serve you still, if you will have me."

"It would be an honor." MacLaren clasped his hand to the Frenchman's shoulder. They embraced the way men do, slapping each other hard on the back.

"Urgh!" Chaumont made a face. "You smell like the devil's arse."

"I swam through the moat to escape the castle. Now I know exactly where the garderobes empty into." MacLaren turned back to look over the lake. "That water was like Marguerite, a beautiful exterior, but underneath, naught but a filthy sewer."

The words were barely out of his mouth before he was pushed hard and he fell gracelessly into the cold clean lake. He came up sputtering, only to hear the Frenchman's laughter. MacLaren bathed in the cold water and emerged the better for it. He pulled himself swiftly up the bank and tossed Chaumont into the water for good measure. It was time to go home.

"Step along now," MacLaren called to his soggy companion. "Come to the Highlands, my friend, and we shall feast like heroes."

❧

Balquidder, Scotland

Shrouded in the winding cloth of the dense mist, a shadowy apparition of a horse and rider stood on the high peak of the Braes of Balquidder. Built into the side of the craggy rock, Creag an Turic, the abandoned tower house of the MacLarens, loomed stark and black against the pre-dawn sky. Below, the small village of Balquidder slept by the shores of Loch Voil. The MacLaren fields lay mostly fallow, brown and grey in the early morning gloom. Without its laird, misfortune and neglect had befallen the clan, leaving it vulnerable to raids from its neighbors. Few clansmen remained, scraping out a living as best they could.

In the valley below, a young boy stood in the doorway of a farmhouse. He gaped up at the ghostly figure and blinked—horse and rider were gone.

"Mama! I seen the ghost!"

"Come away from there, sweetling. What do ye ken about such things?"

"I seen him looking down on us. Do ye think it be an ill omen?"

Mary Patrick sighed. Having your nine-year-old son tell you there is a ghost at the door before you even got your boots on in the morning couldn't be a good sign. She silently said a quick prayer to a few saints for protection and one to the Holy Mother for good measure.

"'Twas the Bruce," whispered Gavin, his eyes gleaming.

"Robert the Bruce is no' riding these hills," said Mary to Gavin's skeptical face. "And even if he is, he's no' going to help ye wi' yer chores. Now off wi' ye. We've much to do if we want food in our bellies."

Somewhere in the ethereal mist, the cloaked figure raced at an inhuman pace… straight for Dundaff Castle.

One

Dundaff Castle, Scotland
June 26, 1347

EVERYONE KNEW ST. JOHN'S EVE, HELD ON THE SUMMER solstice, was a time to be wary. Spirits roamed free, faeries were up to mischief, and betrothals could either be happily made or ruined forever. It took careful planning to ensure all the requirements of the feast were met, lest the harvest be poor and the well run dry. Considering all they had suffered over the past year, the entire future of the Graham clan was hanging on the events of St. John's Eve. It all depended on Aila.

Lady Aila Graham sat on a stone bench carved into the wall in her tower room of Dundaff Castle, looking out of the thick, leaded glass window. Dundaff Castle was situated in the pass through the rocky hills between the town of Carron and the main road to Stirling. An imposing structure, Dundaff was carved into the mountainside on progressively higher levels. The main keep, constructed high on the mountain, was connected through a series of walls, towers, and passageways to the lower bailey.

It was dawn, and the sun's orange glow shone on the town below as the burghers began their usual routine. The steeple of the village church rose prominently, casting its long shadow across the thatched rooftops of the village homes huddled closely together. Aila leaned her forehead against the cool of the glass and closed her eyes, reviewing all she needed to do. As chatelaine of the castle, she had been preparing for this day for months. Nothing could go wrong.

Aila donned a brown work smock and pinned her wimple in place. Her attire was not particularly fashionable, but it was practical and modestly cut, as befitted a woman destined for the convent. Reassuring herself everything was well in hand, she squared her shoulders and walked steadily down the tower stairs. Exiting the tower into the cold, damp mist of morning, a strange tremor of excitement coursed through her. It was going to be quite a feast. Though, she recalled, her mother would never allow her to attend. Aila's pace slowed and her shoulders regained their weight. Still, she hoped this day would represent a fresh start for her clan, away from the pain and grief.

"Good morrow, good yarrow, good morrow to thee." A young lass skipped through the courtyard of Dundaff Castle, the morning mist swirling in her wake. She gave Aila one of her precious bundles and danced away, continuing her song: "Send me this night my true love to see. The clothes he'll wear, the color o' his hair, and if he'll wed me."

A small bundle of yarrow leaves had been pressed

into Aila's hand. It was common knowledge that if a maiden slept with yarrow under her pillow on St. John's Eve, she would dream of her future husband. Aila opened her mouth to call the lass back. She had no need of a husband; she was bound for the convent. Yet the words stuck in her throat, and she watched the girl skip away. She should drop the plant on the ground.

She slipped the yarrow leaves into her pocket.

"Och, Lady Aila." A serving maid, flushed pink with exertion, ran to Aila. "Come ye quick! Laird Graham done and invited more for the feast, and Cook's fashed something fierce."

"How many more are expected?" Aila inquired and followed the maid back to the kitchens.

"Fifty men, m'lady. And they look the hungry sort."

Aila frowned and quickly did some calculations. She muttered in Latin when it came to some more difficult sums, not realizing her thoughts found their way to her lips and unaware of the strange look the maid gave her. This was going to be a problem. Her father had not bothered to send word of any changes to the guest list. The oversight was not unusual, since he rarely spoke to her, most likely a result of the ongoing feud with her mother. Not for the first time, Aila wished her parents would end their silent war.

Aila stepped into the kitchens and was assailed by the heat of the ovens and the welcoming smell of rising yeast and baking bread.

"Lady Aila, Lady Aila," wailed Cook when he caught sight of her. "Fifty more men. What am I to do? I've got precious little grain left, even if I had the time to bake. What wi' the fields being ruined, we'll be short this winter. We'll all die o' starvation." The big man was near tears and wringing his pudgy hands. Cook was excellent with the preparation of food, but he never failed to make the most of any inconvenience.

"No one is going to starve, no' tonight, no' this winter." Aila spoke with more confidence than she felt, given the current situation. Despite Cook's tendency to overreact, his current worry was one of true concern. Without explanation, there had been several accidents of late in which their fields had been burnt. If the destruction continued, it would indeed be a lean winter, but Aila was confident it would be well. How many accidents could there possibly be?

"Send some lads to Carron to help wi' the baking. If the meal be a little late, I assure ye, no one will notice." Aila spoke with brisk calmness and decided a change of subject was in order. "Do ye ken who will be joining us for the feast?"

"'Tis the MacLaren and his men."

Aila's mouth dropped at the mention of MacLaren's name. Her heart skipped a beat then thumped wildly as if to compensate for the missing pulse.

"MacLaren? MacLaren is here? Are ye certain?" Memories hit her like a hot blast from the ovens. The last time MacLaren had entered the castle walls, he had brought news of her only brother's death. Her brother had led the contingent of warriors from Dundaff to join King David's ill-fated campaign against the English. The Scots had been hard-pressed at Neville's Cross. Attempting to turn the battle, the Graham clan, known for their fierce valor, had charged the field, only to be cut down by the longbow.

The Grahams suffered grievous losses. Aila's brother, uncles, cousins—all dead. The Scots fled, King David was captured, and the fragile unity of Scotland, forged under Robert the Bruce, dissolved.

And now MacLaren was here again? Aila fervently hoped his presence was not a sign of some new calamity. Though perhaps Graham meant simply to invite MacLaren to thank him for his service to the clan. She had heard a rumor that MacLaren was the one who had snuck back over the border to retrieve her brother's body from English soil and bring him home for proper burial.

Aila pushed aside the pain of her loss and focused on the task at hand. She would probably never know why her father had invited MacLaren, but at least she could make sure he was properly fed. She gave additional instructions to Cook and sent some lads to prepare sleeping quarters.

"Lady Aila," a castle page addressed her with solemn self-importance. "Laird Graham requests yer presence."

Everything stopped. No one moved. The kitchen, for the first time in Aila's memory, was silent. The last time she had been called before her father, he had told her of the slaughter of her clansmen and the death of her brother. Despite standing in the heat of the kitchens, a chill crept up Aila's boots and slithered all the way to her fingertips.

"By the saints," murmured Cook. His eyes were filled with fear.

"Continue preparing for the feast," Aila said quietly, though her throat had gone as dry as their burnt fields. "'Twill all be well."

Aila followed the page to the main keep and the domain of her father, Laird Graham of Dundaff. Why would her father summon her? Had MacLaren come once again to leave ruin and grief in his wake? Worse yet, had her father discovered what she had been doing every morning? What would he do to her if he had? Her stomach flipped in a mean, queasy roll. Her father had never been unkind to her, but neither had she ever given him cause. Laird Graham was a large gruff man who could intimidate seasoned warriors with ease. If he was now angry with her...

Aila entered her father's solar with some difficulty, since her feet grew heavier with every step. Confirming her fears, MacLaren stood next to her father. The two imposing men stared at her, saying nothing. This could not be good. Her father folded his large arms across his massive chest and turned to MacLaren.

Aila was struck at the change in MacLaren. She had known him years ago when he had been a friend to her brother. The warrior now before her hardly resembled the braw, cocksure young man who had left Scotland to fight the English in France. He looked older, his slate eyes cold. A red scar carved a wicked path from the corner of his left eye down to his chin.

"Well?" demanded her father.

MacLaren looked her up and down in a manner that brought heat to her face.

"Aye, I'll have her."

Aila's mouth dropped open, and she stared at one, then the other. MacLaren frowned and turned to Laird Graham.

"Ye've no' told her then?"

"I've told no one," replied her father. "Watch yer back, laddie. I warrant there will be some what will take offense to yer marriage."

Marriage?

Two

"WHAT DO YE MEAN, 'MARRIAGE'?" AILA'S VOICE squeaked. What was happening?

Her father spoke with authority. "I mean ye to marry MacLaren here. He's a good lad and will be kind to ye." Graham gave MacLaren a hard look. "Or ye'll be answering to me, laddie."

"Aye, m'lord."

"But I'm for the convent…"

Her father sighed. "Nay, lass. Since yer brother, along wi' most o' our kin, died at Neville's Cross, unless I sire another son, ye stand to inherit all my holdings. I'll no' be giving all of Dundaff to the Church, no' wi' Barrick as abbot. He'd be turning out my tenants afore I was cold in the ground. Nay, I owe more to our clan than that. And I'll be damned if I let that bastard McNab have ye." Graham's voice raised and he pounded his fist in his hand. "Now, we are to the Church."

"Now?" MacLaren and Aila spoke as one.

"Aye, children, let's be done wi' it."

"But, father, I canna… Ye dinna mean… marry

him?" It was unfortunate that coherent speech chose that moment to abandon her. Aila felt slightly dizzy, as if the air in the room had gone thin. MacLaren was uncommonly large, his even larger claymore strapped to his back. This man could not be her future. She was going to be a nun. She had been promised to the Church as a young girl, and a new convent and monastery had been built on her dower lands—lands that would be given to the Church. Marriage was not possible.

"Daughter," said Graham in a low voice that resonated with danger, "I say ye will marry MacLaren, and marry ye will." Graham looked at Aila, then MacLaren, as if daring either to brook opposition. "'Tis time to be wed."

In numb silence, Aila followed her father as he limped across the courtyard to the tower chapel, MacLaren directly behind her. She sensed his presence behind her and knew he was staring at her. A shiver went up her spine, and the nape of her neck tingled.

As they crossed the courtyard, a tall, attractive knight Aila had never seen before fell into step with MacLaren. He spoke to MacLaren quietly in French, and though it was not good manners, Aila strained to hear their conversation.

"How did it go with Graham?" asked the tall knight.

"I'm getting married," replied MacLaren evenly, as if it were an everyday occurrence.

"What, now?"

"*Oui.*"

"Are you ready for it?"

"No."

"Will you go through with it?"

The question remained unanswered as they entered the chapel tower and marched up the stairs. Aila followed her father blindly, feeling naught but a hazy bewilderment. At the landing before the chapel door, Laird Graham left them to speak privately with the priest. Aila turned to MacLaren, her future hanging on his answer to the French knight.

MacLaren looked appraisingly at Aila, causing her once again to fluster. Men did not look that way at her. Everyone knew she was bound for the convent. Besides, she knew there was nothing in her appearance that would interest a man. Her kirtle was plain and modestly cut. A white linen wimple covered all of her hair and wrapped around her chin, revealing nothing of her mass of red curls. Her face she knew to be plain, her ivory complexion hiding none of the freckles no amount of buttermilk could wash away. Worst of all, at least according to her mother, she had grown much too tall.

MacLaren continued his assessment in a manner most unchivalrous. It would have been more modest to look away, but with a rising sense of indignation, Aila squared her shoulders and met his gaze. Perhaps if he saw her undesirable features more clearly, he would change his mind about proceeding with the union.

"Aye, we'll be wed," MacLaren answered in Gaelic with a tone of finality.

Aila's knees gave way and she stumbled to a bench beside the chapel door. How could this be happening? This could not possibly be real. Surely she would awaken soon. She felt the lump in her pocket and pulled out the yarrow plant, staring at it suspiciously. She knew St. John's Eve was a dangerous time, for mischievous spirits were abroad, but she hardly thought a little plant could be quite this magical. What was in this thing?

Aila put her head in her hands, her mind having difficulty keeping pace with all that was happening around her. Up until this morning, her life had been utterly predictable. She knew her duty well. She was to tend to her ailing mother until she passed, and then she would take her vows. Her mother! Saints above, her mother would be furious to find her married. Her ears burned thinking of what her mother would say. And how could she possibly explain this to the sisters of St. Margaret's? What would her mentor, Sister Enid, think?

Trying to focus her thoughts, Aila considered all she knew of this man her father wished her to wed. MacLaren had returned to the Highlands less than a year ago, after spending many years in France fighting against the English. He must have been successful, since he had been knighted for valor and brought back a considerable force of seasoned warriors. She also knew that MacLaren's clan had suffered during his five-year absence, and he returned to find there was not much left. Aila's thoughts were interrupted by the laughter of the French knight.

"Faith, man, not like that, I pray," said the French knight to MacLaren in a jovial tone. "You cannot intend to enter the house of our Lord wearing naught but a blanket." Apparently, the French knight took issue with MacLaren's Highland garb. At the well-dressed Frenchman's chastisement, Aila thought to remove the simple smock she used to cover her silk kirtle.

"I'll leave it to ye to be concerned wi' fashion. I'll no' compete wi' ye on that score," MacLaren answered without concern.

"Few men can, to be sure," replied the Frenchman immodestly.

Since the men were paying her no heed, Aila took a moment to make her own assessment of the two knights. They were both tall, well-formed, and moved with the fluid grace of skilled warriors. The Frenchman was a wee bit taller and slimmer. He was richly dressed in the latest court fashion and stunningly handsome, as he was clearly well aware.

Despite the Frenchman's fine looks, it was MacLaren who held her gaze. MacLaren was dressed in the rough attire of the Highlander. His large plaid was belted at his waist and thrown over one shoulder, pinned to his linen shirt. It was not a garb worn frequently by her clan, but living on the border of the Highlands, she was accustomed to their style of dress. The plaid revealed his lower legs and, occasionally—she noted with a sudden skip of her heart—a glimpse of a muscular thigh.

Aila swallowed hard. MacLaren was as tall as her father, with broad shoulders and a powerful presence. Yet where her father was large and barrel-chested, MacLaren was more lean and muscular. His black wavy hair fell about his face in an unkempt manner, framing his gray eyes, cold as granite. She had spent her entire life preparing for the convent, praying with the sisters, studying the scriptures. Nothing had prepared her for this. MacLaren turned toward Aila and caught her staring. He raised an eyebrow, and this time she had the decency to turn away with a blush.

"Come now, children," Graham said, bursting back onto the landing, his large frame dominating the small space. "The priest is ready to proceed."

Moments later, Aila was in front of the altar, standing beside Sir Padyn MacLaren. Father Thomas, the elderly priest who served Dundaff, recited the order of marriage from memory, though in his dotage he could remember little else. Aila was speeding toward a precipice and would soon fall if she did not act quickly. She tried to think of what to do, but her brain seemed to move at the speed of day-old porridge. She prayed for guidance but received no discernible answer. She glanced around, desperate for someone to come to her aid, but the elderly priest prattled along, oblivious to her concern. Her father stood, looking determined, the tall knight seemed quite amused by the whole scene, and MacLaren did naught but stare grimly down at her.

The priest reached the point of asking MacLaren the covenantal questions of marriage, which he answered in the affirmative without any hesitation. Yet his grasp on Aila's hands tightened until she gasped. He released her instantly, a flash of surprise flickering across his otherwise expressionless face. The priest posed the same questions to her. She looked at her father, who gave her a curt nod to proceed. Still she hesitated. Aila waited for some sign as to what to do. MacLaren said nothing, but gently claimed her hands, his hands rough, yet warm. Looking up at MacLaren, she was captured by his gaze. Though his face remained expressionless, his eyes told a different tale. She guessed there was much behind the cold mask he wore.

"Do you take this man?" the priest asked again. Aila gathered the frayed edges of her courage and took a deep breath.

Three

MACLAREN LOOKED DOWN AT THE WOMAN HE WAS about to marry as she struggled to find an answer to the priest. She appeared to be as happy to be standing at the altar as he was. Perhaps she would say no. A twinge of relief crept through him at the thought. *Go on, lass, turn me down.*

He glanced at Chaumont and wished he had not. The bastard was grinning like a fool, obviously taking vicious delight in this turn of circumstance. Chaumont had proved his courage and skill in the crucible of battle and earned his place as MacLaren's second in command, yet the Frenchman had an irritating habit of always finding amusement in life, often at MacLaren's expense. Chaumont was most decidedly laughing at him. Perhaps with good cause. MacLaren wished he had not been so adamant in vowing never to marry. After his disastrous engagement to Marguerite, he'd sworn he would never trust another woman. And now here he was at the altar. Well, trusting and marrying were two distinctly different things.

MacLaren turned back to glare at his reticent bride. The proposal he'd received from Graham yesterday was most unexpected and one he could ill afford to refuse. As part of the proposed alliance, MacLaren was to fight against Graham's enemies, and in return, Graham would give MacLaren his daughter Aila in marriage. More importantly for his clan, MacLaren would get her dowry. Graham needed warriors; MacLaren needed land. It was a fair trade. Aila's fortune would provide for his clan.

Whatever his personal feelings on the matter, MacLaren knew his duty. He had returned from France to find his clan impoverished, his herds raided, his fields fallow. He had done what he could to rebuild, but he needed coin for the clan and additional land for the knights he had brought back with him from France. His men deserved their reward. Aila's dowry, along with the hope of inheriting all of Dundaff someday, amply provided for all.

The wench only needed to say "aye." MacLaren scowled down at Aila, waiting for her to give her answer. Behind him, Graham cleared his throat and glared at his only offspring. Aila blanched but continued to dither. Since there was naught to do but wait, MacLaren took another good look at his maybe bride.

Aila was a bit tall for a lass but had a trim figure, at least from what he could tell from her modestly cut kirtle. A large white wimple covered all of her hair, and she was a bit long in the tooth to be still unmarried. He quickly did the math based on what he recalled from his friendship with her brother;

MacLaren was twenty-six, which would make Aila about twenty-two. Old for a first marriage, but if she had been intended for the convent, it would explain why she had not married earlier. Her face was pleasant, and he could find no obvious fault with it, except the poor lass looked terrified. She looked up at him, and the green of her eyes caught his attention. His stomach did a sudden flip. Odd… must be marriage did not agree with him.

He continued to gaze into her eyes, unable to turn away. With sudden clarity, he decided he did want her to consent to the marriage. The longer he looked into her eyes, the more certain he became. He took her hands in his, enveloping her cold hands with his warm ones. Her lips parted, and her eyes widened. A tingle flushed through him, warming places he thought long dead. Everyone else faded away. *Marry me.* He gently rubbed the palms of her hands. *Marry me.*

"I do."

A slap on the shoulder brought MacLaren back to reality. Chaumont was smiling like a fox in a henhouse. MacLaren scowled. He was not sure what had come over him. He could not possibly be weak enough to be tricked again by a woman's beauty. Not again. Never again. He glared down at Aila. He was not sure what power she thought she could wield over him, but he would have none of it. She was his wife by Church and by contract, nothing more. He would do his duty by her. His heart would not be touched.

With a bow to the altar and a curt nod to the priest and Laird Graham, MacLaren led Aila outside. Best not to look at her. Might fall into the trap of those eyes again. They were quite remarkable eyes, but no matter. He would not be deceived again.

❧

Blinking dazedly into the sunlight, Aila walked out of the chapel tower on the arm of her new husband. What had happened? Was she truly... married?

"Fire!" The yell came from a lookout on the castle wall.

"Fire on the fields!" The cry was taken up by watchtowers throughout the castle. Without a glance at his new bride, MacLaren took off, running down to the lower bailey, with the French knight close at his heels. Aila's father hobbled behind.

"Go at 'em, lads!" bellowed Graham to his new son-in-law as they ran ahead. "Saddle me a horse. We'll get the bastards this time!"

Aila stood alone, watching them run away, wondering when she would awake from this most-odd dream. With a bland smile, Father Thomas shuffled out of the tower.

"Father." She acknowledged the elderly priest as he came up beside her.

The old cleric smiled and took her hand with a squeeze. "There's a good lass, Molly."

"No' Molly," said Aila a little louder, leaning over to yell into the old man's ear. "I'm Aila, Aila Graham... er... MacLaren."

"Lady Aila?" asked the priest with surprise. "Why I have a message for ye, I do." He pulled a folded parchment from his robes, handed it to her, and continued to shuffle along his way.

Wondering who could have possibly written her, Aila broke the seal. The brief contents had been dictated by Sister Enid, her dear friend from St. Margaret's Convent.

> *My Dearest Lady Aila,*
>
> *I am writing to warn you against falling away from the path of righteousness. I am deeply concerned that you may soon be pressured to marry. Remember you are promised to Christ alone, so take great care to remain true to your commitment to the Most High Lord. I fear the ungodly may try to lead you astray, so I urge you most fervently to take your final vows and join the convent with all possible haste. In this regard, the abbot and I are of one mind. I hope to embrace you soon as a fellow Sister in Christ.*
>
> *Your friend in the Lord,*
> *Sister Enid*

Aila read over the missive twice, trying to understand its contents. A horrid sinking feeling gripped her, and her stomach dropped as if plummeting from the tallest tower. Had she done wrong by marrying MacLaren? How could she have defied her father? Her neatly ordered world was shaken all to pieces. What kind of man was she married to? For a moment in the chapel, he had looked at her in a way no one had before. In his eyes, she believed she had seen interest, kindness, maybe even compassion. Yet when she had consented to the marriage, he turned away and ignored her once more. What was she to do now?

Despite it being unladylike, Aila sat down on the chapel-tower stairs and put her head in her hands. It was all too much. Around her, the castle dwellers and village burghers went about their daily business, oblivious to her distress.

"What is she doing?" Aila heard the whispered question as someone passed her by.

"'Tis Lady Aila, probably deep in prayer," answered another. "She's verra pious, bound for the nunnery, ye ken."

"Aye, she'll make a fine nun," replied the other as the voices faded from hearing. Fortunately, no one heard the pitiful moans of the ever-pious Lady Aila.

❧

MacLaren and his men joined Graham's forces and sped toward the fire to douse the flames and pursue the culprits. To avoid panic, Graham had tried to play off the arsons as accidents, though the soldiers knew the truth, and many others were starting to suspect. MacLaren doubted Graham could keep this secret much longer.

Though permanently injured, the Dundaff laird insisted on joining the party. Grievously wounded at the battle of Halidon Hill, John Graham would fight no more. Merely walking was a struggle. MacLaren considered it rather game of Graham to even attempt to ride. Out of respect, MacLaren remained with his new father-in-law, though he would have preferred to be among the group of faster riders. He was impressed Graham actually made the journey, since his old wounds clearly pained him.

When they arrived at the smoldering field, the fire had been doused, and the destruction was minimal.

"Good work, lads," Graham's big voice boomed. To MacLaren he said, "We'll get that bastard McNab next time."

MacLaren searched the scene, but no evidence to the identity of the raiders could be found. He was at a loss as to why anyone would do this. Raiding another clan's livestock he understood, perhaps a little too well. But what benefit could there be in burning another man's fields? Graham was convinced his neighbor McNab was behind the attacks. MacLaren preferred to be more certain before initiating a clan war.

"With respect, my lord," said MacLaren quietly to Graham, "how do ye ken for sure it be McNab responsible for the attacks?"

"McNab sent a message, offering to help me against my enemies, demanding Aila's hand in marriage in return," Graham said with disdain.

"Is this no' the same offer ye made me? Why are ye so convinced o' his guilt?"

"Do ye ken what that McNab clan has done?" Graham asked, his thick brows furrowed. "They feigned friendship wi' Wallace and then betrayed his men to the bloody English. They fought against Bruce and only supported his cause after he had won. Bruce was right to strip McNab of his most of his holdings. Should have left him naked in the Highlands, I say, but the abbot interceded, more's the pity."

MacLaren considered Graham's logic but remained unconvinced. The current Laird McNab was too young to be guilty of the sins against Robert Bruce or William Wallace. That past generations of McNabs sided with the English was hardly enough evidence for condemnation. MacLaren was all too familiar with the fickle loyalties of the aristocracy to be overly shocked by the behavior. Still, someone was burning the fields, and even if McNab was not the culprit, he was at least trying to profit from it.

MacLaren opened his mouth to continue the debate but stopped, noticing Graham's pained expression. Laird Graham was a proud man, one who had earned the respect of all true Scots. He had always supported the call for freedom against the English and had personally fought for both Wallace and Bruce. His wounds were badges of honor in MacLaren's eyes. Indeed, MacLaren held the Graham laird in high regard.

"I see your point, m'lord," MacLaren agreed. "Our work is done here. I suggest ye take yer men back to Dundaff while my lads and I ask the crofters if they saw anything notable."

"Verra good, lad." Graham smiled, looking somewhat relieved. "Our fortunes will turn wi' ye, my son."

MacLaren watched the Dundaff laird ride away.

Son.

No one had called him that in a very long time.

Four

AILA GRAHAM REMAINED ON THE CHAPEL STEPS UNTIL it seemed pointless to continue to do so. Despite her world coming to an end, everyone else's continued to move along, and eventually she got up to join them. It was still St. John's Eve, and this unexpected and inconvenient marriage had put her behind schedule.

She worked with efficiency to ensure all the preparations were proceeding as planned. She consulted again with Cook, conferred with Pitcairn, the steward, and supervised the building of large piles of wood that would serve as the bonfires for later that eve. As she focused her attentions back on the familiar task of managing the castle, the events of the morning faded like a confusing dream. It seemed so unreal.

Remembering a promise, she dashed to the main solar to help one of her young students, a merchant's daughter named Sara. She looked over some arithmetic problems with the girl and made some corrections. It was Aila's responsibility to teach the pages their letters and sums in the most relevant languages of

Gaelic, English, and Latin. It was not her responsibility to teach girls, but she enjoyed it, and as long as it was done discreetly, no one knew to raise a fuss.

Hamish, a new page and foster from the powerful Campbell clan, saw Aila in the solar and stopped, asking, "Do we have lessons today, m'lady?"

"Nay, Master Hamish," replied Aila.

"Then what are ye doing?" He looked confused. "Ye're no' teaching that wench, are ye?"

"Hamish," replied Aila sharply, "this dinna concern ye. Go assist Pitcairn if ye are without employment."

"Wait till my father hears o' this. He says teaching women is nothing but a waste. They have no head for it," the lad said with a smirk.

Aila glared at him. The truth that he was being taught by a woman did not seem to interfere with his prejudice.

"Hamish, get thee gone," Aila repeated with all the firmness she could muster.

"I'll tell my father to talk to Laird Graham about this. He'll put a stop to it," boasted the lad, puffing up his chest. Aila considered the ramifications of his threat. Her father did not know she was spending time teaching girls. If he found out, would he stop her? She reckoned he would do anything if demanded by the Campbell. She folded her arms across her chest. Hadn't enough been taken from her today? She looked down at Sara, who looked up at her with big, forlorn eyes. Would this arrogant pup rob a poor lass of her only means of education?

"Hamish, ye will no' tell anyone," said Aila with warning in her voice.

"Or what?" mocked the lad, overconfident in his position. He was from a powerful clan, one whose alliance they needed, but his bravado was too much. Something inside her snapped.

Aila opened her mouth, and out poured the vilest curse she had ever heard her mother utter. Hamish's mouth dropped. Sara started. Hamish turned white.

"Well then," she said briskly, "'tis St. John's Eve, much to do."

She walked from the solar, wondering what had come over her. Well, someone needed to put that little brat in his place... but she never thought it would be she. From Hamish's reaction, neither did he. It was not like she would actually ever carry out such a threat. Honestly, she didn't even know what a scrotum was.

The midday meal approached and with it another requisite visit to her mother. Aila dreaded revealing to her mother that she had married. How on earth could such news be delivered? She respected her father, but it seemed rather cowardly of him to run away rather than facing Lady Graham's wrath.

In an attempt to calm herself, Aila focused on Latin grammatical rules, a trick she had learned during her studies to deal with unpleasant situations. Unlike most girls, Aila had benefited from an extensive education, since her mother planned for her elevation in the Church. Latin had been a primary lesson, since it was the language of the scriptures. In her youth, she had asked why the Bible was not translated into English but was told in shocked, hushed tones that such thoughts were heretical.

Aila muttered Latin verbs, Latin nouns, and even tried a little Italian. Nothing helped. She trudged up the tower stairs as if she were mounting the steps to the gallows. Taking a deep breath, Aila entered her mother's domain.

"Good day, Mother," she said in a voice she hoped was not too loud nor too soft, too cheerful nor too gloomy.

Her mother was wrapped in fur and reclining in a high-backed, padded chair. Her wheat-blonde hair was arranged in an ornate style, plaited high on her head and held in place with jeweled pins. Lady Moira Graham had been a stunning beauty in her youth and still retained much of her looks. A nervous-looking lady's maid stood behind her, while two serving maids laid out the midday meal on an ornately carved table in front of her. The sitting room was filled like a priceless heirloom labyrinth with expensive objects displayed on delicate tables placed around the room.

The faint smell of perfume hung in the air, rising from the dried lavender and rose water liberally sprinkled over the fresh rushes covering the floor. Colorful tapestries hung beside one another across the outer stone wall of the tower room, covering the window openings and making the air hot and stale, giving the room a stifling feeling. Daylight effectively banished, the room flickered with the dancing light of numerous wax candles, too many to count.

Lady Graham frowned at her daughter, the expression marring her beautiful face. "Ye're late," her mother stated, her voice cold. "Yer lack of attention to yer responsibilities and fidelity to yer own kin is disappointing. I had certainly expected better from ye than to make the entire household wait until ye decided to deign us wi' yer presence."

"I apologize, Mother." Aila took her seat across the table. The wedding had put her behind schedule, but Aila recognized that mentioning it would hardly help her case.

"Ye apologize, do ye? And ye believe that an adequate recompense for yer discourteous, disrespectful behavior?"

Aila did not provide a response, as none was required, and turned instead to the maids. "'Twill be all for now, thank ye."

At their dismissal, the maids vanished like smoke in a sharp wind. Once they were alone, Aila pulled her chair around the table and moved her food so she was sitting next to her mother. It was only then Lady Graham removed her hands from beneath her fur cloak, revealing her disfigurement. Her bony fingers were red and swollen at the joints, her hands twisted into immovable fists. Aila cut the meat in the trencher into bite-sized chunks and began to feed her mother. Lady Graham reached with both hands to drink from her goblet and would have spilled had Aila not caught it. Her mother made a small sound that might have been anger or frustration or shame, and grudgingly continued to allow Aila to feed her.

Aila knew it was mortifying for her mother to be unable to do for herself and attributed much of her mother's bitterness to that fact. Lady Graham took great pains to prevent anyone, particularly her husband, from knowing her condition, which had slowly and painfully worsened over the years. Lady Graham was a proud woman, though her life had begun simply enough, the daughter of a merchant. She learned early in life to use her beauty to its best advantage, and her hand in marriage had been much sought after. She had even been betrothed prior to meeting Graham. But Sir John Graham, then the heir to Dundaff, made a richer prize, and Lady Graham's father made a tactical change of alliances.

Once their midday meal was finished, the servants entered again to clear the table, and events proceeded along predictable lines. Lady Graham complained bitterly about the poor quality of the laundry, the taste and selection of food, the insufficient number of candles, her husband's neglect, and that inexcusable cough from a terrified maid. She gave multiple commands as to the particulars of the St. John's feast and admonished her daughter to return to her tower before the burghers from Carron arrived.

"I dinna want ye exposed to that sort. Dirty, disease ridden the lot o' them."

"Aye, Mother," replied Aila without attending to what her mother was saying. Her mind spun, trying to find a way to gently broach the subject of her marriage.

Marriage?

Heavens above! She did not have words to explain it to herself, let alone her mother. Her mother was adamant Aila join the convent and had already determined that Aila would be abbess. It was a life Aila had long ago accepted and expected. It was the only future she had ever known, the only option she had ever been given. Aila sat on the bench, nodding at the appropriate times without really listening, as Lady Graham ranted about something.

"Sooth, child, where's yer smock?" chastised Lady Graham, turning her critical eye on Aila. "Dinna be ruining yer fine kirtle now."

"Sorry, Mother, I must have left it at the chapel," replied Aila without thinking.

"Chapel? What were ye doing there? Father Thomas does the morning mass at the Church and mass at our chapel at eventide, does he no'?"

She was caught. How was she going to explain being in the chapel? Aila chewed her bottom lip, looked at her hands, glanced at her mother and back down at her hands. Several clever lies crossed her mind. But no, there was no escaping it now. She held onto the bench for support.

"I was getting married."

Silence filled the room as her mother, two maids, a serving lass, and the ghillie carrying a pitcher of wine all froze and stared at Aila.

"What did ye say?" asked her mother in a hoarse whisper.

The room was utterly silent as five sets of eyes stared at Aila. Drums pounded in Aila's ears, and she was dimly aware it must be her own heartbeat. The room grew unbearably hot, and she resisted the urge to run for the door, her knuckles turning white as she held onto the bench with a death grip. She knew she must speak, and when she did, it sounded small and far away, as if she was watching events unfold from afar.

"This morn, father took me to the chapel where I married Sir Padyn MacLaren. Father said that since I am now his sole heir, he'd no' have all his inheritance go to the Church. So I... we were married in the chapel by Father Thomas."

All heads now turned to stare at Lady Graham. Her face went white with frozen horror, yet remained eerily silent. She stared at Aila for what felt like an eternity. Aila began to wonder if the shock of such an announcement had caused an apoplexy. Then Lady Graham's face flushed red, and her features twisted into fury as she took a deep breath. Aila gripped the bench even harder and prepared for the onslaught.

"How could ye betray me like this? After all I've done to give ye a good life. I would ha' ye be abbess, but no, ye treat my love wi' contempt. How could ye... I dinna... how did... Argghhh!" Moira Graham was reduced to sputtering her words yet still managed to curse with such ferocity the ghillie dropped his pitcher. The maids swarmed to help clean the splattered wine while attempting unsuccessfully to calm their lady. Aila remained seatèd, the one point of calm in a raging sea.

"And him," said her mother with a sneer when she regained intelligible speech. "How could yer father make this decision wi'out even consulting me? He'll regret this, I swear to ye he will. And ye will, too. Married. Ye ken nothing o' what that means. And to who? A nothing, a nobody, an opportunist come to claim yer inheritance."

Her mother's derogatory assessment of MacLaren roused Aila to speech. "But, Mother, remember

MacLaren is laird o' his clan now and was knighted fighting the English in France. Dinna forget what our family owes him for his kindness toward our kin what fell in battle."

Her mother dismissed Aila's defense with a snort and a toss of her pretty head. "If I wanted ye to be married, ye'd be married to royalty, maybe even David himself."

"King David is being held by the English in the Tower o' London," Aila reminded her mother. But Lady Graham would have none of these petty realities and continued to berate Aila for getting married, using such vitriolic language it made Aila cringe.

"Ye belong to him now." Her mother escalated to the point of shrieking. "He can do anything he wants to ye. Anything! Ye ken? I canna protect ye. Go. Sleep in the bed ye made. I doubt ye'll be liking it overmuch. Go now! I canna stand the sight o' ye. Go, all o' ye. Now!"

Eager for release, the servants ran down the tower stairs and flew in every direction to spread the news. Aila followed slowly behind and was soon to discover that castle gossip spreads faster than fire on the fields. As she emerged from the tower, Mrs. Haden, the washer woman, came running across the courtyard and, much to Aila's surprise, wrapped her strong arms around Aila, giving her a smothering hug.

"Och, m'lady, forgive me," said Mrs. Haden, letting Aila go. "I'm so excited about yer marriage to Laird MacLaren. Such a fine young lad he be. He wa' knighted in France, ye ken. Looks right braw." Mrs. Haden sighed and looked up at nothing in particular, a wistful smile on her face. "I recall when I were first a bride. My Haddy and me had quite the time afore the bairns came." Mrs. Haden looked back at Aila with a mischievous smile. "Ye will, too, if ye ken my meaning."

Aila had no idea what the laundress meant, but the stout woman seemed to require no reply and walked off humming. Before Aila could consider the woman's odd behavior, more castle dwellers came to offer their well-wishes, and even Cook left his kitchens to squeeze her hand in his massive fist.

"God bless ye, Aila. I was so worrit for ye. Ah, such good news," said Cook, wiping his eyes with the corner of his apron.

Cook was not alone in giving Aila warm sentiments and congratulations. Hopes were raised as the news of Aila's marriage spread through the castle and to the town of Carron below. It had been a long winter after the grievous tidings of their losses at the battle of Neville's Cross. So many men had left to join the young King David; so few had returned. The Scots were a pragmatic folk. While an alliance between Aila and Sir Padyn MacLaren was not prestigious, it did give the Grahams the one thing they lacked— seasoned, battle-tested warriors. That alone was reason enough for celebration.

Yet one in the castle was not pleased when news of Aila's wedding reached him. Indulging in a moment of anger, he flung his goblet, which hit the far side of the room, whiskey splattering the wall. Taking gulps of air, he tried to silently regain his composure before anyone could note his reaction, but his body shook with the effort required to contain his fury.

With the firm resolve of a man long acquainted with deception, he tightened his grip on his emotions, pushing them beneath the surface of the mask he wore so well. Despite his outward appearance of calm, rage seethed within him like a bottled tempest. Seeing the whiskey dripping down the wall, he moved quickly to clean it, noting as he did the container from which the spirit flowed. It was a finely crafted bottle, inlaid with red jewels around the neck. Grabbing the vessel, he walked over to his private chest from which he pulled a smaller bottle. He had intended the special contents of the small bottle for Laird Graham, but these were desperate times. He admired the small bottle in his hand. *'Tis the lovely thing about poison; it takes so little to leave a man dead.*

He liberally poured the contents of the small bottle into the larger jeweled carafe, smiling at his cleverness and MacLaren's impending demise. He paused for a moment, considering what might happen if Aila should also drink the poison, but rejected the notion with a shrug, confident Aila did not drink whiskey. Satisfied with his reasoning, he rang the bell and told the servant to deliver the gift as a wedding present later in the evening. MacLaren's marriage to the Lady Aila was going to be much shorter than anyone anticipated.

Five

MACLAREN RECEIVED REPORTS FROM HIS MEN, WHO had questioned the nearby crofters. No one had seen anything. Most were gone to the town of Carron for St. John's Eve, and those who had stayed behind were too frail to be outdoors. Whoever had perpetrated the brazen daytime attack had chosen the time and place carefully to minimize the risk of detection. He called for his men to mount up, and they began the journey back to Dundaff.

Though unsuccessful in their hunt, MacLaren's men were pleased to be active again, and they rode back to the Graham stronghold in good humor. Of late, MacLaren had directed his men to plant his fallow fields, and while his men would follow any command, they were weary of playing farmer.

MacLaren had returned from France last autumn with this band of war-weary soldiers and landless knights who had followed him in his campaigns against the English and continued to follow him now. MacLaren rode in silence, Chaumont by his side. The men behind him talked and laughed freely, engaging in the easy banter of men who knew each other well. Most had been his companions for years in France. Though many were from other clans or even other countries, they had become his friends, his family, his clan. He would do anything for them—including marriage.

"We have cause to celebrate, lads," Chaumont said with a smile. MacLaren knew where this was going and concentrated on the dirt path ahead of him.

"MacLaren has taken a wife." Chaumont was enjoying the moment with unabashed glee. His proclamation was greeted with stunned silence from the men. MacLaren gritted his teeth for what was to come.

"MacLaren married?" asked one man.

"But he declared he would ne'er wed," said another.

"It canna be so."

"Who did he marry?"

"The lovely Lady Aila Graham," replied Chaumont in his smooth voice.

More silence.

"Heiress to all of Dundaff," Chaumont added.

Cheers shook the leaves from the trees. Men gathered around MacLaren, celebrating his—and to large extent their—good fortune. MacLaren accepted their felicitations with stoic resolve. It was certainly good news for his men, but MacLaren was unsure his fate was equally bonnie. Worse yet, MacLaren found there was no end of advice to be given to a man newly married. Even men who were confirmed bachelors now seemed experts in the field of matrimony. As they continued back to Dundaff, MacLaren was assailed by their enthusiastic, if not helpful, comments.

"'Tis important ye master her early so she dinna give ye no strife," said a gangly youth MacLaren felt sure would kiss the feet of any comely lass who gave him but an ounce of notice.

"Ho, ho! Big talk from a lad what's more afeard o' the lasses than the English," mocked Rory, a stout fighter who had been married for as long as MacLaren could remember. He gave MacLaren a knowing nod. "Treat her fair now, lad, and she'll do right by ye."

"Nay, a woman will bring ye naught but aggravation." This was from Gilbert, who had left his wife and three children to join MacLaren's campaign in France, only to return several years later to find he had acquired two more bairns. He had endured much hazing from his fellow soldiers about the amazing strength of his seed, which could impregnate his wife from hundreds of miles away—twice.

"Now, Gilby, Meg is a right fine lass," said one man.

"Aye, we all think so," rejoined another, followed by the bawdy laughter of the group.

"Plague take ye all!" spat Gilbert.

When the laughter subsided, Chaumont, who had been riding quietly next to MacLaren, listening to the questionable marital counsel of the Highland warriors, decided it was time to contribute to the conversation. "You all seem to be full of advice, most of it bad, and none of it addressing what is most important in a marriage." He spoke in his rich, smooth voice, the ever-present spark of humor in his eyes.

"What might that be?" MacLaren asked warily. He wasn't beyond tossing him in another cold loch if he felt the need arise.

"I speak of your husbandly duties in the marital bed."

This got the attention of the men, and they rode in silence, listening to what the Frenchman might say on the topic. "You know it is your responsibility to give her pleasure so she can give you children." The Highlanders nodded. It was well known only a woman well pleased in the bedroom could conceive a child. Those who had never heard of this particular axiom also nodded wisely, believing the Frenchman to be an expert on all such matters.

Yet MacLaren remained a skeptic, both of the statement's truth and Chaumont's humor. "Do ye really ken that be true, or is it an old wives' tale?"

Chaumont smiled broadly. "I am sure it is a tale told by many wives." More laughter rang forth from the men. What followed was more advice from the men on the subject of happily bedding a wife, which ranged from the crude to the poetic.

After a while, one man turned to Rory, saying, "Do ye no' have a dozen bairns? Ye must know how to keep a wife well pleased."

"That I do, laddie, that I do." He lowered his voice as if sharing a great secret. "I'll tell ye how to give the greatest pleasure a lass has ever known."

The men leaned in their saddles, straining to hear the old man's words.

"Take a bath."

◦⟋◦

Aila was overwhelmed and touched by the expressions of joy and celebration from those in the castle. All sorts of people, including many her mother would have found unacceptable, came to offer their congratulations. Their joy was contagious, and she soon shared their excitement about the union. Perhaps she had done the right thing after all. Soon the maids came swarming back, insisting Aila return to the tower to be properly bathed and dressed for the return of her master.

Her maids prepared her bath and worked to modify a silver gown to be more in keeping with the current court fashion. The reality of her union to MacLaren began to sink in. After the bath, the maids attempted to tame Aila's wet, curly tangles into long ringlets.

"Och, m'lady," said Maggie, one of the maids, "ye ne'er told us ye were to be wed."

Nobody told me either.

"And such a man," said another maid.

"'Tis verra braw," said a third.

"Aye, verra." The maids all made happy humming noises.

"Too bad about his face. What an ugly scar."

"Gained fighting against the English," Aila reminded them, though in truth she did not know how he had received the scar and was unsure why she needed to defend him.

"Aye, m'lady," the maids acknowledged. They finished without further discussion and sent her up to dry her hair in the sun.

Alone with her thoughts, Aila stood on the turret with her face to the sun. Pushing aside the doubts and worries, she considered what it might be like to be married to such a man as MacLaren, who had risked his life to bring back the body of her dear brother. To

MacLaren, who was knighted in France for fighting valiantly against the English invaders. To MacLaren, who had been her brother's friend and whom she had secretly idolized in her younger years. She smiled, remembering her childish fancy. She had secretly watched the young MacLaren, thinking he was the most handsome lad she had ever seen. She had planned to marry him at the age of five, until she realized "nun" meant "no man."

Aila's smile broadened. MacLaren's growth to manhood had done nothing to diminish his appeal. She wondered if his choice in brides had been motivated solely by the size of her inheritance, or if he felt any particular regard for her. The thought of MacLaren wanting her gave her a sudden flush. He had looked into her eyes with such intensity, as if he was the first person to truly see her. Her smile waned as she remembered how he had acted after they had wed. What would it be like to be married to him? Would he be kind or harsh? Questions tumbled in her head.

Si qua ergo in Christo nova creatura vetera transierunt ecce facta sunt nova.

The scripture came unbidden to mind. *If anyone is in Christ he is a new creation, the old has gone, the new has come.* A new beginning? That would be nice. She breathed deeply of the promise in the air. Closing her eyes, she enjoyed the warmth of the sun. It was St. John's Eve.

Anything was possible.

Returning to the castle, a multitude of questionable pieces of advice ringing in his ears, MacLaren decided it was time to meet his wife. Chaumont intercepted him and refused to allow MacLaren to seek her until he was washed and dressed "properly."

"I dinna come to court her. I've already married her," MacLaren said, arguing he did not bring the garments Chaumont deemed necessary.

"I've yer clothes here," chimed in Braden, his squire. MacLaren glared at Chaumont with suspicion.

Chaumont shrugged. "I may have given him a few packing suggestions."

After MacLaren was dressed to Chaumont's satisfaction, MacLaren was directed to Lady Aila's tower, being warned several times to go to the third floor—not the second, but the third. Lady Graham, it was whispered, resided on the second floor. He wondered at the emphasis but dutifully passed the second floor and continued on to the third. He stood on a small landing before a heavy oak door, wondering what he was supposed to say to his bride. The opportunity had emerged so quickly, he barely had time to think about it, except that it presented a resolution to a problem.

Graham's proposition for MacLaren to marry his daughter provided MacLaren with much-needed land and fortune from her dowry. And if Graham was to sire no more children, MacLaren would inherit more than he had ever dreamed of owning. The marriage fulfilled his responsibilities by providing support to his clan and land for the knights who followed him. It was the right thing to do, but as he had made his quick decision yesterday, he had considered only Aila's land and Aila's money, not actually Aila herself. Prior to Marguerite, he had taken his knightly vow of purity seriously and so had little experience with women.

Now, as he stood outside the door, he felt... what exactly? Intimidated? Nervous? He shook his head to bolster his courage and his pride. Such nonsense. *You've bedded a countess; you can bed her. People get married every day. This is nothing more than a common business transaction, like buying an apple at the market.* With that romantic thought, he knocked on the door and, without waiting for a reply, opened it.

The room was clean and, apart from a great curtained bed, rather simply adorned. A brush and copper mirror lay on a small table beside the bed. A chest sat at the foot of the bed, and a washing tub, still filled with water, had been placed by the window alcove. It appeared he may have interrupted her in the middle of her bath, yet the room was neat and orderly. And nothing in the room resembled the frightened-looking lass he married that morn. He was unsure of what to do next. There were no tapestries on the walls and nothing of a personal nature to provide him clues to her disposition. Feeling an odd mixture of relief and disappointment but seeing no point in standing in an empty room, he went back to the staircase. Noting the stairs went farther up to what he guessed was the turret, he decided to take a look and orient himself to the terrain that may soon be host to his next battle.

He bounded up the stairs, thinking of strategy, and reached the top of the turret before he realized he was not alone. He froze at the unexpected sight. A woman, dressed in nothing more than a linen chemise and a plaid wrap that hung loosely about her arms, was standing in profile, gazing at the valley below. Her figure, which he strained to see in the sunlight through the thin chemise, was perfect. The wind swirled around in teasing gusts, pressing the fabric to her skin, revealing her curves and then billowing out the material once more. In the late afternoon sun, her hair seemed to reflect the sun's rays with no lesser brilliance, shining like red-hot embers, as if her long ringlets were emanating a light of their own. The wind played with her hair, swirling it around her. She closed her eyes and arched her back into the sun.

MacLaren's mouth fell open. He was reminded of the sirens who led men to their deaths. This one could certainly lead a man to destruction. Since he was a man newly married and she had not yet seen him, he endeavored to leave before notice. His boot scuffed the floor. She turned at the sound and made a small gasp, covering her mouth with one hand, her chest with the other. MacLaren also gasped. The beauty before him was none other than his wife.

Six

Saints above, but she was beautiful. MacLaren stared at his wife, and she stared right back at him. He tried to think of something to say, but his mind grew ever more blank as the awkward silence continued. He was seized by the compulsion to kiss her, rejected the idea, but then remembered that with this lass, he had the right. He walked slowly toward her, the desire to thread his fingers through her hair and press his lips on hers growing with every step.

"Sorry, sir, ye startled me. I dinna ken you were there," Aila finally said. She chewed on her bottom lip, her eyes growing larger with MacLaren's approach.

"Hmmm," said MacLaren, because it was all he could think of to say.

"I have been remiss in not stating this earlier," Aila's words tumbled on top of each other, her voice a little high. MacLaren drew nearer and reached out to touch her. Nothing could stop him now. "Please let me express my deepest gratitude for the return o' my beloved brother."

Nothing but that.

Painful memories came flooding back, and MacLaren's arm dropped along with his desire. He remembered the night he returned to the battle ground of Neville's Cross. There had been so many dead. It had taken hours, crawling body by body to evade capture, before he found the remains of William Graham. Will had been a good friend, quick with a sword, faster on a horse. It should not have ended this way. If only MacLaren had arrived in Scotland sooner.

When MacLaren heard of King David's advance into England, he followed his path, intending to join his forces. He met the Scots when they were in full retreat. All he could do was to protect their retreating flanks and avoid a rout as they crossed back into Scotland. He had been a day too late. One day earlier, and he could have helped to turn the tide. Or maybe he would have joined his friend in the sleep of death.

He nodded to Aila, accepting her words, and turned his focus to the waning sun casting its long shadows across the landscape. The vista from the tower was impressive, providing a view of some of Graham's extensive lands. Awkward silence threatened to engulf them again, and MacLaren recognized it was his turn to say something.

"'Tis a highly defensible position," he stated, showing his appreciation for the castle's design.

"Pardon?"

"Dundaff. 'Tis well built. Good visibility. Ye winna be able to take her by surprise."

"Oh… aye," said Aila, looking a bit confused.

"So…" He voiced the first question that came to mind. "Ye were meant for the Church?"

"I was destined for the Church from an early age. My mother's dream was for me to be an abbess. But wi' her poor health, I was needed here. I was waiting until my brother took a wife who would act as chatelaine of Dundaff in my stead, but then…" She turned toward the waning sun now setting to her left. "But then ye came." She turned to him with a tentative smile, looked down the length of him, blushed, and turned back to the battlements.

MacLaren noted her appraisal of his person with some interest and wondered if he had passed inspection. Uncommonly conscious of his appearance, he was glad to be clean shaven and freshly bathed. At Chaumont's insistence, he had abandoned his Highlander's garb in favor of the attire he was accustomed to wearing while in France. Instead of his kilt, he wore snug-fitting russet-colored breeches tucked into black leather boots. Over a linen tunic, he wore a formfitting surcoat of dark green that hung to mid-thigh.

The coat had cost him a considerable sum and was a fine piece of work, embroidered with gold thread along the edges and held together with gold buttons down the front. He recalled, with some repulsion, he had commissioned the coat to wear to the French court, in large extent to impress the Countess Marguerite. Both the countess and Laird Graham's daughter had been born into higher rank and privilege than he, and he wondered if Aila also thought herself beyond his touch.

"Ye seemed reluctant to wed this morn," MacLaren said, edging closer to his suspicions about her pride.

"I was surprised." Aila gazed over the green valley below. "I have always been destined for St. Margaret's." She turned to him. "Have ye ever had yer life change in a moment? And everything ye thought ye knew was gone, altered forever?"

"Aye, I have experienced something o' the like." Indeed, his whole world had been shattered with the blink of a traitorous eye. Perhaps her hesitation was not a rejection of him, but rather shock and surprise. He could understand that.

MacLaren was trapped once again by a pair of green eyes. He moved closer to her, keeping his eyes on hers. He reached out and softly stroked the side of her face. Her eyes widened, and her breathing increased with the quick rise and fall of her chest underneath her thin chemise. Bedding her was his duty. He was certain he would be diligent with his responsibilities.

Aila's eyes broke from his and fluttered around, as if looking for purchase, before landing on the sleeve of his surcoat. "Ye've changed yer clothes since this morn."

"Aye," said MacLaren, his arm dropping by his side, his suspicions raised once more. He wondered if his current attire was more to her liking. He did not wish to elevate false expectations in her. Best to set her straight now. He did not wish to deal with a fractious wife.

"May I ask why ye made an offer for me to my father?" Aila's voice was soft, and MacLaren noted she once again was chewing on her lip.

"Graham proposed the alliance to me. I accepted."

"Oh."

"When we return to Creag an Turic, I rarely have

occasion to wear such as this." MacLaren watched for Aila's response.

"Creag an Turic?"

"My home... and yers now, too. 'Tis no' so grand as Dundaff." MacLaren was disappointed at the look of panic on Aila's face.

"But I canna go wi' ye. I must stay at Dundaff. I canna leave my mother."

MacLaren's jaw set, and he fell back upon the mask of grim determination he was so accustomed to wearing. It was as he expected. She would never accept him.

"I'm sure yer mother will miss ye greatly. Forgive the intrusion, m'lady. I'll let ye continue wi' yer dressing." He gave a short bow, turned on his heel, and left.

❧

Laird Archibald McNab arrived on horseback to the meeting place. The appointed glen was far removed from any known road or path and would provide the necessary privacy for the occasion. McNab swung down easily from his horse and wrapped the reins around a low-hanging branch, stepping into the secluded glen surrounded with dense forest. The wind swirled around the trees, picking up leaves and debris, hitting McNab in the face. He squinted and put up his hand to shield himself from the angry gust.

When he opened his eyes again, a man was standing before him. Startled, McNab jumped back, putting his hand to his sword hilt. The man merely gave him a caustic smile. It was he alright, dressed in a roughly woven peasant cloak and cowl he had obviously used to sneak unnoticed from Dundaff. McNab cleared his throat and tried to regain his composure. He did not like this man, this traitor of his own people. He would use him, surely, but he had no love for a man who would accept coin in exchange for his loyalty.

"Did yer laird receive the message?" McNab asked. He had drafted what he considered to be a very polite offer for the Lady Aila in return for his protection against the marauders.

"Aye, but dinna plan yer wedding to that Graham wench any time soon."

"Why no'? What other choice does he have? "

"He decided he'd rather have MacLaren for a son-in-law and married his daughter off today."

"What? How can this be?" McNab accused the cloaked man. "Ye said he'd have to give Aila to me. Ye said it would be easy."

"Dinna worrit yer head o'er MacLaren. I'll take care o' him. He'll be dead before morn. But ye need to remind Graham o' why he has no other choice than to form an alliance wi' ye."

"How could ye let this happen? Ye said the lass would tell us if Graham tried to plan a marriage wi' another."

"Do ye wish to whine like a wench or do something about it? I have a plan, if ye're man enough, which I doubt."

"What would ye have me do this time?" asked McNab with suspicion. The traitor had been helpful in giving information on the movements of Graham's men, giving McNab the ability to set fire to the fields without risk of being caught. It was supposed to be easy. He had not planned for MacLaren to be involved. Shame he had to die.

The traitor held out his hand. Disgusted, McNab handed over a bag of coin. The hooded man made a show of opening the bag to count his bribe, enjoying the insult the action delivered. At length he appeared satisfied, saying, "Graham's soldiers stay wi'in his walls tonight. While he sleeps away the night, ye need to burn all ye can. Remind him o' what he needs to fear."

"But tonight? I canna go out tonight. 'Tis St. John's Eve. The spirits are out tonight. And if I burn too many fields, my own clan will suffer."

The hooded man laughed without humor. "Ye decide what sort o' a man ye are. Are ye afeared o' the faeries? Or are ye a warrior? Me thinks ye are what everyone always said about ye. Worthless."

McNab reached for his sword, but the man simply faded away back into the trees.

The traitor smiled and strode away. *Stupid, stupid man. Does he really believe I would betray my clan for naught but a few coins?* He set a quick pace back to the castle. *Ah, but this is sweet. Graham will wake tomorrow to find MacLaren dead and more o' his precious fields burnt. He'll be forced to wed Aila to McNab. Then, when the timing is right, I'll kill the weasel McNab and that fat bastard Graham. I'll say I slayed McNab trying to protect the life of my laird, but alas he died in my arms, asking me to carry on in his stead. Then I'll take Aila for myself. I hope McNab winna have her breeding by the time I get her, but no matter. If it be so, I'll drown the bairn in the loch.* He chuckled, looking up at Dundaff, perched high on the rocky cliffs in the distance. *Patience, patience, and all is mine.*

Seven

Aila remained on the turret looking at the empty space that had once been her husband. He had not offered for her. He had not wanted her. Her father had arranged the marriage, though for what purpose she was still unaware. Her face still burned where MacLaren had touched it. No one had ever touched her like that. She had been aware of a sudden desire for more. She wanted to feel her whole body pressed against his. She shook her head at her own shocking response to him. Perhaps it was a good thing she would not be a nun.

Though she supposed it should not have been a surprise, the thought of leaving Dundaff was a shock. This place was all she knew. Her mother needed her. Her people needed her. It was her home. MacLaren's reaction to her concerns had been dismissive. She did not understand him. His feelings seemed to fluctuate, sometimes kind, sometimes cold; they were a rather unstable lot.

The sun was low on the horizon. It was St. John's Eve at last. The burghers of Carron walked up to

Dundaff for the festivities, their torches forming a line of lights up the steep path to the castle gates. A tremor of excitement coursed through her. This would be the first time she attended a feast or even ate in the Great Hall.

Walking down to her room, Aila was accosted by various servants and lady's maids. Soon they were swarming around her, preparing her for the banquet, chattering and clucking like mother hens. Lady Graham's own personal attendant, Treva, arrived to do her hair. As the skilled woman plaited and crafted her hair, Aila wondered if her mother had sent Treva, or if the valued attendant had come on her own.

At one point, she was left alone with the taciturn woman and seized the chance to voice her concerns. "Treva, I may need to live wi' Laird MacLaren," said Aila.

"I expect so," returned the lady's maid.

"My mother depends on me. I am concerned for her welfare."

"I've been serving Lady Graham for twenty years now. I warrant I can care for her." Treva stopped her work and looked directly at Aila. "Dinna worrit yerself now. Yer mother winna starve."

"Thank ye, Treva. I'm much relieved." And she was.

With wide grins, the maids came back into the room. They had completed the alterations to the gown and were clearly proud of their work. Senga entered, carrying a fine carafe with red jewels, saying a ghillie had brought the whiskey from a well-wisher in the castle for their wedding night.

Aila took the red-jeweled bottle and admired the craftsmanship before placing it on the side table. Everyone seemed so happy to rejoice in her marriage; Aila was truly touched.

"Look at ye now. I ne'er kenned to see ye a bride," said one maid as she affixed the veil.

Nor I, thought Aila.

"What a night ye'll have tonight," said another, and the maids giggled in response.

"Ye'll be wi' child in no time."

Child?

Aila's mouth went dry. Of course a man would be wanting heirs; why hadn't she thought of it before?

"Aye, he'll have ye breeding soon, t'be sure." Because her future had consisted only of the convent, she had given little thought to marital relations between man and wife. How did a man impregnate his wife? Would he want to do that to her? Tonight? Her heart beat faster. She glanced at the whiskey on the table. She never drank potent spirits, but perhaps tonight she would make an exception. The women around her all seemed to be more knowledgeable on the subject, and she wished for some basic clarification. It should be the role of her mother, but Aila knew better than to request help from that quarter. Despite her curiosity, she was embarrassed to admit ignorance to her servants, and they finished their work before she found the right words.

Dressed to the satisfaction of her maids, she felt like an entirely different person, one she knew not. Her ladies stepped back and looked at her, smiling. Maggie even had tears in her eyes.

"Ye look verra bonnie, m'lady."

For once in her life, Aila believed it to be true. The bodice of her silver kirtle had been lowered and made more formfitting, revealing cleavage that had never before seen the light of day. The full skirt of her gown had been modified to add a short train. Over the kirtle she wore a sleeveless surcoat, open at the hips, pale blue in color and richly embroidered. It fit snug across her chest and was tied tight with silk ribbon, giving those never-before-seen parts of her some added lift. Low on her hips she wore a gold belt from which her small dagger hung. Her hair had been plaited and styled on the top of her head, falling in auburn ringlets down her back. A gold circlet mitre was placed on her head and held a gauzy veil that delicately framed her face. She felt exposed with her hair loose… and excited… and free.

The maids discussed whether she should go down on her own or wait for an escort. To Aila, who had never attended meals in the Great Hall, it felt wrong to arrive without an invitation. MacLaren would surely escort her or send a ghillie at the very least. She dismissed her maids with a smile and watched out the window, tapping her toe as she waited for her escort. This was going to be quite a night.

MacLaren prepared for the evening meal with some reservations. Aila's reaction had been disappointing, yet perhaps the lass needed a little time to adjust. Or maybe she would try to have him killed, like another beautiful woman had once tried to do. He shook off those unpleasant thoughts and took an emerald necklace out of a wooden box. It had been his mother's and now would go to his reluctant bride. He may not have as many worldly goods in comparison to her father, but he wanted her and her kin to know he could still impart gifts of value.

Looking down at his attire, MacLaren regarded it with disgust. The fancy clothes, the expensive gifts, it all reminded him of the last time he had courted. His jaw clenched. He would not play the fool again. He changed back into his Highlander's garb. He was a MacLaren and proud of it. His lady wife best accustom herself to her fate.

"*Slàinte!*" called a man when MacLaren entered the Great Hall.

"*Slàinte mhath!*" MacLaren returned, wishing him good health. A goblet of whiskey was pressed into his hand, and MacLaren made his way through the crowd to the high table.

"*Slàinte mhor!*" yelled another man, not to be outdone by wishing all present great health.

"*Slàinte mhor a h-uile là a chi 's nach fhaic,*" called out Chaumont. The Scots cheered. Being in Scotland less than a year, Chaumont's grasp of Gaelic was tentative at best, but he had managed to memorize certain phrases such as, "Great health to you every day that I see you and every day that I don't." It went a long way toward improving his acceptance in the clan. He walked up to MacLaren with a wide grin, and the two men sat down next to Graham at the high table.

"Arrogant bastard," muttered MacLaren, though the corners of his mouth twitched momentarily in an upward direction.

"True on both counts, I'm afraid," Chaumont

responded with great cheer. "Careful now, wouldn't want folks to see such an undisciplined show of emotion."

MacLaren, who had just taken a sip of whiskey, choked, trying not to laugh, and was barely able to avoid spraying the table. When he was able to talk, he cursed Chaumont with great creativity and felt much more himself.

Chaumont's smile faded as he noticed MacLaren's choice of dress. MacLaren was wearing his thick pleated plaid, belted around the waist and thrown over one shoulder, a large broach pining it to a linen shirt dyed saffron yellow.

"How could you betray me like this?" Chaumont asked, his expression pained.

MacLaren was confused by the question. He cursed Chaumont on a regular basis, but Chaumont had always laughed back at him. "How have I offended ye?"

"By abandoning all sense of fashion—what on earth are you wearing?"

MacLaren raised his cup to his friend. "I am a Highland laird. 'Tis best my wife and her clan ken it well."

Chaumont stared at MacLaren's bare knees and shook his head.

"You look like you're wearing your bedroll."

"Conveniently, it can be used as that. 'Tis quite comfortable," MacLaren added.

"Yes, I think we all can see how comfortable you are."

MacLaren snorted but shifted to a more modest position.

The feast was brought out by young lads, first to Graham, then MacLaren, and then the remainder of his guests by order of importance. Graham acquitted himself well, providing the roasted meat of sheep, fowl, and wild pigs. Venison pies were in abundance, as were salmon, haddock, and cod. Pastries, bread, and cheese were brought out on large trays, along with plates of wild cherries and roasted apples. Of course whiskey flowed like water, along with wine, cider, ale, and mead. As the first course was served, MacLaren looked around for his missing wife, hoping to see her soon.

"Where's your bride?" whispered Chaumont.

MacLaren sliced through his meat with a hard slash of his knife and said nothing.

"She did look a bit on the terrified side this morn. Perhaps you've scared her away," Chaumont continued. "Though I am certain any bride would look the same when they saw you as groom."

"Attention, my friends, yer attention please." Graham stood at the table, and the room filled with people hushed into silence. "Many blessings to ye this St. John's Eve. Though many of us have borne great losses this past year, still, together we have survived. And now we have reason to celebrate. Tonight I introduce to ye our neighbor, Sir Padyn MacLaren. He has recently returned from France, where he fought valiantly against the Sassenach devils. He is here with his men, seasoned warriors all. And I announce to ye tonight, an alliance between our clans in the marriage of Sir Padyn to our own Lady Aila."

Shouts echoed in the hall as people got to their feet to cheer. MacLaren stood and acknowledged their enthusiasm for this union. If only he could feel the same. He would feel a lot better if Aila was sitting obediently beside him. Where was she?

By the time the dessert was presented, MacLaren realized—with the familiar ache of betrayal—that she would not be coming to the meal. Though no one had said anything about it, he could only imagine what they must be thinking of him. She had publicly rejected him at his own wedding feast. His anger increased while the sense of humiliation grew, though he took great pains to keep it behind a cold mask of detachment. He considered finding her and dragging her forcibly down to the meal but decided that would create an even greater scene, providing more interest for the gossipers.

Chaumont was in fine form, talking and laughing and endearing himself to as many people as possible. He even started telling heroic stories about MacLaren's time in France. MacLaren knew his friend was trying to divert attention away from the reality of Aila's absence. At the end of the feast, the entertainment emerged. Jugglers and acrobats proceeded to entertain, yet to MacLaren, their amusing antics were a mockery of his shame. He wanted nothing more than to leave this public arena of humiliation, but to leave would be to admit he was hurt by her rejection. Defeat was unthinkable. He had never surrendered in battle, and he would not now.

Just as MacLaren was considering murdering the juggling clowns to put an end to the nightmare that was his wedding feast, the musicians struck a lively tune, and before long, the men began spirited attempts at dancing. For partners, they grabbed their wives or unmarried lasses or one another, and soon the rushes were flying. Chaumont was swarmed by interested lasses, and he promised to oblige each of them in a dance of whatever sort they were most interested. MacLaren watched grimly while Chaumont danced with polished perfection. Taking a short break from his partners, Chaumont sat by MacLaren, the absence of a certain lady looming large.

"No need to sulk in your drink. Come, dance, do whatever you please. There are more than enough bonnie lasses for us all."

"I warrant ye feel different, but there be some problems bedding a wench canna solve," grumbled MacLaren.

"That may be true, my friend," Chaumont replied with a sly smile, "but it fails more agreeably than most."

The corners of MacLaren's mouth twitched again. "Go, my friend, let me no' keep ye from yer quarry."

Before Chaumont could find another partner, the musicians took a break, and folks began to wander outside. MacLaren walked from the banquet hall, thinking about his mother's necklace still in his sporran. What a fool he had been to think he had anything that cold-hearted wench wanted.

Outside in the courtyard, the large bonfire was lit with a great whoosh of light and heat. The priest said prayers to St. John, requesting blessings for the coming harvest. Others brought cattle to walk sunwise around the fire to bring good luck and prosperity. After the circling, some of the spryer young men took to jumping over the flames.

"What on earth are they doing?" Chaumont asked.

"Heathen ritual," muttered an old man at his side. "They jump o'er the flame as a sacrifice to the gods. Ought no' be done!" The man tottered off to complain to the priest as another young buck braved the flames to the appreciative gasp of the crowd and squeals of delight from the young females. Not to be outdone, some of MacLaren's men joined in the jumping.

"It seems to me this fire jumping has more to do with winning favor from the lasses than any heathen gods," said Chaumont to MacLaren with a wry smile. "And a brave thing to do, wearing a skirt."

"'Tis called a kilt," MacLaren answered in a growl.

"Whatever you call it, with naught underneath, 'tis a good way to get your bollocks burnt."

A tall, thin man with long silver hair walked toward the fire, people moving out of his way.

"Please tell us a story," begged a child.

"And what story would ye have me tell?" asked the man with a slow smile.

"The ghost!" exclaimed several children at once.

"Ah, the ghost. They say a lone figure in a hooded cloak, riding a pale horse, has been seen roaming these woods in the wee hours o' the night." At the sound of the storyteller's rich voice, people moved to hear him, the elderly given spaces on benches placed around the fire. The silver-haired bard paused, waiting for people to settle. The fire popped, sending a cascade of orange sparks high into the night sky, the dancing flames casting flickering shadows on the stone walls of the bailey. A hush fell over the crowd.

"Our good King Robert Bruce," began the

storyteller, "after winning freedom from the tyranny o' the English, was no' long to enjoy his victory. His success was no' wi'out sacrifice, and having met much hardship fighting for the freedom o' the Scots, he took sick in his later years. Realizing he would no' recover from his illness, he repented the sins of his youth and fervently wished he had been able to go to the Holy Land to make war upon the Saracens as penance for his actions. Thereby, he requested his closest friend and strongest warrior, the Good Lord James Douglas, to carry his heart to Jerusalem.

"Thus, after the death of Bruce at Cardoss, his heart was taken from his body, and being embalmed, was placed in a silver case and worn around the neck o' the Lord Douglas. He took the heart o' Bruce as far as Grenada, Spain, but there was cut down by the Moors. The body o' this brave warrior was found atop the silver case, protecting the heart o' his king wi' last his breath. Sir Simon Lockhard, now called Lockheart, carried the heart o' Bruce back to Scotland, where it be buried below the high altar in Melrose Abbey.

"Yet some say the spirit o' Bruce canna rest wi' his dying wish left unfulfilled and his heart no' in the Holy Land. Many a Scot ha' sworn they seen him in the mist in the wee hours o' the night, wearing a white cloak and cowl and riding a pale horse so swift no human rider can catch him."

Confirming the storyteller's ghost story, people gave witness, telling their own experiences of seeing the ghost. Robert the Bruce must be quite restless, thought MacLaren, with all the reported sightings. Music started again in the lower bailey, and people continued the dancing. The fire would burn all night, and many would stay awake till dawn, celebrating and keeping watch to protect the castle from wandering spirits.

MacLaren decided he had stayed long enough and walked slowly to the base of Aila's tower. Best to slip away now before anyone could suggest doing some of the more public traditions of the wedding night. The last thing he wanted was to confront Aila with a bunch of her happy kinsmen standing nearby. He had plans for that treacherous wench, ones that were best done without witnesses. She had humiliated him in front of her clan and his. He would see that she paid dearly for her defiance.

Eight

AILA WAITED. AT FIRST SHE STOOD IN THE MIDDLE OF the room, anxious for the knock on the door, not wanting to sit and crumple her gown. After a while, she grew weary of standing and leaned against the wall. As the evening progressed, she finally sat at the window, watching for someone to come fetch her. She wondered why it was taking MacLaren so long. After more time elapsed, her anticipation and excitement faded, and a new reality began to dawn. Could it be she would not be invited to her own wedding feast? A soft knock on her door made her jump, and excitement rushed through her, only to be dashed again when Maggie entered the room.

"Brought ye a tray o' food, m'lady," said Maggie without looking Aila in the eye.

"I was planning to join them in the Great Hall."

"The food's been served, m'lady," said Maggie in a small voice. "They are finished wi' the meal and are having the entertainment now." Maggie began to set the tray of food on the stone bench across from her, but Aila shook her head.

"Thanks for thinking o' me, but I'm no' hungry."

Maggie took the tray and crept out the door.

Aila sat on the cold stone bench, listening to the faint strains of music wafting up from below. They would be dancing now. Her breath fogged the glass, and she idly drew people dancing on the misty window pane. She wondered if MacLaren danced, celebrating his newfound fortune. It was all clear now. He didn't want her. He only wanted her inheritance. A tear slipped down her cheek as she tried to focus her mind on her picture, anything but thinking of MacLaren's disregard.

Light from the bonfire reflected through her window, flickering in her room like a funeral pyre. A lump formed in her throat and her stomach tightened into a heavy knot. She tried to choke back the emotion, but more tears slid down her cheeks. Her mother had forbidden Aila to eat in the hall; her father had never intervened in her behalf. Her father did not want her. Her husband did not want her. She was alone. It was nothing new, but somehow MacLaren's rejection felt oppressive, and she struggled to draw breath. She started to sob, unable to hold back the tears, which streamed down her face. Years of isolation and loneliness came rising to the surface. Without anyone there for comfort, she held herself, thin and weak against the onslaught of grief.

～

MacLaren stood at the base of Aila's tower, rigid as the steel of his sword. He took several breaths of cold night, trying to regain his calm so he did not act on his impulse to wring her neck.

"She'll not be able to give you children if you kill

her tonight," said Chaumont from behind him, as if reading his thoughts. "And I warrant you'll have a hard time collecting her dowry, too."

"This is why I wished never to wed. Women are at best an aggravation, at worst a harpy from the bowels o' hell itself."

"I understand your engagement to Marguerite did not end well."

"No' end well? That deceiving whore killed my cousin and tried to have me killed, too." MacLaren glowered, pointing to the scar on his cheek.

"Perhaps it has occurred to you that one bad apple should not keep you from the barrel?"

"They be no' apples, for their fruit be naught but poison," responded MacLaren, his voice dripping with venom.

"And your mother?"

"Was a saint."

"Naturally."

"He chose well, my father. I wish I could still seek his counsel."

"What do you think he would want you to do now?"

"Take care o' the clan," MacLaren answered without hesitation. "And that's what I mean to do. Come, Chaumont. Let's take the fight to the enemy tonight." MacLaren turned away from Aila's tower and strode toward the lower bailey and the stables.

"What and miss your wedding night with your bride? Once you've calmed down, you should go talk to the mademoiselle."

"I've no stomach for cruel, manipulative wenches. I'd rather a sword in my face than a knife at my back."

Chaumont shrugged and joined MacLaren in rounding up the men. MacLaren's troops were none too happy at the prospect of leaving the cozy fire and the feminine companionship they had found. With so many of the Graham menfolk gone, the lasses were plentiful and looked at the MacLaren warriors with hungry eyes. Separating one from another would be a challenge. His clansmen also balked at leaving the safety of the stone walls and bonfire. Who knew what eerie creatures roamed free this night? Only a great fool would venture forth on this night of all nights.

MacLaren refused to give a command, rather invited any who would join him to come. Despite their grumblings and misgivings, MacLaren's warriors, to a man, eventually followed him into the wild darkness.

"If I get caught by a faerie, I expect ye lads to come back for me," said one man.

"Not me," replied Gilbert. "If I get captured by some beautiful fey creature, let me go. Bid my wife *adieu*."

MacLaren spread out his men to cover as much territory as possible. Graham had extensive lands, so it would be impossible to guard it all. MacLaren made some guesses and concentrated more men toward the north. If McNab was behind the attacks and was man enough to leave his own walls on St. John's Eve, he would not want to travel far before being able to flee to safety. MacLaren considered it unlikely anyone would be out tonight. But if one had the guts, it would be an ideal time to attack without risk of being caught, since only a fool would stray from the safety of the fire on St. John's Eve. *A fool like me.*

MacLaren spent the better part of the night lying

concealed in a ditch carved by a small burn. Nothing happened. During the long, cold night, his mind had ample time to wander. And wander it did, all over Aila's body. He remembered in exquisite detail how her chemise had clung, the shape of her body, the blazing ringlet hair. The more he tried not to think of her, the more his mind turned traitor, and he imagined her again, this time without the chemise. He tried reminding himself she had publicly humiliated him and would no doubt use her beauty to betray him again and again. It was a pointless exercise. His mind would not be tamed, and soon he decided he was a simpleton to be lying outside in the dirt when he could be lying with her, gaining a much more sweet revenge.

The more he thought on it, the more a desire to return to Dundaff burned within him. Why was he lying in the mud when his beautiful bride lay in bed waiting for him? Her soul may be vile, but her body was not. And truly, what more did a man need? He was about to call the men to return to the castle when a soft noise drew his attention. He peeked above the dirt embankment; torches were headed his way.

Aila woke early. So early, many would call it the dead of night. Somehow she had fallen asleep on the stone bench, and she stood gingerly, her body cold and sore. Some wedding night. The groom had never bothered to show. She felt like a mouse battered by a cat all night and then discarded, not even worthy enough to kill. Her mother had been right all along; men brought nothing but pain and rejection.

The red-jeweled bottle of whiskey still waited for her wedding-night celebration. Perhaps a draft now would do her good. She walked slowly over to the bottle and took out the stopper, breathing in the contents. Instantly she pulled back as the unfamiliar alcohol fumes hit her like a restorative. Making a face, she put the stopper back into the bottle.

Though it was the wee hours of the morning, she generally awoke at this time. With growing anticipation, she decided to follow her normal routine and do what she usually did at this time of the morning. She had thought this lost to her, but since MacLaren was not here, there was no one to stop her now.

With some difficulty, she shed her fancy clothes, and in the dim light of the moon, she donned a pair of men's breeches, leather boots, and a thick woven shirt belted at the waist that hung almost to her knees. Over this she put on a pale blue silk cape that had once been her grandmother's but had long since faded into grey. Aila valued the old, tattered garment for its inner layer of thick wool, which kept her warm from the chill night air. She quickly spun her hair into a bun and attached her head covering, pinning the hood of her cape to the wimple so it obscured her face from view.

Moving on soft feet, she descended the staircase and stole through dark corridors as silently and confidently as a cat. Through her daily excursions she knew all the hidden passages about the castle. Exiting the tower, she skirted the courtyard, keeping in the shadows to avoid the sentry's eye. Most of the revelers had gone to sleep, many simply sleeping on the ground, but a few stood guard by the bonfires, ensuring the flames did not wane till dawn.

Aila crept silently past the guards and then plunged into darkness again, entering the enclosed staircase to the lower bailey. Exiting the tower stairs, Aila slipped quietly into the back door of stables and walked down the short corridor past the stable master's quarters, turning right into the long corridor of the main stables.

"Good morn to ye, lass," said the old stable master, who was tightening the leather straps of a saddle onto a tall horse. The stable was warm and cozy, lit by the glow of a single lantern.

"Good morn to ye, Fergus. Lovely day for a ride. How's he doing this day?" Aila walked up to the misty gray stallion, who nudged her softly. Aila responded to his affectionate greeting by stroking his silky nose. The stallion twitched and pawed the ground.

"He's ready to run," said the old man with a smile. Shadow was a fine piece of horseflesh, the best in the stables. He had been her brother's charger. The horse had returned from war uninjured, but would let none ride him. After repeatedly tossing some of the castle's finest riders, Laird Graham decided Shadow was no longer trustworthy as a warhorse but still kept him for stud. Aila was more persistent and gradually restored the high-spirited horse's trust.

"Shall we ride today?" Aila murmured to her mount, taking up the reins and following the stable master's slow but steady steps down the long corridor of the stables. Fergus had worked the stables for so long, no one knew his real age, including Fergus himself. He was thin, his shoulders bowed with age, yet his hands still had the strength of a young man's. His skin was like tanned leather, creased yet worn smooth over the years. The animals responded to his calm presence, and Aila always felt at peace when she was with him. Fergus never asked if Aila had permission to ride, and she never asked him not to reveal her equestrian habits. They both knew she did not, and he would not.

"I dinna think ye'd come, ye being married and it being St. John's Eve and all," said Fergus.

"And yet ye saddled him anyway."

The old man shrugged and led the way with his lantern to the end of the stables. In a dark corner, the last stall stood vacant. On the sides were heaped broken bits of saddle, discarded bits of iron, torn leather straps, and pieces of rope. Fergus entered the stall and moved two boards leaning across the back of the stall. Aila smiled. This was her brother's legacy to her. Her brother Will had taught her to ride and allowed her to ride still.

The stable master pushed the back of the stall, which swung open noiselessly, revealing a large cave hewn into the rock. The cave was cut out of the side of the mountain and opened into a large room with a sandy floor. Toward the back of the cave, the walls narrowed into a corridor. A thick iron gate barred the passage to a tunnel cut into the stone. Fergus held up the lantern and Aila unlocked the gate, walked Shadow through, and locked the gate behind her.

"Take care now, lass."

"Thank ye, I will."

The stable master shuffled back to the stables, taking the lantern with him. He closed the secret door to the cave and plunged her into blackness. Aila was accustomed to the dark and waited for her eyes to adjust to the faint fluorescent glow of the minerals in the cave wall. She led her mount through the cave tunnel, which sloped down the mountain.

The passage had been cut generations ago as a secret exit from the castle in times of siege. At some point, the passage was considered unnecessary and blocked by debris and large rocks. As a boy, Will had chanced to overhear their father speak of the tunnel and sought it out with his best friend, Duncan, the son of Pitcairn the Steward. They worked together to clear the rocks and reopen the passage, and the stable master turned a blind eye to the proceedings. For many years afterwards, they would sneak out in the early morn for carefree rides across the heath, relishing their freedom.

After Duncan died in an accident at the lists, Will gave in to Aila's begging and allowed her to come with him, teaching her to ride and challenging her to keep up with his breakneck pace. Those had been the best times of her life. Though Will and Duncan were now gone, she still guarded their secret. She and the stable master were the only ones who now knew the tunnel had been opened.

After a slow walk through the dark tunnel, Aila and Shadow reached the mouth of the cave. The entrance to the cave was concealed by a large slab of rock and thick bushes, which blended so well into the landscape, it was almost impossible to find. Aila stepped into the silver light of the moon and swung onto Shadow's back in a fluid motion. She breathed deeply, enjoying the scent of the night, the breath of freedom.

Aila did not worry about being seen, for people rarely left the roads in these parts, and certainly no one would be out tonight. Many said the hills were haunted with the ghost of Robert the Bruce, but in all her nocturnal rides, Aila had never seen any such ghost, so she didn't give much credence to the story. Shadow stamped impatiently on the ground, and with the barest touch of Aila's heels to his flank, they were off, Aila hanging on tight for the wild ride down the slope.

When they reached the heath, Aila gave Shadow full rein, and they flew across the plain. She reveled in the experience, moving in concert with the magnificent beast as if they were one. Riding through the night wilds, the exhilaration coursed through her veins, pure and free. It was the only time in her day, particularly after the death of her brother, that she was truly happy. Riding Shadow made her feel close to him again, as if he was racing alongside her, and she urged Shadow even faster.

With Shadow's speed, Aila was able to cover a lot of ground in the several hours she allotted for her ride. She traveled first to the convent of St. Margaret. She stopped on a hillside, looking down over the peaceful community, the place that until yesterday would have been her home.

St. Margaret's and the nearby monastery were relatively new communities, built to a large extent through the generosity of the Grahams. They were

located on Graham land, though it had been designated as Aila's dower lands and would go to the
Church when she took the veil. That is, it would
have gone to the Church, but now the lands belonged
to MacLaren. Would he continue to support the
communities or demand the nuns leave? Aila sighed.
More questions, and her mind was already full of
them. She needed to run.

Aila headed north toward more isolated fields and
the lands of MacLaren toward the west and McNab
toward the east. Pushing Shadow faster and farther, she
forgot her sad marriage and put aside nagging questions of what she should do next. She was free, and it
was enough for now.

The pre-dawn fog was dense, and it made common
noises sound odd. She reined in Shadow to listen to
the strange noises. Was that mournful wail someone
screaming? Tales of beasties that roamed the hills
came flooding back, and she began to think, with
some trepidation, this ride had been most unwise. The
sound grew louder, but in the fog, she had difficulty
determining from where it came.

Without warning, two figures on horseback raced
from around a large bolder and came skittering to
a halt. One held a torch; the other screeched like a
banshee. *I'm dead,* thought Aila and screamed at the
ghostly apparitions. Like an avenging angel, another
figure appeared out of the mist. It was a mounted
warrior, his mighty claymore raised high. Aila's mouth
dropped open, her scream died in her throat, and her
heart stopped. It was MacLaren.

Nine

MacLaren silently watched from his hiding place in the burn as the two figures ambled closer, each carrying torches.

"Och, 'tis the ghosties," gasped one of MacLaren's men.

"I warrant ghosties dinna carry torches," whispered MacLaren. "Watch 'em, lads; these may be the raiders we're looking for."

The unknown riders emerged from the tendrils of mist. Though MacLaren was confident these figures were not phantoms, still a slithery feeling ran down his spine. Did faeries carry torches?

"I canna believe we got talked into this. Set something ablaze, and let's be done wi' it," said one of the figures. "This night gives me the creeps."

Not faeries. MacLaren's confidence rose. Human meddlers he could handle. He stepped onto the road and drew his claymore. The ringing of steel on steel sliced through the night.

"Stand down and drop yer weapons," MacLaren commanded.

One of the ghostly figures shrieked and dropped his torch. Both riders spun round and raced away.

"To me, to me," hollered MacLaren, and his men emerged from hiding to run to his aid. MacLaren commanded some to put out the small fire that had started where the torch had landed and the others to follow the raiders into the mist. Rory brought the horses, and MacLaren mounted quickly to lead the chase. MacLaren rode after them blindly into the dense fog. Fortunately, one of the raiders continued his unmanly screeching, and MacLaren followed the sound as best he could until he spotted the faint light of the remaining torch.

MacLaren was closing in on the raiders when he rounded a large rock and found his quarry stopped before him. He raised his sword to end the chase and was startled by the eerie sight of a third apparition that had appeared in front of the two men. The ghostly figure rode a pale horse and wore a grey tattered cloak and cowl, its face concealed. Unlike the first two raiders, this one carried no torch.

MacLaren stared at the figure, wondering if the stories of the ghost of Bruce had been true. At least he was man enough not to scream like the two raiders, who were making quite a din with all their yelling. Heedless to the danger MacLaren might pose, the two men turned and rode back past him into the night. Cursing this new ghostly figure that had caused him a moment of inaction, he yelled at some men to follow the raiders while he and Chaumont chased this new apparition. The figure spun its horse and took off at a gallop.

Fighting fear, he spurred after the strange creature, determined to discover its identity, whether of this world or the next. The fleeing figure was fast, very fast. Indeed, he had rarely seen the like and struggled to maintain pace. Once free of the trees, they reached the marshes, where horse and rider broke into full speed through the treacherous bog, forcing MacLaren to conclude the man was either very sure of his path or an utter fool. Speeding faster despite the risk, MacLaren suddenly pulled up on the reins, stopping short. That horse—he had seen it before. He was sure it had been William Graham's mount. He had seen it last wandering the field of battle, searching for its fallen master. MacLaren swallowed hard, his heart beating with exertion, and watched the rider race in the direction of the Graham fortress, disappearing into the mist.

"What was that?" Chaumont caught up, breathing hard. MacLaren stared into the eerie gloom where the ghostly figure had disappeared.

"I dinna ken."

MacLaren returned to his men and discovered the two culprits had gotten away. He was a fair tracker, so he decided to wait the short time until dawn to continue the pursuit. He also decided, with strong encouragement from his men, to light a large fire so as to ward off any other wandering spirits. Even Chaumont did not mock the plan or laugh at the superstitious Scots. Instead, he lent an able hand to collect firewood. Not until the sentries were in place and the fire's warmth was familiar and comforting did MacLaren start to feel more himself.

"What was that thing?" asked Chaumont.

MacLaren shrugged.

"Were we chasing a ghost?"

MacLaren stared into the flames. He had no answer to Chaumont's questions. "I think next year I'll keep by the fire on St. John's Eve."

Chaumont and his men readily agreed.

Shaken by the chase, Aila returned to Dundaff by way of the tunnel. She was still trembling when she unlocked the iron gate and walked Shadow into the cave. She wondered if her heart would ever slow down. Her face was stung by branches that had whipped by; her whole body ached. Never had she been more terrified. MacLaren had looked like a demon spawn.

She relocked the gate and entered the stables, surprised to find no lit lantern hanging on the stable wall as was Fergus's custom. She also wondered why the old man did not come shuffling to meet her. Perhaps he had gone back to sleep, since it was still early. She stabled Shadow in the gray light of the early hour, not wanting to wake the old man. She shuddered, as if icy fingers trailed down the back of her neck, and she struggled to regain her composure. She worked quickly with a growing desire to be gone.

Completing her task with speed, she walked down the long stable corridor and around the corner to the side entrance, where a strange sight stopped her cold. A crumpled figure lay on the hard-packed dirt floor in front of Fergus's room. She held her breath and edged closer. It was Fergus, a gash to the back of his head. He lay motionless on the ground, and blood pooled around the open wound. She gasped and ran to him, kneeling beside him, but he lay still, his eyes closed, his cheek cool to the touch. Her stomach lurched and sank like stone. She froze, unable to move, unable to scream.

From around the corner came the creaking of the main door of the stables. She stood to call for help but noticed an iron bar lying beside the old man. One end was bloodied.

Aila's heart pounded and her mind whirled. She had never known anyone besides Fergus to be in the stables at this time. The sound of spurs drew louder, and the orange glow of a lantern grew brighter. What had happened to the stable master? Was it an accident, or had he been...? She could not draw breath; her vision narrowed. Was the approaching person a friend... or a killer? The clinking footsteps drew closer to the side passage where she stood. She was frozen in place.

Turris fortissima nomen Domini ad ipsum currit iustus et exaltabitur.

The name of the Lord is a strong tower; the righteous run to it and are safe. The verse from Proverbs ripped through her mind in a flash, with an emphasis on the word "run." Whether or not her mind understood the command, her feet got the message, and she bolted to the side door. When she closed the door behind her, it squeaked loudly. Unsure whether the unknown person had heard the noise, she ran to the tower staircase that led back to the upper bailey. Inside the tower, she was once again in total darkness, and she flew up the spiral staircase.

Halfway up the tower, she paused to take a breath, wondering how long she had held it. Her lungs burned, and she panted, gulping for air. Below her, the ominous sound of spurs clinking up the circular stairs grew louder and a faint orange glow was visible. Panic clutched at her gut like talons, and she stumbled up the stairs in a frenzy.

Reaching the top, she broke into a sprint across the courtyard to her own tower and raced up the stairs, not stopping until she reached her room. She bolted her door and ran to the window. Below, a cloaked figure shined a lantern first one way then another. The figure looked up at her tower, and Aila fell to the floor to avoid being seen. When she finally had the courage to look again, the cloaked figure was gone.

Ten

AILA WAS STARTLED BY THE SOUND OF SOMEONE TRYING to open her door, the bolt clanking. Aila cowered on the floor, frozen in place. How long she had been there? Had it been minutes or hours? She wanted to raise some alarm but feared leaving the safety of her room. Had the strange man gone back down to the lower bailey, or had he come into her tower? Was he even now standing outside her door? Had he killed Fergus and was waiting for her to answer the door, so he could do the same to her?

"Ye there, m'lady?" came the familiar sound of the maid.

"Och, aye," breathed Aila, much relieved; yet as she stood, she found she still wore the shirt and breeches. That would be difficult to explain, so she stripped off her clothing, stuffing it in her trunk, and slipped on her chemise. Aila opened the door to Maggie and Senga.

"Are ye… available, m'lady?" asked Maggie in a whisper.

"Aye," returned Aila, a bit confused.

"Is the MacLaren still sleeping?"

Now Aila understood. They naturally thought her husband would have eventually come for her. "Nay, he is no' here."

"Verra good," said Maggie, bustling into the room. "We've come for the sheets."

Sheets? Was it washing day already? Aila had too many other concerns to figure it out. Maggie and Senga stripped back the blanket on the bed and stopped, looking down at the sheets.

"Oh," said Senga.

"Oh my," said Maggie.

What could be the matter? Aila stood beside them and looked down at the plain white sheets. She could see nothing amiss. What was wrong here?

"Um, m'lady," stammered Maggie, blushing pink, "did ye sleep elsewhere last night?"

"On the bench," Aila admitted, wondering why they would ask that.

"The *bench*?" Maggie sounded incredulous.

"Aye."

Both maids stared at her then walked over to the window and to examine the bench. This was getting odd.

"Ye and MacLaren on the bench?" asked Senga.

"MacLaren was no' here last night."

"Oh!" Maggie said brightly with a big smile. She paused, and her smiled faded into a frown. "Oh."

Grim-faced, Maggie and Senga helped Aila dress in her normal attire, working efficiently and avoiding her eye. Senga lapsed into silence, but Maggie nervously chattered about nothing in particular. Occasionally, she would give her mistress a look of sympathy. Aila was lost in her own thoughts until Maggie stumbled upon something that caught her attention.

"What did ye say?" asked Aila, unsure of what she had heard.

"I said the stable master ha' gone and fell and broke his head."

"Fell?"

"Aye, they found him in the stables. I probably ought no' tell ye, but my brother is a stable lad, and he says po' auld Fergus must ha' been reaching for a bridle, and that's why he got up on the chair."

"Chair?" asked Aila weakly. There had been no chair near the body.

"Aye. The chair was crushed beside him. Must ha' broke, and that's what caused the fall. Ye feeling all right, m'lady? Ye look right pale. I shoud'na have told ye. These things are no' for lady's ears." Maggie brushed Aila's hair and affixed the wimple. "Father Thomas came to give the last rites, 'cause he is breathing verra poorly."

"The stable master still lives?"

"Aye, but they canna wake him, and I warrant the good Lord will be calling him home soon. There now, ye look right bonnie." Everyone in the room knew that to be a lie. Senga and Maggie gave their curtsies and headed toward the door. Maggie glanced back, giving Aila one last look of pity before she left.

Pity. In all her years at the castle, Aila may have lived a restricted life, but never before had she been the object of pity. She picked up the copper mirror and gazed at her reflection. Back in her plain kirtle and white wimple, she looked more familiar but rather bedraggled. Her eyes were red and swollen with dark circles underneath. Her cheeks were scraped and scratched. She was married to a man who despised her. She put down the mirror, the copper heavy in her hand. She had seen enough.

Aila put her hand to the side of her face, as if by holding her head still, her thoughts would likewise stop spinning. Over and over, the image of the crumpled stable master flashed before her eyes. Could it have been an accident? She shook her head. There had been no chair; a metal rod, yes, but no chair. But what could it all mean? Aila sucked in a gasp of air, shocked by a sudden realization. Someone had altered the scene to make it look like an accident. It could mean only one thing. Somewhere in the castle was a killer.

She alone knew the truth. No... she was not alone, one other person knew—the murderer. But who could it be? Why would anyone do such a thing? More importantly, had he seen her? Was he waiting even now for her to emerge from the security of her tower?

Her mother was right. Marriage was a hell on earth. Why had she consented to this nightmare? Feeling she had nothing left to lose, Aila resigned herself to endure her mother's triumph and slunk down to her mother's chambers.

From her regal, fur-covered chair, Lady Graham regarded her daughter with cold resentment. With a flash of her eyes, Lady Graham dismissed the servants, and they fled for the door. Aila's shoulders drooped further, and she focused on the black tips of her shoes.

"Come here, child." Her mother's voice was uncharacteristically soft, and she reached out to Aila with concern. Aila ran to her and buried herself in her mother's arms, beginning to cry once again. Holding on tight, Aila was enveloped in soft fur and warm velvet. She inhaled the soft scent of rose petals, and it brought back memories of long ago being cuddled by her mother. It was a comfort she had not known for a long time, and it soothed her soul.

"What did he do to ye, child?" Lady Graham finally asked, her voice soft and worried.

"Nothing," Aila said, her voice choked. She wiped the tears from her eyes and tried to gain control of herself.

"Ye can tell me, child. What did that bastard MacLaren do to make ye cry?"

"He did nothing, Mother. He ne'er came for me."

"What do ye mean, Aila? How did he hurt ye?"

"He dinna hurt me. I dinna see him at all. I wasna invited to the feast, and he ne'er came for me last night. But in the stables—"

"What?!" Lady Graham stood up so fast, she tossed Aila onto the floor, landing her flat on her bottom. "He dinna come for ye? He rejected ye on yer wedding night? How dare he treat me this way! I will no' be ignored!" Lady Graham tried to take a step, but the pain in her feet caused her to sit back down with a grimace. "Aila! What in heaven's name are ye doing on the floor? Get up and go fix yer face. Ye look a mess."

Aila picked herself off the floor, brushing the rushes from her skirt, and washed her face in the basin as commanded.

"Now sit down, shoulders back. We dinna wish the servants' tongues to rattle." The servants were ushered back into the room to present the food and then commanded to leave once again.

"Now we must consider what to do," said Lady Graham as she accepted a bite of food.

"But, Mother, there's naught I can do. I'm married now." Aila wanted to tell her mother about what had happened in the stables but feared this might only provoke a new bout of anger. Her mother would be furious if she knew Aila had been out riding. Lady Graham flashed Aila a wicked smile, and all thoughts of confiding in her mother vanished.

"Married, yes, but consummated, no. Ye've got options, my dear, until he beds ye."

"Oh?" Aila's eyes widened.

"I ken it be time ye joined the convent."

"But the wedding…" Aila was still not sure she understood.

"Since that fool of a husband ignored ye last night, the abbot can have the marriage annulled." Realization struck Aila. Her mother was right; the abbot would be certain to champion her request for an annulment, particularly since the convent and his abbey were built on her dower lands. The Church would not be likely to turn away her inheritance. Besides, Sister Enid had written to encourage her to avoid marriage and take her vows. She valued the nun's opinion, so it must have been a been a mistake to agree to the marriage.

Her mother stopped eating for a moment and gave her daughter a penetrating glance. "Ye dinna want to stay married to such a man, do ye?"

Aila sighed. She had wanted to be married to him, very much at one point. But now… she thought of his rejection. "No, Mother," said Aila sadly, "I dinna want him for my husband."

"Good. 'Tis all settled. Ye'll go to the convent today and ask for sanctuary and an annulment."

"But, Mother, how will I get there? 'Tis not the day I usually visit the sisters, and I doubt they will let me go on my own." Aila went with an armed escort to visit the convent once a week, but those trips were arranged in advance. To leave the gates, she would need the permission of her father, or perhaps now, her husband, and she had no idea if they would grant such a request. Too bad she had not thought of this earlier. She had ridden past St. Margaret's this morning. She could sneak out the secret passage, but the stable would be too crowded during the day to leave unnoticed.

"I could leave at night," Aila started to say.

"Nay, child. Ye must leave today, as soon as possible, before that ugly brute of yers gets his hands on ye."

Aila was about to respond that MacLaren was not at all ugly, but wisely swallowed the comment and said, "But how can I leave the castle?"

Lady Graham smiled at her daughter. "Watch and learn." She ushered the maids back into the room. Maggie and Senga gathered the food tray and spread out a clean tablecloth.

"Maggie," said Lady Graham slowly, causing the maid to jump and cringe.

"Aye, m'lady?"

"How is that beau of yours?" Lady Graham asked, her tone suspiciously sweet. "Is he no' one o' our soldiers who guards the gate?"

"Aye, m'lady," replied Maggie, nervously fidgeting with the hem of her sleeve.

"Does he have duty today?"

"Aye. He begins his shift after Matins," replied Maggie, confusion clear on her face as she glanced from Lady Graham to Aila.

"And where is yer young suitor now?"

Maggie's eyes grew large. "I dinna ken."

"How verra odd, for I swore I heard him talking wi' ye outside my door no' too long ago."

All the color drained from the maid's face. "Oh, m-m'lady, I be so s-sorry."

"Dinna worrit yerself," said Lady Graham, her voice smooth. "I ken young love. Why are ye no' married?"

"Well... I..."

"'Tis yer lack of dowry, no? Well, I'd like to help ye. Bring me the chest." Aila brought her mother the small chest of cedar and polished brass and opened the lock with a small key that hung around her mother's neck.

"Here are ten coins, my dear," said Lady Graham. "Will that no' provide for yer dowry?"

Maggie gasped. To her, it was a considerable fortune. "Thank ye, m'lady. I dinna ken what to say."

"'Tis how I reward my faithful servants who help us in our time of need. Ye do wish to help us, aye, Maggie?" Maggie nodded her head vigorously, eyeing the stack of coins on the table.

"That's a good lass. All I need from ye and yer

beau is a soldier's tunic and guaranteed safe passage from the castle."

"Nay, m'lady, I coud'na. My Brody will no' accept a bribe."

"I'm no' bribing Brody. I'm dowering ye, and I'm ashamed at ye for suggesting different," said Lady Graham, her voice once again harsh. "I only supposed ye'd wish to help Lady Aila to reach the safety o' the convent afore her husband returns for her. He surely has no love for her. I shudder to think o' what he may do to her once he gets her back to that pile of rocks he calls his home. I suppose it be nothing to ye if poor Aila is beaten, thrown in the dungeon, or worse."

Maggie was not the only one in the room to look horrified. "Nay, m'lady." Maggie gulped. "Do ye ken he will treat her badly?"

"I've heard his cruelty has no end. His public rejection o' her will be only the beginning o' his shameful treatment o' her. 'Tis yer choice, Maggie. Aila's life is in yer hands. I wish to protect my daughter, and I'm willing to reward all who do."

Senga spoke up. "I ken the way to the convent. I can lead her there safely."

"Thank ye, Senga. I need two tunics. What do ye say, Maggie?"

"Aye, I'll help ye," said a wide-eyed Maggie, looking at Aila.

❧

Events were moving much too fast. Dressed in a soldier's tunic and trews, her hair somehow crammed into a cap. Aila walked down to the lower bailey with

Senga—also dressed as a soldier—by her side. Her mother's description of her peril had convinced not only Maggie but Aila of the necessity of this plan. Above all, she wanted to seek guidance from Sister Enid. Since her friend had written to encourage her to avoid marriage and take her vows, Aila guessed Sister Enid would be in full support of this plan.

When they entered the stables, chaos reigned. The stable master still lay on his death bed with his family and many who worked in the stables around him. This left the stables ill-staffed and hectic. Aila was glad to be in disguise. She still didn't know if the person in the stable had seen her, or if he wished to do her harm. Retreating to the safety of the convent seemed a good idea.

"What d'ye want?" snapped the assistant stable master as Aila walked in the door.

"Swift mounts to carry an urgent message," Aila replied, trying to keep the hood of her traveling cloak covering her face and her voice low.

"Alright, alright, keep yer breeches on. I'll be wi' ye in a minute."

"I'll help ye," said a young stable lad, rushing up. Aila recognized him as Maggie's brother, who must have been alerted to the plan.

"Go find him a good horse," Aila said, nodding to her maid. "I'll choose my own." Aila walked directly toward a particular stall. If she was indeed leaving Dundaff forever, she could not leave Shadow behind. Saddling him quickly, she backed Shadow out of the stall to find Maggie's brother standing there aghast.

"Nay, m'lady," he whispered. "Let me find ye a more suitable mount."

Aila looked the nervous lad straight in the eye. "I'll be taking my brother's horse." The stable lad looked around. The others were all busy with other work, not heeding them in the least. He simply nodded and walked away.

So far, so good, thought Aila as she tied a small bundle of clothes to the saddle, mounted, and rode toward the main gate.

"Messengers from Lady Graham," called Aila to the gate guard, wishing to be gone but cringing internally at the lie.

"Permission granted," called back the voice of the guard, most surely Maggie's beau. She hoped they would have a good marriage and passed through the portcullis. Reaching the other side, she breathed deeply. She was free.

Eleven

AILA STRUGGLED TO HOLD BACK SHADOW, AS HE WAS accustomed to being given free rein once outside the castle. Her maid would never be able to keep up with her, so Aila constrained her mount to a more sedate pace. Having traveled to the convent many times, Aila hardly required an escort, but her mother liked the idea of having someone with her on the journey. Senga must have been swayed heavily by the sight of gold when she boasted she knew the way to the convent, for several times she would have led them astray had Aila not set her right.

By the time they reached St. Margaret's, Aila was in quite a state. She doubted her reasons for coming and wondered if she was doing the right thing. She felt guilty for sneaking away from her new husband and even more guilty for marrying him in the first place. She turned it round in her head but could not decide who had the greater demand on her loyalty: her father, her mother, her husband, or the Church. Utterly confused, she stabled her horse and sought out her spiritual advisor and friend, Sister Enid.

The Sisters of St. Margaret were trained to be concerned only with the things of God and renounce worldly interests, but the sight of Lady Aila, wearing soldiers' garb and muttering broken fragments of different languages as she wandered dazedly through the convent, raised more than one eyebrow. Aila was a wreck by the time she finally found Sister Enid sitting in the gardens.

"Aila?" asked the nun with surprise. Sister Enid was a middle-aged nun with sharp, discerning blue eyes, a warm smile, and the faintest of accents borne from her native France. Her hands had become stiff and painful over the years and now were so deformed she was no longer able to write. Her spiritual guidance was still frequently sought both in person and by courier, though now she used a scribe to respond to the letters.

"Sister Enid." Aila collapsed at the nun's feet and began her anguished tale. "I've made such a mess of things. I dinna get yer missive until after I married MacLaren, but he dinna come for me, so I can still join the sisters if the abbot can get an annulment, which Mother says he will, due to the dowry. Oh, and the stable master was murdered, or at least he will be once he dies."

"Saints above," exclaimed Sister Enid. "Clearly a lot has happened since I saw you last. Come sit here beside me and be still."

"But, Sister, I need to ask for sanctuary."

"You are in trouble?"

Aila nodded vigorously.

"Have you prayed for guidance?"

Aila slowly shook her head.

"These walls cannot protect you as well as the Lord. Breathe your prayer and be still."

Though her mind was racing, Aila tried to do as her friend suggested, using the breath prayer she had been taught. *Lord Jesus Christ,* she prayed as she inhaled, *have mercy on me,* she breathed out. As she focused on her breathing, she became more aware of her surroundings. They were sitting on a stone bench by the wall of the convent. Before them was the garden, with lines of vegetables, mostly beets and turnips. There were rows of dark, rich soil, too, freshly tilled for more planting, and the smell of dark, rich earth. The birds chirped around her, singing their cheerful songs. She became more mindful of the garden and felt more centered and peaceful.

"Now please tell me what has brought you here today," said Sister Enid.

Feeling considerably better, Aila began to relate the events of the past day. Sister Enid listened without comment except to remind Aila to breathe. Aila told her everything—the wedding, receiving Sister Enid's letter, her talk with MacLaren on the turret, his rejection of her on their wedding night, the secret passage, MacLaren's chase, the attack on the stable master, and her escape from Dundaff. When Aila finally finished, she was still unsure what to do but was relieved for the cathartic experience of telling all.

"Well now," said the nun. "That was a lot to tell. Why do you think your father would have you marry so suddenly? And why to MacLaren?"

"I dinna ken," said Aila, thinking back on events. "Though father did say to MacLaren that some may no' be pleased wi' the marriage. And he said he woud'na let McNab have me. I wasna able to ask any questions, since my father left right after the wedding to put out the fire."

"Fire?"

"There have been some accidents of late, and some fields have been burnt. Folks seem concerned about it, but I dinna give it much…" Aila's eyes opened wide as she considered new, frightening scenarios. "Could we have been attacked?"

"It seems a possibility."

"Then maybe my father needs MacLaren for the warriors. MacLaren is most ferocious." Aila remembered him appearing out of the mist like the devil's own, sword raised high. "But woud'na someone tell me if we were attacked? Shoud'na my father ask me if I wanted to form an alliance with the MacLaren clan?"

Sister Enid raised an eyebrow.

"Well, he should," said Aila indignantly.

"Tell me about the stable master. You say the maid said it was an accident?"

"Aye, but I dinna ken seeing a chair, like she said. What I saw was the bloodied end of an iron bar. Someone was in the stables wi' me, but I ran. Maybe I should have called out for help, but I was so scared."

"Did this person see Fergus?"

"He must have. He had a lantern, and he walked right by him."

"What did the person do when he saw Fergus?"

"Nothing. He chased me up the stairs."

"Aila," said Sister End, patting Aila's hand with her gnarled one, "I think in this case you were right to run."

"Ye ken he was the killer? Gone back to the stables to make it appear an accident?"

"'Tis a mystery," said the nun, her eyes gleaming. "There is much ado at Dundaff to be sure. I have something else to tell you, too. I did not send you that missive."

"Ye dinna? Then, who?"

"Who would profit from your entering the convent?"

"Surely a person o' the Church woud'na deceive me."

Sister Enid smiled again, waiting patiently and saying nothing.

"Oh, Sister, surely no' the abbot..." Though even as she spoke the words, her suspicions were raised. Father Barrick served as the abbot for the region, residing at the abbey about five miles away. The abbot was a large, gruff man who made Aila feel most uncomfortable. Perhaps it was because she had never before known a priest to carry a sword and wear armor under his robes.

"Or someone who wished ye to leave the protection of Dundaff."

Aila put her head in her hands with a groan. "I've acted the fool."

"You're not foolish. You're unaware of the lengths to which a person will go for his own gain."

Aila looked at her friend as if for the first time. She knew very little about this woman's history or what had brought her so many years ago from her native France. "How far would they go, Sister?" Aila asked softly.

"Aila, I fear for you. You are an heiress now. I wonder you never thought on that."

"I ne'er kenned I would inherit more than my dowry.

After my brother, there were my uncle and cousins who would inherit before me, but they died, too." Aila shook her head, realizing her thinking had been much too small. "I thought only of my own grief, my own daily responsibilities, no' of what it all meant."

"Well, clearly someone has been counting your worth."

"What am I to do?" Aila asked plaintively, but Sister Enid was quiet once more and waited. Aila took a deep breath. She was a woman grown, and it was time she started acting the part. "So we ken my father may have arranged a marriage to gain MacLaren's warriors. We ken someone struck the stable master and made it look like an accident, though we dinna ken why. We ken there be someone who sent me a false message to try to get me to leave Dundaff and enter the convent. And someone may be putting fire to the fields. The question is, where will it be safest for me to be?"

"Indeed, is that the question?" asked Sister Enid. "I was more wondering why, when danger is all around, you decided to stop praying."

Aila gave an embarrassed shrug. "I guess I was too distracted by all that's happening."

"Has not the Lord always spoken to you through the scriptures? Listen again, Aila. You need divine guidance more than ever." Sister Enid struggled to her feet and shuffled away slowly, leaving Aila to ponder her words.

Aila's mind was again in turmoil, but she returned her attention to her breathing. *You're not a child anymore. 'Tis time to grow up.* At first, nothing came to mind, but then she remembered the stories of the women in the Bible—the strong and confident good wife in Proverbs, Ruth, who stayed with her mother-in-law against the odds, the women who stayed at the Cross when the disciples ran.

Si enim nunc silueris per aliam occasionem liberabuntur Iudaei et tu et domus patris tui peribitis et quis novit utrum idcirco ad regnum veneris ut in tali tempore parareris.

She pondered the verse from the book of Esther. It was the story of a beautiful Hebrew girl who became Queen of Persia. Esther risked her life to tell the king about a traitorous plot and saved her people from annihilation. *And who knows but that you have come to royal position for such a time as this?* The quote was the encouragement Esther received not to remain quiet but to tell the king the plot.

With sudden insight, Aila recalled she had not told her father what had happened to the stable master. It was surely information he needed to know. Aila breathed deeply, gaining a new sense of confidence. She had been thinking only of herself. She needed to think on what was best for her clan. She stood and walked with sure steps out of the garden. Going back to Dundaff would be difficult. It would require an embarrassing confession of her flight, and she would probably be punished by her father or her new husband… and after that, her mother would kill her. But for the first time since her surprise wedding yesterday morn, she had a purpose, and she knew what she must do. She smiled wryly, remembering what Esther had said when she agreed to her mission: *If I perish, I perish.*

Aila caught up quickly with Sister Enid, who had not gotten far on shuffling feet. "I'm going back to Dundaff," Aila announced with surprising confidence.

Sister Enid smiled. "God's speed, Lady Aila."

"Thank ye, Sister." Aila knelt before the nun to kiss her gnarled hands.

"I'm pleased you received the guidance you sought. But perhaps before you return, you may want to consider your dress?"

Aila looked down at her soldier's garb and gasped. "Merciful heavens! I will change directly. Thank ye again." Aila ran back to the stables where she had left her horse and her clothes.

Aila found Senga in the stables. The maid had already changed back into her kirtle and was in deep conversation with a lad who looked to be a courier. When told of the decision to return to Dundaff, Senga was visibly distressed. She urged Aila fervently to stay, pleading with her, reminding her of the punishment they both would suffer. Aila gave the maid leave to stay at the convent, not wanting Senga to be punished unfairly for a mistake that was not hers. Though Aila persisted in her determination to return to Dundaff, it was unnerving to see her maid so distraught. In the end, Senga decided to return with her, though she made it clear she was quite ill-pleased.

As Aila mounted her horse to leave, the courier mounted quickly and brushed her out of the way in his haste to leave the stables. Surprised and irritated by his rude behavior, Aila watched him gallop away, resisting the urge to ride after him and give him a stern talking to or, better yet, nudge him off the road. She sighed, suppressing her uncharitable thoughts, and reluctantly accepted the easy walk that appeared to be Senga's top speed.

Twelve

MacLaren and his warriors trudged back through the castle gates that afternoon after a long night. When dawn had restored their courage, they had tracked the trail of the two raiders northward until they reached the border of McNab's land. It seemed Graham was correct in suspecting McNab was the culprit behind the arsons. It had been a strange, cold night, but MacLaren was satisfied to have prevented the burning of more fields and to have found the likely culprit. There was still much to do and McNab's cowardly attack must be answered, but MacLaren's thoughts frequently wandered to his new wife. MacLaren was tired, dirty, and hungry—hunger that had little to do with food. He sent Chaumont to give a report to Graham. It was time he dealt with his wife.

This time MacLaren did not stop to make himself presentable before going to her. He was protecting Aila's clan from starvation this winter, and she could damn well deal with the dirt. MacLaren burst open the door to her chamber without knocking, but much like the last time he had entered the room, it was devoid of habitation. MacLaren growled. *Would it be too much to ask for her to be waiting in her room so I could ravish her senseless?* No, of course not. She was doing this on purpose to drive him insane. Now he would have to go search for her, which would make him look even more the fool.

A maid with an armload of linens obscuring her face entered the room.

"Where be my wife?" he barked at the maid. She dropped her linens and stared at him, horrified. Honestly, he knew he was a little dirty, but he could not look that bad.

"She's… I dinna ken," squeaked the maid. That was clearly a lie. What was going on here? He walked toward her with determined intensity. She shrank away until she had backed against the wall.

"Where be my wife?" He spoke slowly, but his voice rose with every word, saying "wife" with a menacing snarl.

"G-gone, m'lord," stammered the hapless maid, who burst into tears.

"Gone? What do ye mean by gone?"

"She's gone to St. Margaret's. I'm so s-sorry, sir," choked the maid between frightened gasps.

That his wife had gone to visit the convent did not seem overly upsetting. Yet the maid was acting so guilty, he was sure there was more to the story. Patiently, he watched her sob and shake until she calmed down a little and looked up at him once more. She cringed, and he wanted to know why.

"What is yer name, lass?" he asked in a calm tone.

"Maggie," she replied in a small voice.

"Now, Maggie, tell me why my wife went to the convent."

Maggie looked furtively right and left as if trying to find a way to escape. MacLaren took another step forward, placing his hands on his hips, one hand by his dirk.

Maggie's eyes opened wide, and she began to tell all. "She went to St. Margaret's, sir, to ask for yer marriage to be annulled so she can join the convent."

"What?!" MacLaren grabbed the maid by her arm and dragged her down the stairs and across the upper bailey, ignoring her wails. Was Graham trying to play him false? This spectacle caused quite a stir in the castle, but MacLaren cared not and continued to drag the maid to Graham's study, where he found the old man sitting in contentment, a glass of whiskey in one hand, the bottle in the other.

"What's this?" Graham stood and glared at MacLaren.

"Tell yer laird what ye told me," growled MacLaren to the maid. Chaumont, Warwick, and Pitcairn, roused by the commotion, burst into the room.

The poor maid shook, saying, "L-lady Aila went to St. Margaret's to seek an annulment and join the convent."

"Impossible," roared Graham. "I've no' given her leave."

"S-she went d-dressed as a soldier."

"This canna be," said Graham and looked to his Master of Arms, Warwick. "Go find her."

"I dinna ken what yer playing at Graham, but I'll have none o' it," growled MacLaren. It was the same deceit, the same trickery the countess had played on him. He was being betrayed once again by someone he trusted. MacLaren shook with the effort it took to prevent himself from doing the old man harm. Chaumont stood between him and Graham, as if to prevent MacLaren from doing something rash, which, he might at that. The last man who had betrayed him, MacLaren had killed.

"Have no' our clans always been allies?" MacLaren seethed. He felt his control slip, and molten rage coursed through his veins. "I dinna seek yer daughter. I tell ye the truth, if ye were being attacked, I would have fought for ye. All ye had to do was ask. Ye dinna need to offer yer daughter as a bribe. But ye offered an alliance, and I accepted. Have I no' kept my word? I'll no' be deceived. I'll no' be having ye treat my men, who are willing to die for ye, wi' disrespect. And I'll no' tolerate betrayal from anyone."

"Exactly what are ye accusing me of?" snarled Graham, his face turning red. "Did I no' give my daughter to ye in marriage afore ye spent more than an hour in my home? This be nonsense. My daughter woud'na defy me."

"Then why did yer obedient daughter leave?"

"I tell ye, she'd ne'er leave."

A breathless Warwick returned with the sad news that Aila had not been seen by anyone that day. She had even failed to provide the pages their lessons. Graham sighed and his shoulders slumped. "Maggie," said Graham in a soothing voice, as if he were calming a spooked horse. "Why did Aila leave? Tell us the truth now, lass."

"L-lady Graham told me Aila would be hurt bad by the MacLaren and we had to get her to safety or he'd lock her in the dungeon and most horrible things would happen to her."

Graham sank down in his chair with another sigh. "Thank ye, Maggie. That will be all."

Maggie dashed from the room like a lost soul released from purgatory.

"My wife, gentlemen." Graham crossed his arms across at his massive chest. "I fear we've fallen victim to her conniving ways. Dinna worrit yerself, I'll get Aila back."

MacLaren shook his head. He used to know whom to trust, but he no longer felt secure in his own judgment, let alone others'. "I'll ride to St. Margaret's to find her. If she comes wi' me, I'll return. If no', I'll be taking the lads home."

"Go," Graham commanded Warwick and Pitcairn. "Bring her back to Dundaff."

"And if she's claimed sanctuary from the abbot?" asked Warwick.

"I'm her father, her kin. What's she need to claim sanctuary from? Bring her home."

"I swear I'll find a way to return her to ye, my laird," said Pitcairn in a soft voice.

"Good man," said Graham. "I know ye will no' fail me."

The men left Graham's study, each knowing if Aila had been granted sanctuary from the abbot, there was very little any of them could do while she remained inside the cloister. But if she were ever to leave, she was fair game.

❦

Aila plodded along the dirt path, her maid straggling behind. The ride seemed to take forever and tested Aila's resolve. Her decision made, she wanted to be done with it. The long ride back to Dundaff gave her too much time to consider her fate. She was fairly certain her actions warranted some sort of punishment, but was not sure what that might be. MacLaren wouldn't really lock her in a dungeon—would he?

Pushing aside frightening thoughts, she focused on her calming breath prayer. They were walking through dense forest now, thick brush on either side of the road. The sunlight filtered through the trees, and Aila appreciated the beauty of it. They sauntered along steadily, the clopping of their mount's hooves muted by the packed dirt road.

Abscondita est in terra pedica eius et decipula illius super semitam.

Aila pondered the verse from the book of Job, wondering what it could mean. *A trap lies in his path.* Perhaps her decision to return to Dundaff would be more perilous than she expected. Perhaps there were those at Dundaff who planned to do her harm. Or maybe there would be detractors, like her maid or her mother, who would discourage her from doing what was right. She sat tall in her saddle, determined not to let fear weaken her resolve to return.

Corripiat me iustus in misericordia et arguat me oleum amaritudinis non inpinguet caput meum guia adhuc et oratio mea pro malitiis eorum.

Men have hidden a snare for me. They have set traps for me along my path. Aila considered the verse from Psalms. Perhaps the snares were her old nemeses, indecision and fear, that eroded her confidence, challenged her faith, and robbed her of joy. No, she would not give in to fear. Shadow nickered and pranced, pulling at the bit. Aila leaned forward to stroke his neck. He was impatient to be free to run. She was too, but since her maid behind her rode at a snail's pace, that was not an option. Besides, she was determined to enjoy the day, at least until she reached Dundaff.

Aila was so focused on her self-motivational musings, she was knocked off her horse and hit the ground hard before she knew what was happening. She lay on her back in the road. A man on top of her pinned her arms to the ground and leered at her. She was so shocked, she wasn't even afraid. Lying motionless she gaped at him as though he were an apparition. What had just happened?

Shadow's high pitched shriek slammed her back to reality. The horse reared and sliced through the air with his hooves, striking the man's head above her. The forest erupted in confusion. Men were shouting, emerging from the bushes. The man on top of her crushed her to the ground with his weight, holding his bleeding head and screaming. She pushed the man off of her, rolled to the side, and got up, running. More men appeared before her, and she swerved off the road into the brush, beating a path as fast as she could through the dense foliage. Branches sliced at her, tearing her gown.

Her head snapped back as merciless fingers grabbed her wimple and dragged her backward. Screaming in pain, she struggled to break free from the pins, but she was almost back to the road before she escaped. Shadow continued to buck and paw at the men who surrounded him. Aila ran into the trees, men shouting behind her.

"Get the wench. After her. Hurry!"

"Enough of this. Shoot the damn horse."

Aila froze. Not Shadow. Not her brother's horse. She turned and ran back to the road.

"No!" Aila screamed and dashed between Shadow and the archer taking aim.

A tall man stepped forward and pushed up the archer's arm, causing the bolt to soar into the sky.

"Lady Aila," said the tall man with a bow. "How good of you to join us."

Aila was surrounded by ten men. Senga stood at the side, eyes wide, her arm being held by one of the men. At the lecherous looks of the men, Aila felt unbearably exposed. Her gown was torn and dirty, her wimple gone, her hair unleashed and flowing down around her in fire-red ringlets. She had been attacked by robbers.

"I have no coin to give ye," she stammered.

"Ah, but yer father does," said the leader with cool detachment. The leader was dressed in a dark brown surcoat, tan breeches, and a black cloak that was pinned at the shoulder and hung down to his brown leather boots. His dark hair was cropped and his face covered by a beard also trimmed short. In different circumstances, Aila might have found him attractive, but as it was, decidedly not. He appeared vaguely familiar, and she stared at him, trying to place the face.

"Archie McNab?"

"'Tis laird now, since my father's death."

"I'm sorry for yer loss." Aila responded before she remembered this was no time for social niceties.

"And I for yers," replied McNab, but he smiled when he said it. "I've come to take ye home, Aila."

"I was going home. There be no need to knock me

from my horse." Aila's sense of indignation rose. Even she had her limits.

"No' to Dundaff, my lady." McNab slowly walked to her. "To my home."

Aila opened her mouth to argue with McNab, but behind her, Shadow spooked again, rearing up against the men who had tried to grab the reins.

"Stop!" said Aila, rushing to Shadow's side to calm him. "Ye're scaring him."

McNab watched while Aila calmed the beast. "I'll make ye a deal. Ye may ride yer mount, but ye must come wi' us and do what we say, or we'll shoot yer horse out from under ye, ye ken?"

Aila nodded, though she could not understand why McNab would wish to abduct her. She remembered her father's comment about McNab. Was he going to ransom her? How did she get in this predicament? With a sudden flash of clarity, she remembered the verses. Enemies set a trap on the road. It wasn't metaphorical; it was an actual trap set on the real dirt road. She looked heavenward and could only imagine the Good Lord's aggravation at her stupidity. Somehow it struck her as humorous, and she began to laugh. Knowing this was hardly the appropriate time, she tried to suppress the urge, which made her laugh only harder. Aila giggled uncontrollably as McNab helped her back into the saddle.

"Is she daft?" whispered a man to his laird.

"As the future mother of my children," replied McNab, "I certainly hope no'. But whatever the state of her mind, her inheritance more than makes up for a little madness. Dinna ye agree?"

Thirteen

MacLaren and his warriors, along with Warwick, Pitcairn, and several soldiers from Dundaff, rode to St. Margaret's to find the wayward Lady Aila. The two clans had similar goals, but distrust had sparked between the groups, and they regarded each other with wary caution. An unspoken, fragile truce emerged as they rode along. MacLaren took the lead with his men, Pitcairn and Warwick with the lads from Dundaff following behind.

Though sunset was still hours away, the skies darkened, and a storm threatened. MacLaren chose a challenging but more direct route through the forest instead of staying along the main path. By the time they were within sight of the convent, the heavens had opened, and rain was pouring down in sheets. The wind whipped them mercilessly, cutting the chill through their wet garments.

The hard ride through the wet weather had effectively dampened MacLaren's anger into resignation. By the time he reached the convent, he wanted naught but resolution. Either she would agree to stay his wife, or he would go home. At this point, a nice warm fire in his own hearth sounded mighty tempting. MacLaren reached the large oak door of the main hall, illuminated by a flash of lightning, and had to pound on the door to be heard over the booming thunder. Eventually, an ancient nun opened the door and led the drenched party to a large room where they were offered food and drink.

MacLaren, Chaumont, Pitcairn, and Warwick requested an audience with the Reverend Mother while the rest of the men gratefully accepted the nuns' hospitality. The four men followed a young nun—MacLaren's mouth set in a grim line; Warwick scowling and well-armed; Pitcairn saying little but watching everything with a careful eye; and Chaumont, tall, smiling, and elegantly dressed even as he sloshed down the corridor. The four men crowded into Mother Karine's small study, looking like awkward oafs next to the Mother Superior's tiny frame.

"I'm here for the Lady Aila MacLaren," said MacLaren possessively.

"Lady Aila was here earlier, speaking wi' Sister Enid, but she left many hours ago. Is there a reason why ye ken she would be here still?"

It was not the answer MacLaren nor any of the men had expected to hear. They stood silent, looking all the more uncomfortable.

"Perhaps ye would like to speak wi' Sister Enid?"

The men agreed and were led to her cell, having even more difficulty squeezing into the smaller space.

"We seek Lady Aila." This time it was Warwick who spoke in his low, gravelly voice.

Sister Enid looked concerned. "Lady Aila was here earlier, but she returned in the afternoon with her maid. Has she not returned to Dundaff?"

"Nay."

"And did you not meet her along the road?"

"We came overland, Sister."

"Ah, that explains it," said Sister Enid, her face relaxing. "You must have missed her."

"Ye're sure she be going back to Dundaff?" asked MacLaren suspiciously.

"Most assuredly, yes," replied Sister Enid, studying MacLaren's Highland garb. "Would I be correct in assuming you are Sir Padyn MacLaren?

"Aye." Thunder crashed again, louder and closer.

"Considering the poor weather, you and your men are welcome to stay the night and return to Dundaff in the light." It was a sensible suggestion, but MacLaren was anxious to lay eyes on his elusive wife.

"Nay, we'll be going back," said MacLaren. A giant clap of thunder shook the building.

"It will be black as pitch out there," said Warwick slowly. "Are ye're sure Lady Aila returned wi' enough time to beat the storm?"

"Yes, I would say so."

"Sister, Lady Aila is verra dear to us all. Are ye certain she be safe at Dundaff now?" Pitcairn spoke with a soft voice.

"Where she is now, I cannot say for sure. I do know she left for Dundaff many hours ago with her maid, Senga."

"Then it's settled." Pitcairn spoke with relief. "We gratefully accept yer hospitality, Sister Enid."

"Ye may stay. I'll return," said MacLaren over the sound of hail beating a staccato rhythm on the roof.

"I don't cherish losing my way in the dark and ending up in a bog," said Chaumont, looking up as the hail beat down louder.

MacLaren sighed. He was losing this fight. The others were right. Aila was most likely curled up by her warm fire, mocking him for riding all the way out to St. Margaret's in a storm for naught. He was tired and hungry, hungry for real food this time. The thought of a hot meal and soft bed sounded heavenly. MacLaren reluctantly agreed to stay, and the men returned to the hall to fill their empty stomachs.

After a hearty meal, MacLaren once again sought Sister Enid, finding her reading in a room designated as a small library. Books were stacked on shelves, revealing a nice collection for such a small community. Sister Enid looked up from her reading and smiled a welcome to him.

"How did ye find my wife today?" MacLaren asked, not exactly sure what he needed to know.

"She was rather upset when she came to see me," began Sister Enid.

"She wasna by any chance wearing a solder's garb?"

"Yes, she was." Sister Enid motioned for him to sit in a nearby chair, but MacLaren remained standing.

"Was she planning to request an annulment and join the convent?"

"Why did you not visit her on your wedding night?"

MacLaren looked away. He had not thought this nun to be so direct. There was no delicate way to answer this question, and he was not about to talk about his fear of betrayal with anyone. "I went hunting the men who are burning Graham's fields." MacLaren's gaze snapped back to hers. "And you dinna answer my question. Was she going to join the convent and ye changed her mind?"

Sister Enid studied him with shrewd interest. "You're not a man who trusts easily."

"I am often correct in my judgment, and it saves time," answered MacLaren caustically. This nun was nipping at all sorts of tender spots.

"You've been disappointed in life."

"Disappointed?" said MacLaren with a snort. "That's one word for it."

"You blame God."

"Nay, I blame the whoring wench who deceived me." The words tumbled out of his mouth before he could remember how to speak to a nun. "Forgive my language, Sister. I forget myself." Sister Enid remained quiet, looking at him expectantly. MacLaren sighed and sat in the chair opposite her. "I may have wondered what I've done to offend my Lord that misfortune would befall me."

Sister Enid was silent for a while before saying, "Suppose you took your knife and plunged it into my heart. What would be the outcome?"

MacLaren's mouth dropped open and his brows furrowed. This was not at all the answer he had expected. "I'd be condemned to hell eternal."

"It would be wicked, and I'm not suggesting it as a course of action, mind you, but would it be possible for you?"

"Aye, if I favored hell."

"Suppose you did such an act. Would my death be a judgment on me or the result of sinful action?"

"The fault would be mine alone."

"Just so. Sometimes it is the innocent who suffer the consequence of sin along with the sinner."

"But why does the Good Lord no' protect the innocents?"

"Say you tried to strike me and your knife was changed to a feather so it could not harm me, and you were held back by angels unseen so you could not reach me."

"I would say ye were miraculously protected," replied MacLaren, still not understanding why the nun pursued this course.

"Now let's say anytime anyone tried to harm another, this would be the result. What kind of world would it be?"

"A kindly one."

"Granted. But if it is no longer possible for people to sin, even sin greatly, would they still be free to choose their actions?"

Now MacLaren was beginning to understand. "Nay, they would be slaves."

"Giving people free will means giving them the power to hurt others."

MacLaren thought about this for a while in silence, the steady tapping of rain and occasional pop of the fire the only sounds in the room. "'Tis still a hard thing to be hurt by those ye trusted," MacLaren said softly.

Sister Enid's eyes were filled with compassion. "Logic may help to explain, but it rarely heals the wounds. Talk to Him about your pain," she said, motioning to a crucifix hanging on the wall behind her. "I believe He knows what it is to be betrayed." The nun stood up slowly and shuffled from the room.

MacLaren spent a long time staring at the image on the wall. When he finally sought his bed, he felt, if not peace, at least a calm that had evaded him for a long time. He fell immediately into a deep sleep.

Aila raised her hood against the rain and bent over, trying to shield her face, and blindly followed the man ahead of her. They had plodded along, traveling northeast, and had crossed out of Graham territory. The rain was relentless, and Aila was soaked and shivering. She tried to think of a way to escape, but with riders ahead of her, thick brush on either side, and a crossbow at her back, there was little chance of that. By the time hail started pounding her head, she did not care where they were going; she just wanted to get there soon.

Thunder rumbled, ominous in the distance. Aila recalled the story of Esther, the inspiration for her decision to return to Dundaff, but could not recall any point where Esther was kidnapped. The whole situation was unbelievable. What did McNab think he was doing? She remembered him as a lad, not much older than her brother. She had seen him several times at different fairs her mother had liked to attend when Aila was a girl. Aila had many happy memories of going to the fairs, her mother strutting about on her father's arm, looking resplendent in her finery. Of course that was before the illness crippled Lady Graham and she had taken residence in the south tower, never to leave.

The Archie McNab she remembered was a skinny kid with black, scraggly hair and hungry eyes. He often followed along behind the other children, watching silently as the other children played, never joining the group and never being invited. Everyone knew the McNabs were late to join Robert the Bruce and had been punished for their lack of patriotism. Most of the clans, the Grahams included, had nothing to do with the McNabs, though in fact they were neighbors. The clans had never fought with each other, perhaps because the difference in power between the clans was substantial. What could McNab possibly be thinking?

Even after the scourge at Neville's Cross, surely her father had enough soldiers to devastate whatever forces McNab could muster. Yet, to be honest, she had no idea what kind of numbers that would be or even how many warriors her father currently had. She knew very few returned, but after hearing of the fall of her brother, she had not paid heed to the rest. Was her clan really in such a dire state they could no longer protect themselves from the likes of McNab?

Aila was relieved when they reached the clearing of a small hamlet. Men circled around to have some sort of meeting as another horseman rode up to take her reins. She strained to listen to the conversation but could hear nothing over the thunder and pounding rain. A decision made, the men dismounted and began to lead their horses to the village stables situated next to an inn. She breathed a sigh; it appeared they would stop to get out of the rain and the dark.

Her spirits rose. Surely in the public inn there would be someone she could call to for help. Her hope was short-lived. The men seemed to already have considered that possibility and led her around to the back. When she entered the servants' entrance, there was nobody to be seen but McNab's own men. She was led through the kitchen, up the back stairs, and down a dark hallway. A door was opened, and she was unceremoniously shoved across the threshold. Alone in the dark, the lock clicked behind her.

She was trapped.

Fourteen

AILA STRUGGLED TO SEE HER NEW PRISON WITH ONLY the dim light from a small window slit covered in animal skin. Feeling around with her hands and making use of occasional flashes of lightning, she discovered she was in a simple upstairs bedroom. A bed, small table, and one chair were the only furniture. Taking off her soaked cloak, she huddled in the lone chair. Firewood was laid in the stone hearth, but the men had not thought to leave a candle, so she had no way to light it. She began to shake in the chill, dark room and looked longingly at the wood. She was damp through, cold, and hungry.

After a while of waiting, she got up to ensure the door really was locked—it was. She pounded on the door and yelled for help, though she doubted anyone could hear her over the din of the storm. Still, it was worth the effort. She pounded on the floor and on both walls of her little room. Nothing. She screamed some more until her throat grew dry. Exhausted, she collapsed back into the chair, and within minutes, began to shiver.

Blankets were on the bed, but wary of her predicament, did not want to undress and get into bed. Soon, though, she was too cold to care and stripped quickly out of her kirtle, left on the linen chemise, and wrapped herself in the blankets. She refused to lie down though and sat back in the chair to await her fate. She didn't understand why she had been brought there or what McNab wanted with her. Although she did not wish for his presence, she might be able to tolerate him if he brought food and a flame.

She did not have to wait much longer. Heavy footsteps approached, the lock clicked, and McNab walked into the room, candle in hand. With gnawing resentment, she saw he had been feasting downstairs while she shivered. He was warm and dry, his face flushed. Worse, he had the smell of roasted meat, which teased her empty belly.

"Greetings, m'lady," said McNab with a mocking smile. "I pray ye find yer accommodations to yer liking?"

Aila only glared from beneath her blanket cocoon. She was warmer now, but such a greeting deserved no response.

"'Tis cold in here. Too stubborn to light a fire, are we?"

"Ye dinna leave me a flame," Aila ground out.

McNab shrugged. "Things here may no' be as comfortable as ye are used to, princess." McNab knelt by the hearth and, using his candle, lit the fire. His back turned, Aila had the sudden thought to strike him senseless and make her escape. She glanced furtively around the room, but it was practically bare. A bed, curtains, a table, a chair—the chair, that's it. Standing up without making a noise, her blankets falling to the floor, she picked up the wooden chair and took a step toward the man hunched over his work.

"That should warm us, princess," said McNab, standing quickly and turning to face her. Aila was now directly in front of him, the chair poised over her head for attack. "Well now," said McNab, taking the chair effortlessly from her hands, "ye'd no' be thinking to knock my head off, no?" Aila backed away from the man. He looked her up and down, and smiled in a cold way. "I do thank ye for dressing for our purpose, princess."

Aila tried to grab the blankets from the floor, but McNab stepped forward onto them, preventing her from pulling them up.

"What do ye want from me?" Aila's voice was so soft the words were barely audible above the roar of the storm. McNab slowly approached and heart pounded. She backed away from him until she hit the wall. He continued until he was but an inch away. She pressed into the wall, trying not to let any part of her body touch his. Not wanting to look at his face, she stared at his chest. He also was breathing fast.

"I want ye, Aila. Or more importantly, yer fortune."

"Are ye daft? My father will kill ye for holding me ransom."

"I'm not holding ye for ransom. I'm holding ye forever." McNab pressed against her and smiled when she gasped. "Ah, ye'll make a bonnie bride."

"Nay!" shouted Aila and shoved him back with all

her might. "Ye cannot marry me. I've already been wed. Ye've surely no' heard the news, but I married Sir Padyn MacLaren yester morn."

"Oh, I ken it, but no matter." He grabbed her wrists and pinned them to the wall. "I claim ye by right o' handfast, and if ye be breeding afore a year's out, ye'll be mine." He held her fast, leaning all his weight onto her wrists, holding her straight-armed against the wall.

Aila's heart beat hard and her mind spun. She must think of some escape from the situation. "Archie, listen to me." Aila tried to sound calm and reasonable. "I'm already married. Ye canna claim me. MacLaren winna take kindly to ye stealing me."

McNab frowned, but only for a moment. "And ye be sure o' that?" McNab leaned over and began planting little kisses on her forehead. She turned her face into the wall.

"He will come for me and kill ye for sure." Aila tried to sound more confident than she felt. After MacLaren's rejection of her on their wedding night, she honestly did not know what he would do or if he would even mount a rescue. Though to protect his financial interests, he most certainly would demand her return.

"If he cared so verra much, why did he no' come to ye on yer wedding night?"

Shocked, Aila turned back to him. "How did ye ken…"

Taking advantage of her open mouth, he claimed it with his, pressing hard against her lips and forcing his tongue in her mouth. Filled with revulsion and shock at the forced intimacy, Aila suddenly remembered a jewel of wisdom bestowed on her by her mother. Jerking her knee up, she slammed it as hard as she could between his legs. Archie McNab howled in pain and dropped to the floor, just as her mother said a man would. *Thanks, Mother,* she thought and fled to the unlocked door.

She opened the door and tasted freedom for but a moment before vise-like fingers closed around her arm and she was yanked back into the room. Aila flew several feet before crumpling to the floor and sliding to the opposite wall. McNab slammed the door shut and doubled over once again in pain.

"That wasna verra nice," he panted, slowly sliding down the door until he was curled into a ball on the floor. The two lay still for a few moments, struggling for breath on either side of the small room. Realizing she was more shaken than hurt, Aila climbed back into the chair. She drew the blankets around her once more, feeling more comfortable to be less revealed. She looked at the figure crumpled on the floor and remembered the skinny boy he used to be, always an outsider, always rejected. She pitied him for a moment, but remembering her current situation and his intentions, her feelings moved swiftly to revulsion. She wanted nothing more than to be away from him, away from this trap. She had nothing to fight against McNab except her wits, and she needed to think with a clear head if she had any hope of escape.

"I'm sorry if I hurt ye," said Aila, hoping to reason with the man, "but I canna agree to what ye want. Our clans have e'er been at peace wi' one another.

Kidnapping me can only end in ruin. Let me go now, and I will no' tell my father or MacLaren what ye've done."

McNab sat up with a grimace and leaned back against the door, still sitting on the floor. "What could they do to me, Aila, that has no' already been done? When Bruce made king, did he no' take most o' our land? It dinna matter most folks, including Bruce, mind ye, allied wi' the English at one point. But no, we were treated as if we were the only one."

"But how will starting a clan war help ye?"

"Was no' supposed to be," McNab shot back. "I planned it out careful. The man said Graham would give ye to me to stop the burning."

"What man?" asked Aila. Had someone put this ridiculous plan into McNab's head? McNab said nothing. Aila's mind continued to piece things together. "The fields! Are ye saying ye purposely set our fields ablaze to force Father to give me to ye?"

"Aye, lass. Good reckoning. Nice to ken our bairns will no' be daft."

"But how could ye?" cried Aila, standing up. "How could ye threaten innocent people wi' starvation?"

"How could I?" McNab repeated angrily and struggled to stand. "'Tis time ye reap what ye sow. When our land was stripped from us, our herds taken, did ye no' ken what would happen to our clan? We starved while ye feasted. We struggled while yer father built up yer fortress. Put in real glass windows, did he no'? Ye ken how many o' my clansman that would have fed?"

"If ye needed help, why did ye no' ask?"

"Ask for a handout? Ye must be daft. After we lost our land, people treated us like we was dirt." McNab walked over to Aila, his eyes gleaming with intensity, but this time, Aila stood her ground. "Did ye ken my father humbled himself and took me to see Laird Graham? My father told him I was a good lad and asked if I could foster wi' him. Yer father said he'd no' take traitorous blood in his house and kicked us out."

"I'm sorry that happened." Aila meant it sincerely. "Ye shoud'na be punished for something yer father did."

Suddenly McNab dropped to his knees before her and took her hands. "Would it be so bad, Aila, to be my wife? I have little for ye now, but once yer father dies, we shall both be rich."

Aila was at first startled and then repulsed by his declaration. "I canna marry ye. I am MacLaren's wife."

"MacLaren!" said McNab, jumping up. "That arrogant bastard, always swaggering around wi' his big sword. All the lasses used to swoon for him." Aila looked away. It was unfortunately an accurate picture of herself as a young lass. "Ye've always looked down yer nose at me. I'm no' good enough for ye, am I?" McNab's voice was chilling, and Aila craned her neck to look back up at him.

"I've ne'er looked down at ye, Archie. Ye've always been taller than me." McNab seemed seem to relax a bit, though he still stood close, holding her hands. "I ken ye be taller than MacLaren, too," added Aila, thinking a bit of flattery could not hurt her situation.

"Truly?" asked McNab, and Aila could see once

again the lonely child, if only for a moment. He shook his head, releasing her hands and slowly removing her blankets from around her. She stiffened but offered no resistance. If it came to a physical fight, she would lose. Her only hope was to reason with him. McNab replaced the blankets where she had found them and sat down on the bed. "'Tis too late now. Come here, Aila. I promise I'll be gentle wi' ye."

Aila shivered again, standing before him in naught but her undergarments. Her heart started to beat faster, and she glanced at the door, but the bed stood between her and freedom. "Dinna be a fool, I tell ye. MacLaren will kill ye for this."

"I'm disappointed by yer lack o' faith in me. But no matter. Ye simply dinna understand. I hope my plan will work for the good o' my clan, but otherwise, I dinna care. I may end up a rich man, I may end up dead on MacLaren's sword, but either way, I can say I died a man. I'm no coward, Aila, I ken my plan may no' succeed, but I'm willing to take the risk."

"But…" Aila struggled to find something to say that could change the man's mind. "Our fathers' differences need no' be ours. Let me go now, and we can still be friends."

"Ah, that's where ye're wrong. One o' the best things about this plan is no matter what the outcome, yer father will ken I bedded his daughter." With a cold smile, McNab stood and walked toward Aila. "I wish I could see the look on the auld bastard's face when he thinks about me between yer legs every night."

Aila gasped, her pulse thumping in her ears, making

it difficult to think. Behind her, the fire prevented her from retreating any farther and illuminated her through her thin chemise.

"Ye're a bonny lass. I'm going to enjoy this," he said, his gaze crawling all over her body. Fast and sure, he reached out and spun her to the wall, pinning her body with his. She tried to fight, but he held her arms firm against the wall and ground his hips against hers, preventing any repeat of her kicking him in tender areas. Innocent though she was, she could easily discern his arousal through her thin chemise. *Help!* She lifted up her desperate prayer. Tears pooled in her eyes. *Help, help, help!*

"We made a deal earlier to save yer horse. Let's make a deal again. Ye agree no' to fight me, and I take ye gentle and slow. I can give ye pleasure, Aila, like ye've ne'er kenned. Or, ye can fight me, and I'll slam ye as hard as ye slammed me. Either way, I'll be pleased. So what'll it be?"

Ait ne irascatur dominus meus quod coram te adsurgere nequeo quia iuxta consuetudinem feminarum nunc accidit mihi sic delusa sollicitudo quaerentis est.

The verse that flew to Aila's mind was odd indeed. Despite her predicament, she pondered it quickly, trying to make sense of it. It was a verse from the biblical story of Rachel, who, not wanting to have her camel searched, refused to dismount, saying it was her time of the month.

"Make up yer mind, sweetheart," McNab murmured as he nuzzled her hair.

"My courses!" shouted Aila.

"What?" McNab jerked back.

"Ye canna take me now. 'Tis my, well… that's why MacLaren coud'na come to me last night, ye ken?"

"Oh." McNab frowned and took another step back. "Aye, that makes sense." Aila held her breath while McNab rubbed his beard and glared at her. He twisted his face, looking disgusted. "I dinna want ye now. Ye'll have to wait to please yer new laird. Besides, 'twill be better for me to bed ye first when we reach home. 'Tis no' like ye're going anywhere," said McNab, as if the delay was his idea.

"Aye, sir," replied Aila meekly, trying not to show her utter relief.

"Dinna forget, I claimed ye as my bride. Ye be mine now, so spend yer night thinking of ways to please yer new master." McNab exited the room with quick strides and locked the door behind him.

Exhausted, Aila collapsed into the chair. She wrapped her arms around herself and started to shake again, which this time had nothing to do with being cold. Despite her current situation, she could not help smiling. Men. Her mother had been right about another thing. They did fear a women's time of the month. It seemed rather silly to her, but she was not complaining. Her falsehood had bought a reprieve, but it would not last for long.

Fifteen

AILA WOKE EARLY THE NEXT MORNING, A HABIT BORN from years of early morning rides. While still wrapped in her blankets, she almost convinced herself this was all a horrible dream. But when the remnants of sleep left her, it was painfully obvious she was still locked in the small room in the inn, her maid snoring beside her. Senga had been allowed into her room shortly after McNab left. Aila had been relieved that Senga was flushed and smelled of wine and meat, so at least she had been fed and warmed. Aila was further grateful her maid had brought food with her. Her meal consisted of naught but porridge, but Aila had been happy for it.

Aila looked around her small prison, with a growing sense of panic. She knew once McNab got her to his fortress, there would be no chance for freedom, and her ploy last night would not stall him much longer. Unless someone rescued her, she might indeed become McNab's wife. Since her marriage to MacLaren was never consummated, if McNab claimed her by handfast and she conceived within a year, she

was caught. A slimy feeling slithered over her. McNab
would certainly do his part to ensure she would be with
child as soon as possible. Motivated by this unhappy
thought, Aila got out of bed and tried the door again.
It remained locked, just like the last half-dozen times
she had checked. She wandered around the small
room, seeking a way to escape. Finding nothing once
again, she sighed and sat down in the chair.

Remembering Sister Enid's words, Aila closed her
eyes and breathed deeply, focusing on her breath.
There must be an escape.

Aut quomodo dicis fratri tuo sine eiciam festucam de oculo
tuo et ecce trabis est in oculo tuo.

"Small is the gate and narrow the road that leads to
life, and only a few find it," she murmured. Standing,
she searched the room again, repeating, "Small is the
gate." She took another look at the window covered
in animal skin. With sudden excitement, she ripped
the skin from the window and tried to peer outside.
The opening was a rectangular slit cut high into the
stone wall. She grabbed a chair to stand on and was
able to stick her head through the hole.

Aila breathed deep. The air was refreshingly sweet
with the fresh smell of rain in the orange light of
dawn. Her room must be in the back of the inn,
since her window faced nothing but thick forest. Aila
squiggled forward a bit more until she was able to
see down. It was a straight drop for two stories. She
experimented with different positions and found if she
turned sideways, she might be able to fit her shoulders
through. Yet emerging head first out of the second-
floor window had fatal repercussions, so she wriggled

back in to consider her options. Casting her eye on the blankets covering her sleeping maid, Aila had an idea.

"Wake up, Senga. I ken a way to escape."

❧

MacLaren woke early and roused his men before the sun broke through the early morning mist. He was impressed when the Graham warriors joined his men to break their fast at this early hour without complaint. Some differences between the two groups of men were plainly evident. Many of MacLaren's men wore their traditional Highland garb, while Graham's men wore mainly breeches and tunics. Of course, Chaumont was the best dressed of the lot, happily chatting at Warwick, who made little effort at continuing the conversation.

MacLaren ate quietly and took the measure of the Dundaff warriors. Graham's soldiers may have been few in comparison to the lands they defended, but they were proud and well-disciplined. Graham's men, Pitcairn and Warwick, were able leaders. Pitcairn was meticulous in his person, neat and orderly. He was observant, watching those around him with a shrewd eye. MacLaren doubted there was much this man failed to notice. Warwick was a large man, gruff in speech and not above meting out physical punishment if he felt his men would benefit from the lesson. He was also abundantly equipped with weaponry. Besides the claymore at his back, he had a thrusting sword at his left side and a mace at his right. Strapped across his chest were several daggers, a war hammer, and an axe. MacLaren had rarely seen the like. This was not a man he wished to engage in a fight.

After the basic meal, Sister Enid, supported on the arm of a younger nun, found MacLaren and wished him a safe journey.

"Thank ye, Sister, for yer counsel last eve," said MacLaren sincerely.

"May you find the peace you seek."

MacLaren nodded. Something had shifted last night, though he would have difficulty saying what. He no longer felt consumed with guilt and driven by anger. Those emotions were still present, but something else was there, too.

"Are you ready to find your skittish bride?" asked Chaumont with his usual good humor.

"Aye, let's be done wi' it," said MacLaren.

"Ladies," said Chaumont with a small bow to the two nuns, giving the younger one a sinful wink.

"Good day to you, Sir Knight," responded Sister Enid, giving Chaumont a wink in return.

The whole party left St. Margaret's by dawn while the sky was still grey. The rain had stopped, but the ground was wet and muddy from its torrent, and thick mist settled in the low places. They cantered along the main road back to Dundaff, the horses kicking up mud in their wake.

As MacLaren rode along, something white in the thick brush drew his eye. Stopping for a moment, he dismounted and pulled the sopping head cloth from the bushes.

"What have you there?" called Chaumont.

"Looks to be a woman's wimple," replied MacLaren. He turned it over and his stomach sank. Inside were several strands of long, auburn hair. "Aila," he whispered.

"What's that?" said Warwick from behind him.

MacLaren showed him and Pitcairn the wet, dirty garment. "Maybe it was Aila's."

Pitcairn frowned. "That could be from any number o' lasses. Who kens how long it has been there?"

MacLaren was going to order his men to look around, but Warwick was ahead of him. "Tracks!" the Master of Arms called from the brush. "Rain has washed them out a bit, but looks like about a dozen men rode through here heading north toward MacLaren's land or…"

"McNab's," finished MacLaren, his stomach tightening. "Let's go."

"Ye warrant the lass ha' been kidnapped?" asked Warwick, his thick brows furrowed.

"Aye, or she left the road a willing party."

'I doubt it," said Chaumont, examining the wimple. "From the amount of her hair she left behind, I warrant this was torn from her head."

Warwick gave quick commands to his men, proving to be an able leader accustomed to instant obedience. A lad was sent back to Dundaff to determine if Aila had made it back to the castle, and if not, to inform Graham of their suspicions. The rest of the party moved to follow the tracks. Warwick proved to be an able tracker, and MacLaren followed behind, anxious to find his bride. He cursed himself for taking his rest while Aila might be in mortal danger. Yet doubt nagged him, and he wondered if the scene pointed to a kidnapping or a conspiracy. Perhaps Aila had been plotting with McNab all along, trying to force her father's hand to allow her to marry him. MacLaren shook his head. He was not sure what to think, but as time went by, he grew increasingly impatient to find his bride. *Let her be safe*, he prayed, turning to God for the first time since the day of his cousin's death.

Graham sat alone. He had been informed that Aila was missing and presumed kidnapped. As furious as he was at Aila's flight to the convent, he was just as concerned for her safety now. Where was his daughter? If McNab had her... Graham growled. Someone needed to kill that traitorous bastard, McNab. He wanted to do it himself, but supposed he would have to leave the honors to MacLaren.

Sighing, Graham rubbed his injured thigh. It ached something fierce today, made worse by a sleepless night. Where was his child? He wished he had spent time with her, gotten to know her, but he had let the division between him and his wife separate him from his daughter. What a fool he had been. Aila was married now. He could not do anything for his daughter but trust her to MacLaren's care. It was MacLaren's responsibility to see to his wife. Just as it was Graham's to see to his.

Graham sighed again. Gossip had ripped through the castle. The rift between Laird Graham and his lady was common knowledge, but this time, her flouting of his authority had gone too far. Graham needed to deal with his wife. He'd rather go to war where merely steel could pierce his armor. The Lady Graham's words were sharper than any blade he had ever known and were wielded by an expert. Still, Graham was no coward. He called for a ghillie to inform Lady Graham to present herself before him and poured a glass of liquid reinforcement while he waited for his lady's arrival.

Presently, a nervous ghillie returned. The lady was not coming, Graham was informed. If Graham wanted to see her, he would have to come himself. Graham's response was extreme, even for a short-tempered man. Bellowing, he hurled his large frame to his lady's quarters, cursing across the bailey and yelling even louder from the pain in his leg with every step up the tower stairs. His reaction gained him much attention from his clan, and many waited around the base of the tower, anxious to hear what he would do to his lady.

"Leave us!" Graham thundered to Lady Graham's maids as he barged into the room, knocking over two delicate tables. The maids were gone before the furniture hit the floor. "Ye've gone too far this time, madam. I swear ye'll regret yer disrespect to yer master."

Moira Graham stared at him from her high-backed chair. She was pale but met his gaze, defiant to the end. "What have I done, my lord, to be rewarded with such venom?"

"What have ye done? Ye sent Aila to the convent, did ye no'? Ye tried to have the marriage annulled!"

"Aye," said Moira, her eyes flashing. "I've taken care o' our daughter, even if ye could no' be bothered wi' the task."

"Och, ye've taken care o' her t'be sure," Graham snarled back, pounding over to her and glaring down. "I arranged her marriage with MacLaren to protect Dundaff, to protect all o' us from starvation.

'Tis McNab burning the fields, trying to get me to give him Aila, ye ken? But I forged an alliance with MacLaren to protect us from that bastard McNab so we can have enough grain to feed the clan." Graham grabbed his wife by her shoulders and hauled her to her feet. "Now Aila's gone, kidnapped, thanks to ye," shouted Graham, shaking his wife. It was too much for Lady Graham, whose feet could find no purchase, and she fell into her angered husband, taking them both to the floor. Both Laird and Lady Graham yelled out in anger and pain, giving the castle dwellers below much to discuss.

"Damnation, woman!" Graham hollered as he reached for her hands to drag her back up. Something felt wrong. He held up her hands to the light, revealing the bony disfigurement. It had a chilling effect on his anger. He held her hands for a long time, saying nothing. Lady Graham closed her eyes and waited.

"Yer feet, too?"

Lady Graham nodded.

"How long?"

Moira opened her eyes and stared at him before answering, "Fifteen years." She blinked away tears and her lips trembled for an instant until she pressed them into a thin line.

"Why did ye hide it from me?"

"I'd rather no' face yer disinterest or yer pity," said Moira, snatching back her hands. "Where be my daughter?"

Graham shook his head. "I dinna ken. I believed ye locked yerself up here because ye were displeased wi' me. Were ye?"

This time Moira shook her head. "Why did ye no' tell me about McNab and MacLaren?"

"Why did ye no' tell me about yer hands?"

Husband and wife sat in silence on the floor, looking at each other as if for the first time. Indeed, it was the first time they had been in the same room for many years. Graham reached out to take her hand and persisted in his task even when she tried to pull away. Pressing the gnarled fist to his lips, he kissed the back of her hand then her wrist.

"Ye were a fool to think this little thing would make me displeased wi' ye."

Moira's eyes shone. Graham tried to stand but struggled with his injury.

"It still pains ye?" asked Moira softly.

"Aye, lass," said Graham, managing to get back into the chair and hauling his wife up into his lap. "A fine pair we are. Ah, but ye're still the beauty I married." Lady Graham returned the compliment with a smile that lit her face.

Those who waited below had a long time to wonder what was happening between their laird and lady. Just as some were suggesting they send a sacrificial lamb to check if the two still lived, Graham appeared, looking surprisingly happy for a man who had confronted his demon wife. Thus, the laird and his lady obligingly provided much conversation in all quarters.

Sixteen

SENGA WAS NOT BEING HELPFUL. AILA STRIPPED THE bed and made her preparations, while Senga hovered, questioned, and protested. Aila remained steadfast in her determination, and Senga became even more panicked.

"But, m'lady, ye canna try to escape. If they catch ye, they'll beat ye for sure and me, too." Senga's words were chilling, but Aila was determined.

"I dinna intend to be caught."

"But m'lady…," whined Senga as Aila tied the sheets and blankets together to craft a makeshift rope. "What are we going to do wi' that?"

"We're going out the window."

"Och, nay, m'lady. We'll ne'er fit."

The window slit was rather tiny. Aila stood tall and threw back her shoulders to bolster her courage. She wished Senga was a little less discouraging. The maid was harping on Aila's own fears and doubts. Yet a brief thought of her experience with McNab the night before and what would be her certain fate if she did not escape now led Aila to act with more courage than she felt.

"I dinna care if I have to strip naked and grease

myself wi' lard, I'm getting through that window," said Aila with determination.

"Aye, m'lady." Senga pouted.

"Now I'll tie off this rope, if ye can move the table next to the window." Aila turned to tie the rope to the bed, when a tremendous crash caused her to jump with surprise. The maid had somehow managed to knock over both the table and chair, sending them clattering to the floor. To make matters worse, Senga shrieked at what she had done.

"Wheesht!" hushed Aila, listening for movement below. Though McNab's men had caroused late into the night, she felt sure no one could sleep through that racket. She waited in silence for footsteps to come to the door. Fortunately, she had underestimated the amount and effect of the drink consumed. She released her breath and continued her work.

Satisfied with the arrangements, Aila turned to her maid with shades of doubt. "I'll go first to see if it can be done. If ye wish, ye may try to follow, but I release ye from all obligation to me. Do what be right for ye, wi' my blessing."

That said, Aila placed the table in front the window, the chair on the table, and stood on them. Saying a quick prayer, she grasped the rope and squeezed out of the window. It was a tight fit, but she was slender and managed to get her head free. Turning sideways, she freed her shoulders. She wrapped the makeshift rope around her hands still pinned in the window shaft and slowly wriggled out of the small opening. Yet as more of her body was freed, there was going to be a problem. She was slipping down the rope facing downward. She hoped she would not fall and break her head, but since there was no turning around at this point, she struggled to free her hips.

Her joy in her success of doing so was tempered by her gown falling down over her head. One of her mother's more colorful curses flitted through her mind. If her skirt was over her head, it was not covering what it ought, as a cool breeze across her backside made shockingly evident. She sincerely hoped no one would see her as she hung, bottom-up, outside her window.

Despite the utterly unladylike position, she continued to hang there for a moment, wondering how to extricate her legs and flip around without killing herself. Deciding there was nothing else to do but try, she pulled one leg free and blushed fiercely beneath her skirt at her indecent pose, hanging upside down, legs akimbo. She quickly pulled her other leg free and then shrieked in spite of herself as she suddenly flipped over, slid down the blanket rope, and landed with a loud "Ow!" on her rump.

Once again she froze, sure that McNab's men would come running any second. Instead, loud snoring came from the nearby window. Moving aside, Senga wriggled out the window and flipped down the rope with a good deal more grace and dignity than Aila had managed. Aila's first impulse was to run into the thick brush and hide, but she could not leave him. She could not leave Shadow behind.

"I'm going to get us some horses," Aila whispered to her maid. "Ye stay hidden."

"Nay," said Senga a little too loudly. "I'll help."

I was afraid of that.

They snuck toward the stables. Entering the wooden structure, Aila was surprised by a young milkmaid finishing her chores and carrying milk back to her mistress. Aila froze, not knowing if the girl would sound the alarm, but the young maid merely curtseyed and continued to lug her pail back to the inn.

Aila found Shadow covered with a large blue and red decorative caparison. She did not bother to take off the large horse blanket before throwing on his saddle. She wanted to be gone. It was past dawn, and though McNab was still sleeping off his drink, the rest of the small hamlet was up with the sun, going about their daily routine. She considered asking for help, but she did not know where these people's loyalties lay, so she decided it would be best to leave as quickly and quietly as possible.

Aila finished saddling Shadow and found that Senga had done nothing to saddle a horse of her own. Aila did it for her, growing more anxious every minute they remained in the village. Without warning, a long line of horses ran behind her and thundered from the barn, Senga chasing them out the doors.

"What are ye doing?" Aila cried.

"Now McNab's men will have to find their horses afore they can catch us."

"But now the villagers will surely wake McNab to tell him about his horses, and he will ken we're gone." Even now, Aila could hear the shouts of the villagers as they tried to catch the fleeing horses. "We must fly!"

Aila ran to mount her horse and bolted from the stables, her maid close behind. Any lead they might have gained through stealth had been eliminated, and Aila prayed it would take a while to round up all the horses.

They had very little time for escape. Shadow pulled against the reins, but she held him back, waiting for her maid to catch up. Even in this dire situation, the fastest speed Senga could muster was a loping trot. On Shadow Aila could easily outdistance McNab, but that would mean leaving the maid behind. Despite the risk, she could not do it. She stopped and trotted back to Senga.

"Here, give me your reins. We'll go faster that way." Senga complained but complied. Aila grabbed the reins and gave a good yank, urging Shadow forward. Shadow and the maid's mount took off at a gallop. She could have gone faster alone, but Aila smiled as they raced, happy to finally be putting distance between herself and McNab.

MacLaren was making progress. After some difficulty, the tracks became deeper in the muddy ground. They mounted and followed the trail through the dense forest at a quick pace. Breaking through the trees, they came to a bluff overlooking the valley below just as the sun chased away the dense fog. MacLaren could discern the small village of Kimlet in the distance and two figures trotting toward them on the main path out of town.

Reaching a clearing, one of the figures turned her head into the sunlight. MacLaren drew a sharp breath. It was Aila. His wife and another woman were going for what looked like a leisurely stroll. He held onto the reins with a death grip and watched his wife stop, take the reins of the other woman's horse, and gallop up the sloping hill toward them. His fear of Aila being kidnapped was replaced with fear of her complicity into her own disappearance. No one looked at MacLaren.

"I'll retrieve the Lady Aila," said Warwick in his low, gravelly voice.

"Nay, she's my wife. I'll do it," said MacLaren. Since she was headed toward them, it wouldn't be difficult to abduct the woman back to Dundaff. Damned miserable excuse for a wife. Perhaps he'd drag her back to the nunnery and demand an annulment himself.

He dismounted and hid in the brush, motioning the men to do the same. No sense giving her an opportunity to escape again. He climbed a low tree branch and waited for her to reach him. She was moving with speed now, and he would have to jump quickly. Flying through the air, he knocked Aila clear from her mount, and she landed on her stomach in the mud. Despite his anger, he was careful not to crush her and hauled her up to her feet. Without warning, she spun around, smacking MacLaren on the jaw with her closed fist.

"Ow!" said MacLaren.

"Oh!" said Aila.

"You left yourself open for that one," said Chaumont. He caught the horses' reins, gentled the spooked animals, and handed the maid down.

"I dinna expect her to hit me," complained MacLaren.

"I imagine she didn't expect you to knock her from her horse," returned Chaumont.

"Then she shoud'na have run away."

"I dinna run away," protested Aila, trying unsuccessfully to wrench from MacLaren's grip on her arm. "Well, I did, but then I was kidnapped and—"

"Ye look mighty free to me," interrupted MacLaren.

"I was escaping, and I need to tell ye—"

"Looked more like an easy stroll."

"Pray, sir, if ye will listen to me."

"I've no need for a woman's lying tongue," MacLaren bit out, his anger barely restrained.

Aila gasped. "But I need to tell ye that—"

"McNab's men are approaching!" came the shout from Warwick.

"That's what I was trying to—" But MacLaren wasn't listening and shoved her toward several of his men.

"Take her back and watch her close. Dinna let her escape again." Without looking back, MacLaren and Chaumont ran into the dense forest to meet their enemy.

MacLaren chased after McNab's men, but on their own land, they had the advantage and hid well, attacking suddenly with stealth and then disappearing back into the forest. Hours passed playing this frustrating game and McNab was nowhere to be seen. MacLaren's uncertainty of his enemy's location gave him cause for concern. He moved Aila's hiding place several times, not wanting her to be able to return to McNab but also not wanting her to be too far out of sight. He left his own men to guard her and her maid. He trusted no one else, least of all his wife.

At midday, MacLaren returned to their resting place and watched Aila from afar. The hunt for McNab had so far been unsuccessful. There had been some minor skirmishes but no significant engagements. MacLaren continued to watch Aila surreptitiously and then cursed himself for doing it. He had too many other concerns, like keeping himself and his men alive, to be worried over a traitorous female.

"I have a job for ye, my friend," MacLaren said to Chaumont. "We are dangerously close to the border tween my land and McNab's. We left Creag an Turic wi' scant defenses. I would be obliged if ye would take Toby and Rorke and check on the welfare o' the clan. I would be grieved to find they had been attacked whilst I chased shadows in the trees."

"Certainly, I will see to their welfare and report back directly."

"Be sure to see to the safety o' Lady Patrick." MacLaren felt a particular burden to see to the welfare of his cousin's widow.

Chaumont nodded with a smile. Chaumont also treated Mary with particular regard, though MacLaren doubted his motives were the same.

"And I'd like ye to take this to the Lady Patrick. 'Tis her portion o' the rents." MacLaren held out a bag of coin. When Chaumont just stared at it, MacLaren took Chaumont's hand, stuffed the bag into his palm, and turned to walk away.

"Wait!" called Chaumont. "I thought you weren't collecting rents this year."

"I'm not. But that doesna mean Mary is no' due her share."

Chaumont shrugged and was gone. MacLaren went back to watching Aila, all the while pretending he was not watching Aila. Aggravating lass. What on earth was he going to do with her? Several charming ideas slid into his head, most of them involving little to no clothing. She was a deceiving wench, treacherous to the core, but his cock didn't seem to mind at all.

Seventeen

Mary Patrick tended the fire over which mutton was roasting on a stake. It had been three seasons since the return of her laird, MacLaren, and the sword of her husband. It hung now on the wall, a silent and daily reminder James Patrick would never return. Somehow the news had not been unexpected. Jamie had been the love of her life, yet his memory had faded over the five years he had been gone. She accepted that she would never again set eyes on her husband. She also could not help but notice that although MacLaren was generous to her family, he avoided all talk of his deceased cousin and seemed to go out of his way to avoid her. The clan's preferential yet awkward treatment of her had given rise to new questions, and shadows of doubt crept into her mind.

A knock on the door made Mary jump up from her stool and chased away her musings. Smoothing her apron with her hands, she opened the door to find Chaumont smiling down at her. The French knight's arrival with MacLaren last year had caused quite a stir within the clan. He was a tall, trim knight, impeccably dressed in a blue silk doublet over a tailored linen shirt. His brown woolen hose fit snugly on his legs, leaving no doubt as to his muscular physique. A dirk, sheathed in an ornately engraved case, hung at his side. All this Mary noticed with a glance, but she was captivated by his face. His light brown hair was trimmed short, and his deep blue eyes twinkled merrily. Mary looked up at his square jaw, long nose, and chiseled features that were handsome almost to the point of being bonnie. He was different than any man she had ever seen in the Highlands.

He was gorgeous.

"Good day, Lady Patrick. I hope this day finds you well." The French knight spoke in a smooth voice with a hint of a French accent, which was at once charming and seductive. Everyone seemed enchanted with Chaumont. Children loved him, men respected him, and many a lass had set their cap to marrying the handsome young man. Mary swallowed hard, instantly conscious of his beauty and poise. She felt rather common and dull in contrast. A few moments of awkward silence followed. Chaumont's easy smile faded and he continued to look at her in expectation.

"Och, aye." Mary said, remembering herself. "Do please come in."

"Thank you kindly," Chaumont replied with a generous smile and followed Mary Patrick into the main room of the farmhouse.

Chaumont looked around Mary's homey domain with satisfaction. Her timber home was much larger than the crofter's huts but still smaller than a true manor house. It had been well built, with a real wooden floor and hand-carved wood trim. The main room boasted a large stone hearth and a long wooden table with benches on either side. In one corner was a steep, open staircase, more akin to a ladder, which went up through a hole in the ceiling to what must be a loft. On the side of the room, an open doorway led to the kitchen in which mutton was roasting over another fireplace. Around the room was evidence of work: a spinning wheel, a loom, reeds for weaving baskets. It had a nice feel, and Chaumont had an odd sense he had come home. This was particularly strange, since Mary's home was nothing like any place he'd ever lived.

"MacLaren asked me to see you regarding some business—" Chaumont began.

"Chaumont!" Mary's son, Gavin, came running through the side door and straight to Chaumont. He stopped short of where Chaumont was standing, and for a moment, looked like he wanted to embrace the legs of the tall knight. He settled for a bow instead, which Chaumont graciously returned.

"Tell me about fighting the English! Did ye e'er get hurt? Did ye ride in tourneys?

"Now, Gavin, dinna be bothering Sir Chaumont," chastised Mary.

"No bother at all," said Chaumont with a smile.

"Faith, sir, I'll wager ye have more pressing matters to attend to."

"Not at all, I assure you," said Chaumont, thinking of MacLaren's search for McNab in the brush. MacLaren could take care of himself; this place was much more hospitable. Gavin took his hand and led him to the bench by the table. When they were both seated, Chaumont began to answer the boy's questions, helping himself to some warm bread and fresh cream butter Mary thoughtfully provided. He could stay here all day.

"Let's see. Fighting the English was always hard work, quite a formidable foe. Yes I've been injured, but by God's grace, never seriously. And yes, I've competed in tournaments."

"I warrant ye were the best." Gavin gazed at his hero with shining eyes.

"I was tolerable, but did you know MacLaren never lost at the joust?"

Gavin's eyes widened. "Ne'er? He must ha' been champion in all o' France."

Chaumont smiled. "He was well known in Gascony, at least. As for champion, there was another knight who was also undefeated in the lists. He was called the Golden Knight because of his beautiful armor. Yet every time he and MacLaren were set to compete, something prevented the match. Once, the Golden Knight withdrew before the tourney due to injury. Another time, MacLaren was forced to withdraw because he was needed to hold a town against the English."

"Who was this Golden Knight?" It was Mary who asked the question, caught up in the story.

"No one knew. Sometimes nobles would fight without benefit of title or name, else their competitors, many of whom owed them liege, would withdraw rather than fight their lord."

"Did my father compete in the tourneys?" Gavin asked.

"Yes," Chaumont replied in a soft voice. "There were few who could best him with a sword."

"How did he die?" Gavin asked the question in a matter-of-fact sort of way. The room was quiet, the question hung heavy in the air.

"He was shot with an arrow from a distance. Caught him in the gap of the armor at the neck." There was more silence as this new information was absorbed by Mary and her son. "James Patrick was one of the best men and strongest fighters I've ever known. Here now, let me see your arm." Gavin raised his arm up for Chaumont's inspection, which Chaumont felt from his wrist to his shoulder, giving him a hard squeeze. "Just as I thought. You favor him, strong in the arms. You'll make a fine knight, just like your father."

Gavin beamed. "Will ye learn me to use a sword?"

"Certainly." A small sound from Mary made him quickly add, "With your mother's permission of course."

"Go now, Gavin, and tend to yer chores," said Mary in a soft voice.

Gavin opened his mouth to protest, but with one look at his mother, he changed his words to, "Aye, Mother," and trudged out the door.

"Thank ye for yer kind words to my son."

"Think nothing of it. Only spoke the truth," Chaumont replied.

"He be at an age where he misses no' having a man about the house."

Chaumont turned to face Mary, who sat next to him

on the bench. She was still relatively young though past the full bloom of youth. He would guess her age to be mid-twenties, about his own age. Her features were pretty, but she had the sturdy, confident look of a woman who had managed an estate and raised a son alone for many years. A fresh glow graced her cheeks, and her lips were full and red. Unlike many married ladies Chaumont had known who adorned their hair with elaborate head coverings, Mary's wavy brown hair was simply pulled back and tied, not with a ribbon, but a leather thong. She was of average build, with an ample bosom and a curvy figure even the plain brown linen kirtle could not hide. Chaumont smiled at her. He doubted her home would remain without a man much longer.

"I'd be happy to teach the boy any of my skills, but first let me acquit myself of the duty MacLaren has pressed upon me." Chaumont drew forth the bag of coin and set it on the table. "Your share of the rents, m'lady."

"Thank ye kindly." Mary's smile fading as she looked the bag. "I kenned MacLaren was no' collecting rents this year."

"Well, not as such." Chaumont shifted on the bench. He was afraid she might ask about this. "But MacLaren says you're still owed your due."

"MacLaren…" Mary still contemplated the bag of coin. An uneasy silence followed. Mary reached for the bag and clenched it so hard her knuckles turned white, before dropping it back to the table. "MacLaren has been quite concerned for my comfort but also quite content to ne'er speak to me. Everyone is verra kind yet…" She looked at Chaumont with a determined intensity that caused him to shift again and give a furtive glance at the door. "I ken there be something I'm no' being told." Mary reached out and touched his hand as it rested on the table. Their eyes met. "I need ye to tell me the truth. What were the circumstances o' my husband's death?"

Chaumont shifted on the bench again. "As I said, he died in battle."

"Aye, so ye said, but I ken there be more. Please, ye must tell me what it is. Did he die a coward? Did he dishonor the clan? All the warriors that returned wi' MacLaren ken it, I can see it in their eyes when they speak to me. They'll ne'er tell me, so ye must." Mary lowered her voice to a whisper. "Did he take up wi' another women? Is he no' really dead, but ye made up the story to protect me from the truth? Can ye no' see, 'tis driving me mad. I can take the bree wi' the bram. Please tell me the whole truth."

Shocked and concerned, Chaumont reached over and took both of Mary's hands in his own. "Dear lady, you must not trouble yourself so. Your husband was a brave man and fierce warrior. He would no more dishonor his clan than he would be unfaithful to your marriage." Chaumont sighed, knowing he must tell her yet still wishing the task had fallen to another. "But you are right there is something you have not been told, though it applies to MacLaren, not to you or your late husband.

"MacLaren fell in love and was engaged to be married to a French countess," Chaumont continued. "To defend her, he made war against three English captains. We were victorious, but your husband, brave to the end, fell in the battle. MacLaren returned to his lady with heavy heart only to find the countess had deceived him and merely used his protection to gain better terms in submitting to English rule. Because he succumbed to her deceit, he blames himself for Patrick's death."

Silence filled the house and Mary stared at him with unseeing eyes.

Uncomfortable with the oppressive quiet ringing in his ears, Chaumont continued to speak. "Though in hindsight, had we not been in Gascony to protect the countess, we probably would have joined the French at Crecy. Personally, that is one battle I'm glad we missed. The English won the day, and hundreds of French knights were put to the sword. Likely us, too, had we joined the fray."

Mary closed her eyes. "So my Jamie is really gone."

"It grieves me to say, but yes."

❧

Mary sat on the wooden bench next to Chaumont. Finally, someone had told her the truth. The truth was her husband was dead. Tears slipped without warning, though she did not know if the emotion was grief over losing her husband or relief there was not some dark secret about his character. Without quite knowing how it happened, she found herself in Chaumont's arms, holding onto him as if he was her one line of safety in a perilous sea. She pressed her face into his chest, trying unsuccessfully to stop the tears. He stroked her hair and murmured something in French that sounded comforting. His compassion only made her cry harder.

When her tears subsided, she attempted to release him, embarrassed for her behavior, but he seemed unwilling to let her go. She sighed and relaxed into the embrace, feeling the warmth of his body and taking momentary comfort in being held. The moment ended, and she was flooded anew with shame at her actions with this man she barely knew.

"I'm so sorry," she said, disentangling herself from his arms, her cheeks burning. "What must ye think o' me?" She avoided his eyes, afraid to see judgment, or worse, mockery.

"I think you are a lady of integrity who is not easily fooled by the deception of others."

Chaumont's brilliant blue eyes were fixed on hers. The feeling of embarrassment subsided and was replaced with another emotion, harder to name but equally intense.

"I know you to be a lady of honor," Chaumont continued. "You remained here on MacLaren land whilst others fled. That is why the clansmen give you honor. Because you stayed true. True to your husband. True to your clan. They give you nothing that isn't your due."

Heat flooded her face and she shook her head, overwhelmed by Chaumont's words. "Faith, sir, I deserve no such praise. I am only a poor farmer's daughter. Ye call me 'lady' based on the actions o' my husband. 'Tis an odd thing, too. I wasna called that whilst he was alive, since I dinna ken he was knighted 'til ye all returned. And truly, I stayed here no' for my great virtue but because I had nowhere else to go." Chaumont's eyes never wavered from hers, and his attention flustered her.

"I am a bastard by birth," said Chaumont slowly leaning closer to Mary. "Named for the place of my mother's death, I haven't even a proper family name. Would you strip my spurs because of it?"

"Nay, sir!" Mary unconsciously leaned closer. "Ye are truly a knight if e'er there was one."

"And you are more a lady than any I've met who shares the title." He was very close now, their lips just a whisper apart.

"Me mutton's burnin'!" Mary jumped from the bench and fled to the kitchen. When out of sight, she leaned against the kitchen wall, hand on her chest, and took several deep breaths to clear her head. *He's just over friendly*, she reminded herself. *And ye are a lonely, auld widow. Ye got little chance o' winning his affection, so dinna become one o' his lovesick fools*. After a few more calming breaths, she stepped back into the main room, the mutton, which actually was burning, utterly forgotten.

"Well now," said Mary, keeping her distance and trying unsuccessfully to appear at ease. "I thank ye kindly for yer… kindness. I winna keep ye from yer work."

Standing, Chaumont bowed low at the waist. "Good day to you, my lady."

It was several minutes after he quit the house before Mary remembered to curtsey.

Walking back up the hill to Creag an Turic, Chaumont stopped and turned to look down at the home of Lady Patrick. He stood for a minute, then ran his fingers through his hair and shook his head. He walked all the way back to the tower house with a smile on his face. Collecting his companions,

Chaumont mounted his destrier and rode back to find MacLaren. His smile never dimmed.

❧

MacLaren was tired of playing games with McNab. He had chased him throughout the day, had a few brief clashes with some of his clansmen, but never found McNab himself. It had been a fruitless, irritating day, made worse by the continuous distraction of his traitorous wife. MacLaren concealed himself in the forest and leaned against the rough bark of a tree, watching Aila. The lady was mumbling strange words, seemingly unaware of the men around her.

"What is she doing?" Chaumont asked.

MacLaren had his blade to his friend's throat before he realized who had spoken. "Chaumont," he grunted and resheathed his sword, focusing his attention back on his wife. "I dinna ken. She's been like that all day."

"Perhaps you hit her harder than you intended."

MacLaren shook his head. "I dinna even ken what language she's at now."

Chaumont listened for a moment. "Greek," he said definitively. "I recall it from my days at the Abbey. You've married an educated lady, at least."

"Aye. Whether she's right in the head is another matter."

"Touched or not, I rather like her."

"Like her? She ran away wi' McNab!"

"You don't know the truth of that. Perhaps you should ask her what happened."

"Humph," snorted MacLaren and stomped off to

finish preparations to leave. He had decided to pull back, since the light was fading, and he wanted to be off McNab's land before making camp for the night.

Soon they were all mounted and on their way. Some of Graham's men acted as rear guard. MacLaren trusted them to do that much, but those guarding Aila were his own men. With Rory in charge, he was confident Aila would not be able to escape. He led the party at a quick pace. He wanted to get back to Graham lands and find a safe place to make camp. His men needed rest and he felt safer in the woods than going back to Dundaff.

Finding a sheltered spot near a stream, they made camp with the efficiency of men accustomed to a soldier's life. Though they had not brought provisions, MacLaren's men were familiar with living off the land, and soon a variety of game had been caught and roasted over an open fire.

Throughout the meal, MacLaren watched Aila from afar, noting how much she ate and how she interacted with the men. She looked a little worse for wear. Her gown was torn and covered in grime, her thick hair she had tried to plait into one long braid down her back, but it stuck out in all directions. Yet she held her head high and her eyes blazed. Both his warriors and the ones from Dundaff treated her with the utmost respect, and she them, which pleased him. Dirty as she was, she was still beautiful.

MacLaren shook his head. It was best not to think that way. She had betrayed him, like he had feared she would. She had made her feelings toward him perfectly clear by refusing to dine with him on their wedding night and running away the next day. His stomach churned to think of being married to such a woman, yet they had made their decision. She had agreed to the marriage, and it had been blessed by the Church. There was only one thing left to do, and regardless of what either of them thought about the situation, it needed to be done tonight.

Eighteen

AILA FOUND HER "RESCUE" FROM MCNAB TO BE quite disappointing. She and her maid were taken on horseback by four of MacLaren's warriors and "guarded" all day long. The soldiers were exceedingly polite, professional, and watched her every movement. Different emotions pulsed through her as she waited for a chance to speak with her new husband. At first, she dreaded seeing him again. His behavior had been so cutting, perhaps her mother was right, and he would be cruel to her once she was in his power. Every time he returned, MacLaren completely ignored her, refusing even to acknowledge her existence, referring to her when speaking to others only as "her." As the day slowly passed, irritation crept in, and soon her anger overwhelmed her fear. After all she had been through in the past few days, to be treated with utter disrespect and accused of running off with McNab was unbearable.

The sun sank low in the sky and with it sank Aila's hopes of making it back to Dundaff that evening. She attempted to stay centered and calm, focusing on her breath or conjugating a variety of calming words. Closing her eyes, she sat on the fallen tree stump provided for her to rest and worked through "peace" then "calm" then "serenity." When Latin failed her, she moved to Italian and then tried to recall what little she knew of Greek and Hebrew. It was of dubious comfort.

When the light started to fade, the entire group moved south and made camp for the night. Aila gratefully accepted the meat provided. At this point, she did not care what was roasting on the stick; she ate ravenously. She met briefly with Warwick and Pitcairn and told them of her kidnap and escape. MacLaren's watchers and the tall French knight, who had gallantly introduced himself as Chaumont, stood nearby. The men listened to her tale without comment, which she appreciated, since explaining why she was out of the castle in the first place was difficult.

While Aila felt more relaxed to be among her own kin, she noticed Senga was not. The maid appeared nervous throughout the day, and when the men came back to camp, she looked increasingly frightened. Aila did not wish to falsely accuse, but her suspicions about her maid had been raised. Having the day to think on her situation, Aila recalled the courier Senga had spoken to prior to their leaving the convent. Could she have given him a message to take to McNab? When the men gave the women a brief moment alone by the stream to prepare for the night, Aila took seized the opportunity.

"Are ye working for McNab?" Aila asked, her voice soft.

Senga looked up at her mistress, clearly surprised, but did not try to hide the truth and nodded.

"Why?"

"I'm sorry, m'lady. It was ne'er supposed to be like this, but now I'm afraid no' to do what he says."

"If ye fear McNab, we can protect ye."

"Nay, no' him, m'lady."

"Then whom do ye fear?" Aila asked, her pulse quickening. Did Senga know the identity of the man McNab had mentioned? Was there a traitor within Dundaff? Aila walked closer to Senga, whispering, "Is there one at Dundaff who has betrayed Graham to McNab?"

Senga nodded, wide-eyed.

"Tell me who." Aila was unsuccessful in her attempt to keep the edge from her voice.

Senga shook her head, unsure.

"I will protect ye." Though Aila knew her present situation did not give her much credence for authority. "But ye must tell me who it is."

"Come now, that's long enough," called a male voice. Aila's chance to speak with her maid ended abruptly with the return of MacLaren's soldiers.

Aila and her maid were taken to the edge of the camp where a bedroll had been prepared. Aila expected to sleep there with her maid and hoped to query her more during the night. Instead, Senga was told to stay, and Aila was led on through a maze of men bedding down for the night to the center of camp. MacLaren was waiting for her. To her embarrassment, she realized he expected her to sleep next to him. Not wanting to create a scene, she gingerly sat on the ground.

"Here," said MacLaren patting the side of his tartan bedroll.

"I'd rather sleep wi' my maid," said Aila nervously.

"Ye'll be safer here."

Aila doubted that. MacLaren was still wearing his linen tunic, but since his tartan was now being used as his bedroll, she guessed he was wearing nothing beneath the blanket. His shoulder-length hair hung down around his face, and he watched her with cold eyes. "And take off that kirtle. It's covered in filth."

"'Tis yer fault if it is," Aila snapped, her eyes flashing.

MacLaren shrugged. "Take it off."

"Nay." Aila glanced around, saying in a whisper, "Yer men will see me."

"Turn away now," called MacLaren in a loud voice, and the men obligingly turned their backs on the couple.

"But ye…" added Aila in a small voice.

MacLaren gave her a hard look and also turned around. Taking advantage of her privacy, Aila loosed her stays and pulled off the dirty kirtle, something she had wanted to do all day. She kept on the linen chemise and pulled her cloak over her as a blanket. Edging onto a small amount of MacLaren's tartan, she lay down with her back to MacLaren, trying not to think of what part of his body the cloth she lay on had covered during the day.

MacLaren wrapped his arm around her and drew her to him. She gasped, enveloped by his heat. He pulled her closer, and for a moment, she wanted to sink back into him, feeling his warmth and his strength. Recalling his treatment of her, she pulled away.

"What are ye doing?" she whispered.

"Putting my arm around ye... wife." MacLaren gently but firmly pulled her toward him so she was lying on her back beside him. He leaned over her, and slipping his hand under her cloak, he ran it along her side to her thigh and slowly began to pull up her chemise.

Aila's eyes widened and she tried to stop the upward progression of MacLaren's hand with her nightdress. "Nay. What are ye doing?" asked Aila in a fierce whisper.

MacLaren sighed. "Yer father offered ye to me in marriage. I accepted. We both took vows before the priest, vows I intend to keep. We both have a responsibility, ye to yer father, I to my men. Whatever our personal feelings on the matter may be, the marriage must be consummated."

It was fortunate Aila was already lying down, since the shock of MacLaren's statement would have laid her flat.

"Here?" squeaked Aila.

"Here."

"Now?"

"Now."

"Nay! I dinna want to," gasped Aila a little more loudly than she had intended. She could not decide what was worse, that MacLaren wanted to bed her now or that the whole camp would know it.

"Come, lass, dinna fight me. I'm yer husband." MacLaren drew her closer.

"But everyone can hear us." Aila was desperate to make him stop.

"Nay, they are all sleeping. They will no' hear a thing."

"I can hear you fine." Chaumont's rich voice floated through the darkness. "Perhaps your bride would like a little more privacy for her first time with you." Aila was utterly embarrassed at the Frenchman's words.

"Aye, Chaumont is right," came another low voice.

"Nay," came another, "'tis best a wife learns her place. If he wants to bed her now, she shoud'na fight him."

"A wife should ne'er fight against her husband."

"Aye," agreed several men.

"But then a husband should not be giving his wife a reason to fight him on her wedding night," said Chaumont again.

"That's enough," shouted MacLaren.

"Lady Aila has always been a good lass. If she's fighting him, I warrant MacLaren's doing something wrong." Aila recognized the voice as belonging to one of her father's men at arms, and she blushed down to her toes.

"'Tis been a while for our laird. Maybe he's out of practice."

"My wife likes her shoulders rubbed. Ha' ye tried that?"

"Ye need to woo her wi' poetry."

"Poetry? Nay, 'tis kisses a lass likes."

"Ah, but where should those kisses be placed?"

"Oh, Lord, take me now," whispered Aila and fervently hoped God would take pity on her and let the ground swallow her whole.

"As ye wish," said MacLaren and rolled on top of her.

"Nay, no' ye!" cried Aila and tried to push him away.

"Dinna hurt the Lady Aila," growled a low voice Aila knew belonged to Warwick.

"He's no' hurting her, just bedding her."

"'Tis hardly the place or the time, lad," said Pitcairn.

"That's enough!" roared MacLaren, standing and pulling Aila up with him. "Get yer cloak." MacLaren quickly wrapped his plaid around him. "Ye want privacy, I'll give ye privacy."

Aila was half led, half dragged out from the middle of camp and into the thick forest. After a short hike, MacLaren stopped in a small clearing surrounded on two sides by large rock formations. A full moon peeked over the trees. It would have been a pleasant night except for the tall Highlander glaring at her.

"Will this be acceptable to ye?" MacLaren asked the question like a statement and proceeded to once again remove his plaid and lay it on the ground for them. Before Aila could think of a response, he grabbed her cloak from her, pulled her down onto the plaid with him, and spread her cloak over them like a blanket. They lay there for a while, not touching.

"I ken ye dinna wish to be married to me," MacLaren began, his voice emotionless. "I ken ye'd rather be wi' another, but we're wed now, and we need to fulfill our responsibilities."

"Ye ken what I feel?" cried Aila, shaking with fear and anger and fatigue. "Ye ken what it is to have yer whole life change in a moment? To have everything ye thought ye understood about yer life to be suddenly, completely different?"

MacLaren said nothing but made no move to touch

her. They lay side by side, watching the moon slowly rise above the tree line.

"I ne'er meant to hurt ye, Aila." An odd tingle went through her when MacLaren said her name for the first time. "Maybe this marriage is no' what either of us wanted, but the truth is we are married now, and we must make this marriage fully legal. I dinna wish to worrit myself about ye running off to the nunnery or wi' another man. After tonight, I'll leave ye alone for a time, if ye wish it."

MacLaren rolled onto his side toward her and softly ran his hand down her side and slowly started to pull up her chemise once again.

"Nay," Aila whispered and tried to push his hand away.

"It would be easier for ye if ye calm yerself and dinna fight me."

"Now I understand ye," said Aila sarcastically even as she shook with fear. "This is the part where ye threaten to hurt me if I dinna lie still."

"What?" MacLaren stopped immediately.

"We can do it gently or no'. Either way, ye'll enjoy yerself. Is that right? Yer just like McNab."

"What did he do to ye?" MacLaren's voice was chilling.

"He tried to… he wanted to… What do ye care?" Aila sputtered, and tears began to run down her face. "Oh, I ken, ye want to know if I may be carrying his child. Well, nay, ye need no' worrit about that. But even if I told ye I was still a maid, ye woud'na believe me. So go ahead, do whatever ye like, I dinna care anymore." Aila turned away from him and sobbed.

MacLaren watched helplessly as Aila cried, wondering what he was supposed to do. He had heard the report that Aila had been kidnapped and how she escaped, yet trust came slowly. Her virginity was rather easily proven, and her lack of understanding in these matters only confirmed her innocence. He patted her awkwardly on the shoulder. He did not know what to do with a crying lass.

"Did ye go willingly wi' McNab?" he asked, trying to sound gentle.

"Nay," Aila answered him through her tears.

"Did he…" MacLaren shifted his position. "Did he try to take yer maidenhood by force?"

"Aye." Aila sobbed anew.

MacLaren's anger burned. When he caught McNab, he would make his death slow and painful. "Tell me ev'ry body part o' his that touched ye, and I'll cut it off and make him eat it before I kill the whoreson." Aila stopped crying and turned to him, hiccupping in a way that almost sounded like a laugh.

"Truly?"

"Truly, m'lady. I'll kill the bastard any way ye like."

Aila tried without success to suppress a smile. "'Tis uncharitable to wish another's death."

"Then I have lived a verra uncharitable life."

Husband and wife looked at each other for a long moment, married yet still strangers to each other.

"What are ye going to do wi' me now?" Aila asked quietly.

MacLaren gave a heavy sigh and rolled onto his back. "I will no' force ye, if that's what ye're asking."

"Do ye mean that?"

MacLaren propped back up on his elbow and looked at her. "I swear to ye on the grave o' my father, I will no' force ye to my bed. May my words condemn me on the day o' judgment if I speak ye false."

"Thank ye," breathed Aila and relaxed into him. MacLaren froze as she cuddled beside him, her head resting on his chest, her knee on his thigh. She was soft and warm, and his body responded instantly. He gritted his teeth and regretted his moment of charity. He had the right to take her, willing or no, but he knew he would not be able to force her. He wanted to touch her auburn hair, to shake it loose from its plait and bury his hand in her mass of curls. Desire pounded through him with every heartbeat, but he kept his hands firmly by his side, not wanting to risk the temptation. She was either completely innocent or a master manipulator—he wished he knew which one.

"Sorry," Aila murmured and started to move away.

"Nay," said MacLaren with a sigh, putting his arm around her gently. "Ye're my wife. 'Tis right ye rest yer head on my shoulder and no' on the ground." He should have let her pull away, but he wanted her close; he wanted her very close. "I dinna ken how soon I would regret my oath to ye."

Aila lifted her head, worry in her eyes, "Are ye going to…"

"Nay, I'll keep my promise to ye. Besides, a man shoud'na have to force his own wife."

"I… I'm sorry."

"Now dinna worrit yerself." MacLaren reached his

other arm around and soothed her head back on his chest. "Ye're a verra beautiful woman. I'd have to be dead no' to notice." He started playing with her hair, slowly unbraiding it.

"Beautiful? Do ye mock me, sir?"

"Nay, 'tis only the truth, as I am sure ye are well aware." MacLaren buried his fingers in her thick hair. He was playing with fire, but despite the warnings his brain kept sending, his body seemed to have a mind of its own.

"My mother has told me the truth, that I am verra unappealing to men."

Could this be true? Could Aila somehow not know how attractive she was? Impossible. MacLaren felt her relax and snuggle closer to him, letting out a contented little sigh. He needed her... now.

MacLaren groaned and pushed her away. "Och, lass, ye're driving me mad. I want ye bad but no' quite enough to roast in hell for ye. Now ye've amused yerself at my expense, and I want something in return."

"Did I do something wrong?" Aila looked at him, wide-eyed.

"I want ye to swear to me ye'll tell me the truth, always, no matter what I ask ye."

"But o' course I'll be honest wi' ye. Ye're my husband."

"Aye, but ye seem most intent on denying my rights, so I'll have yer word on this. I give ye leave to deny me yer body but ne'er the truth."

"Ye shame me, sir." Aila's voice shook.

"Yer word, if ye please."

"I swear to ye, Sir Padyn MacLaren, that I will always speak to ye the truth. If e'er I speak ye false, I release ye from the promise ye made to me this eve."

MacLaren smiled. He rather liked this promise. All he needed now was to catch her in a falsehood, and onto her back she'd go. MacLaren reached over to put his arm around her, expecting her to pull away, but she did not. Encouraged, MacLaren tried to think of a question to trip his wife into a lie.

Nineteen

AILA LAY NEXT TO PADYN MACLAREN IN THE moonlight, her emotions for this man rising and falling with every breath. She didn't know what to feel when she was with him, but even if she had been given the chance, she wouldn't want to leave.

"Why did ye go to St. Margaret's yesterday?" MacLaren's voice was calm and his eyes gleamed at Aila.

Aila took a deep breath. It was time to confess. "I left to ask for an annulment and join the convent. It had always been my mother's wish that I join St. Margaret's, and I have prepared myself to be a nun my whole life. Marrying ye was… verra unexpected. When ye dinna come for me on our wedding night, I feared ye married me only for my inheritance and would treat me wi' cruelty once ye took me away from Dundaff. Forgive me, sir. 'Twas cowardly, I admit."

"Do ye still fear me?"

"Nay, well, no' as much."

"I dinna want ye afeared o' me. I will ne'er treat ye cruel. Do ye trust me?"

The warmth of MacLaren's body radiated to her, drawing her closer. He had given her his word and was honoring it. It was more than her due and she knew it. In her gut, she trusted him. "Aye, I trust ye. Do ye trust me?"

That was another question altogether. "Ye must earn my trust, Aila, and ye have already acted in some ways that make trust difficult."

Aila lowered her eyes. The truth of that statement was undeniable, but still, she would like to have a second chance. She was unaccustomed to being thought of as false, and she disliked the feeling intensely. "I did run to the convent, I admit that. But I was confused. I was there only a few hours afore I realized my mistake and went back home. Or at least I was on my way until McNab and his men abducted me."

"Ye made it to the convent. Ye could have annulled the marriage and joined the sisters. What made ye come back?"

"I talked to Sister Enid, and she told me to pray." Aila hesitated. Other than Sister Enid, she had never told anyone else about her prayers or the verses. "Sometimes when I pray or listen to God, a particular verse comes to my mind. I believe God may use these verses to speak to me." Aila glanced at MacLaren, wondering if he would laugh at her.

"Ye take yer faith seriously, then?"

"Aye, sir."

"Do ye have any verses in mind now?" asked MacLaren softly.

Aila closed her eyes to think, and a verse flashed immediately to mind. "Oh!" She opened her eyes wide.

"What is it?"

"Well I'm no' sure these verses are from God. They may be naught but my own thoughts."

"What is the verse?"

"Fraglantia unguentis optimis oleum effusum nomen tuum ideo adulescentulae dilexerunt te."

Padyn frowned. "Perhaps I should have spent more time studying Latin as a lad. Is it something about love and a mouth?"

"'Tis from Solomon's Song of Songs. It translates to something like, *'Let him kiss me with the kisses of his mouth—for your love is more delightful than wine.'*"

"Well." MacLaren smiled with surprise. "God's will be done."

MacLaren leaned over and gently brushed his lips against hers, sending shivers down her spine. He touched his lips to hers ever so softly then withdrew. Repeating the pattern, he touched his lips to hers again, a little longer this time before pulling away. Aila leaned forward, wanting more. MacLaren chuckled softly. Rolling her onto her back, he kissed her firmly. For Aila, it was a strange sensation, but one she did not wish to stop. At first she just experienced his kiss then slowly started to respond. He made a guttural sound she interpreted as approval and kissed her even deeper.

"Why is it we are waiting to do more?" he whispered as he reached down her chemise to caress her breast. Aila drew a sharp breath at the unexpected sensation of his touch. It was surprisingly pleasurable and filled her with an aching for something more, though for what she could not name. He reached down and slowly drew up her chemise until his hand was on her thigh.

Suddenly, she was filled with pangs of fear, embarrassment, and modesty, mixed with unpleasant memories of her experience the night before.

"Wait, nay, stop, please. I need more time."

"Arrghh!" MacLaren released her and rolled over onto his back, taking a few deep breaths as he looked toward the heavens. "If ye're trying to kill me, lass, a knife to the heart would be quicker and more merciful."

"I'm sorry. I'm no' used to a man's touch." MacLaren said nothing, and she stared at him in the darkness, feeling small. "I thank ye for yer patience wi' me. I ken 'tis hard for ye."

"Ye have no idea how hard," MacLaren growled back.

"I always thought of myself as a nun. 'Tis difficult for me to suddenly become a man's wife."

MacLaren sighed. "Is that why ye refused to come to yer wedding feast?"

"I dinna refuse to eat wi' ye."

"Ye've got a short memory, lass. Have ye forgotten how ye dishonored me in front o' all yer kin by refusing to share yer meal wi' me?" MacLaren's voice was gruff once more.

"I waited all night, and no one came for me." A lump formed in the back of her throat as she remembered the pain of that night.

"What were ye waiting for? An escort to yer own supper?"

"Aye," replied Aila in a small voice.

"Why would ye need that? Why should that

night be different than any other time ye came for a meal?"

"But I'd ne'er eaten in the Great Hall afore." Aila felt defensive and belittled.

"Careful, lass, ye'll release me from my oath wi' words like that." For emphasis, MacLaren rolled back toward Aila and wrapped his arm around her once more.

"I am no' untrue. Ask my father if ye doubt my words." Aila was angry. So angry she wrapped her arm around him and pulled him closer. She had no idea what she was doing, but she needed to be near him.

"I'm warning ye, once broke, I'll no' be giving ye the same promise again." MacLaren drew his hand down her back and cupped her backside.

Aila tingled with delight as new, strange feelings pulsed inside her. "I have always e'er eaten wi' my mother. Ask anyone ye like." He was big and strong and warm and infuriating. She was so aggravated she pressed against him and cupped his bottom with her hand, just to be even.

Lying on their sides, face to face, their lips almost touched as MacLaren whispered, "Aila, what are ye doing to me?"

Instantly, she withdrew her hand. "I beg yer pardon, I… I…" She rolled away from him onto her back. "I'm afraid I'm making ye a verra poor wife."

MacLaren said nothing intelligible but snarled in a manner she took to mean he quite agreed with her.

"Sir?" Aila asked.

"Padyn. If ye're going to torture me, ye might as well call me by my Christian name."

"Padyn," Aila continued. She liked the sound of his name on her lips. If only he felt something more for her than just desire for her inheritance and lust. It would be so much easier if he held any real feelings for her. "Why did ye marry me?"

MacLaren rolled onto his back, and they lay there looking up at the stars. "As I told ye, yer father wrote me, offered yer hand in marriage in exchange for my defense of his lands from the marauders burning his crops."

"So ye married me for my fortune," Aila said dully.

"And the land. I need both for my clan."

"Sounds a lot like what McNab said."

MacLaren bristled. "McNab tried to steal ye away, and we suspect McNab of burning yer fields to force Graham to give ye to him in marriage. Are ye comparing me to that bastard?"

"It is McNab burning the fields. He confessed as much to me."

"Well, that makes it easier. Now I have two reasons to send him to judgment."

"So I'm at risk for abduction by any mercenary that comes along."

"Aye, until ye sleep wi' me," MacLaren snapped. "Then ye'll have only one mercenary to deal wi'. But perhaps that's yer plan. Keep me at bay until a knave comes along ye like better."

"Do ye mean I'm at risk until I... we...?" Aila stumbled on her words, not knowing the proper reference for the act.

"Once the marriage is consummated, and particularly after ye conceive a child, yer marriage to me is sealed."

That made sense. Why had she not thought of that before? "So if we consummate tonight, then McNab canna get me."

"Good night, Aila," MacLaren snarled.

Before she lost her nerve, Aila flung herself on top of him.

"What are ye doing now? Ye ken ye can reject me all night and then expect me to respond to yer latest tease?"

Aila kissed him gently on the mouth, silencing his protests. "I'd rather be yer wife than McNab's." She looked down at MacLaren. The moon reflected in his grey eyes. She had made her decision. She would accept her marriage to MacLaren. He looked at her for a moment then rolled her onto her back.

"Good enough for me. Apparently, where ye are concerned, I have no pride. Now if I start this again, ye're no' going to stop me, are ye?"

"No stopping," Aila said, though her voice wavered. MacLaren reached down again and pulled the linen chemise all the way to her chest then pulled up his own shirt as well. Aila gasped, engulfed by his warm, naked body.

"Stop me now," he commanded.

She closed her eyes and stiffened but made no move to push him away.

Brushing his lips against her, he murmured, "What do ye ken about the act between a husband and wife?"

"Nothing."

"But surely yer mother has told ye something o' what ye ought to ken?" he asked hopefully.

"She said men attacked women wi' animal lusts,

using their bodies to fulfill their own desires. As a result, a woman would become wi' child and often die in the agony of childbirth. Mother said a man would use a woman until he tired o' her then move on to attack another bonnie lass—if ye were lucky. Sometimes a man's lusts ran toward barnyard animals and young boys."

MacLaren stared at her, mouth agape. "No wonder ye are scared of me. Forgive me, but I'm starting to think verra unkindly toward yer mother."

"Ye woud'na be the first."

"Well now, let me try to correct any misunder-standings. First, I am no' a man to run after a wench, or anything else for that matter. I'm married to ye, and ye alone will be sharing my bed. Second, I do confess to some lust, but I hope to make that a mutual feeling. Third, I do hope to sire offspring wi' ye, and I forbid ye to die in childbirth. I'll make sure ye have the best midwife around to attend ye. Is that clear?"

"Aye," said Aila, trying to listen to what he was saying. While they talked, their bodies seemed to take on a mind of their own, rubbing against each other gently at first and now more demanding and urgent. She was not sure what she wanted, but anticipation grew inside her, and she wanted something, now.

"Ah, but ye're sweet," he sighed and pressed against her.

A loud crack of a tree branch broke through the night.

"Hey, Finn. Where was the last signal?" a man's voice pierced the darkness.

Aila and MacLaren froze.

Twenty

"O'er there, I ken. Wheesht now. Their camp must be close."

Aila caught her breath. The voice she recognized. It was the greasy-haired man who had helped McNab kidnap her. MacLaren pressed down so his weight was heavy on top of her. She closed her eyes and held her breath as the men passed nearby in the brush. She could not speak even if she wanted, since MacLaren had also clamped his hand over her mouth.

As the rustling noises drifted away, MacLaren whispered low in her ear, "Ye speak; ye die."

Was he trying to protect her or threaten her into silence? MacLaren stood up quickly, bringing her with him. He belted his plaid, and she threw on her cloak, shivering in the cool night air. A few minutes ago she had been warm and happy in MacLaren's arms. Now she was cold, and any affection he had shown her a few moments before was long gone. Her disappointment was palpable. MacLaren looked furious. His anger matched her own. Why had he put his hand over her mouth? Did he really think she would call out to their enemies or was so stupid she didn't know to be quiet? Either way, it was clear MacLaren did not think much of her.

This was not the time for discussion, however, and she focused back on their current situation. More movement came from the brush, and MacLaren grabbed her and threw the edge of his plaid around her for better concealment, pressing her down and back into the shadow of the rocks. Three more men followed the path of the first two, going in the direction of their camp though not directly toward it. As soon as the men were out of sight, MacLaren started back toward camp, using a more direct route. Aila marveled at how he could move so quietly yet quickly, and she tried to mimic his movements. She was no match for his stealth through the forest, as her occasional misstep and his backward glare made plainly evident.

After a short distance and some unfortunate rustling, MacLaren turned back, and without warning, picked her up and flung her over his shoulder. Outraged and embarrassed, Aila opened her mouth to protest, but remembering the need for silence, choked down her pride and allowed him to carry her back to camp like a sack of meal.

Her ordeal was short, since he moved quickly, and soon they were at the edge of their camp. Everything was eerily silent, as if the forest itself was holding its breath. MacLaren pointed for her to sit by a sleeping sentry. She tried to shake the sleeping man awake but found he could not be awakened. Pale in the moon-light, the man's head fell forward. Dark red blood gleamed at the base of his skull. Aila recoiled from the sentry, a flash of the stable master lying in a pool of blood invading her vision. She struggled to focus back on her current situation. The sentry breathed and she too took of breath of relief; the man was knocked unconscious but alive.

MacLaren was crouched a few feet away, his entire focus on something in front of him. Aila turned to see what had captivated his attention and was startled at Senga stepping gingerly through the camp of sleeping men, collecting their weapons. MacLaren glanced back at Aila, giving her a murderous glare. She forgot she was not afraid of him and shrank back. He motioned for her to hide deep in the underbrush, mouthing the words, "Stay hidden."

MacLaren crawled into the mass of sleeping men and began to silently wake them as he made his way toward the maid, whose back was to him. Aila watched transfixed as MacLaren disappeared from view, lost in shadow. Suddenly, he snapped up like a predator and grabbed the maid, silencing her with a hand over her mouth before she could scream, and dragging her back down into the sea of bodies. Aila held her breath, waiting for something to happen. Everything remained deceptively quiet. Occasionally a glint of steel flashed as the weapons were passed back to the plundered men, who remained still and silent.

Aila stifled a gasp when McNab's men emerged from the brush and crept toward men on the ground, the moonlight gleaming off their naked blades. With a loud battle cry that pierced the night, MacLaren jumped up and charged their attackers, his deadly claymore raised high. The rest of the men followed and pounded into

McNab's men with a torrent of angry steel. The shouts and screams and curses of the men and the clash of sword on sword was something terrible.

Aila shrank back farther into the brush away from the fight. A sharp kick to her side made her yelp in surprise. A man tumbled over her, tripping as he rushed from the forest into the fray. He turned and grabbed her arm, dragging her to her feet.

"I found her!" said the greasy-haired man.

Aila screamed and tried to wrench away from him. He grabbed her tight and jabbed his dagger under her chin. Its icy tip stuck into the tender skin of her neck.

Help! The man dropped lifeless beside her. Shaken, she turned and MacLaren was beside her, the black stain of blood on his blade. More men emerged from the forest, their eyes on Aila, their ultimate prize. Caught in the midst of the battle, fear swallowed her whole. Surrounded by fighting men, nowhere was safe. MacLaren kept her fast by his side, shielding her with his body, protecting her with his sword. Despite her terror, she was impressed by his skill as he felled one opponent after the next.

And then, as suddenly as it began, it was over. A call went out, and McNab's men retreated, disappearing back into the forest. Aila clung to MacLaren as her body shook. MacLaren held her tight.

"'Tis alright now. Ye're safe."

"Thank ye," Aila murmured into his chest. "They would have taken me back to McNab."

"Ye belong to me now. Dinna fear. Ye'll be going wi' no man but me." Though MacLaren's words were at once irritating and comforting, Aila chose to focus on the latter, at least until she stopped shaking and was able to stand without support.

"Nasty business that," said Chaumont, walking up beside them. He was surprisingly well-groomed for a man just awakened from a dead sleep to a fight. He was in stark contrast to the Highlanders who had fought in naught but their shirts or, well, nothings, since their plaid kilts were also used as their bedrolls. Aila pretended not to notice as they belted on their plaids and got themselves dressed.

"What's our damage?" asked MacLaren.

"Some cuts on the men but nothing life threatening, I should think. One of Graham's sentries was killed. This one?" Chaumont nodded at the still form of the sentry beside them.

"Unconscious," MacLaren answered.

"Lucky," replied Chaumont. "And, of course, the maid is gone."

"Gone?" asked MacLaren.

"Yes. Was it not you who killed her?"

"Nay. I held her fast until the fight started, but I left her verra much alive."

"What happened to her?" asked Aila, feeling a bit sick.

MacLaren turned his attention back to Aila, and she could discern no emotion in his cold eyes. MacLaren ignored her question and asked one of his own. "Why was yer maid taking our weapons?"

"I dinna ken for sure... that is, I..." Aila's conversation with Senga at the river came rushing back and she wished she had told MacLaren earlier. "Well, she did confess to me this evening that she was working for

McNab, but she was afraid of someone else. McNab also mentioned someone had been giving him information. I think perhaps there may be someone here who is working for McNab."

Both men stared at her. MacLaren's cold eyes flashed with anger. His voice was deceptively soft. "Ye kenned there be a traitor in our midst, but ye dinna tell me?"

"I was… ye were interested in other things, and I, that is, I rather got distracted, and I forgot." Aila winced, recognizing how inadequate that sounded.

"Foolish wench! Ye could have got us all killed. Rory! Watch her." Snarling, MacLaren stalked away.

An older warrior took her gently by the arm. "Come sit here, m'lady. Ye've no doubt had yerself a fright."

The man's gentle words formed such a contrast to MacLaren's harsh tone that tears welled up in her eyes. She brushed them away with impatience, frustrated she had allowed this man once again to make her cry.

Seething with every step, MacLaren followed Chaumont to the body of the maid. Why had Aila not told him this information about the maid before? And how had McNab's men found them? Had they been tracked? The man in the brush spoke of a signal being left, and MacLaren recalled that Graham's soldiers had formed the rear guard as they left McNab territory. It could have been any one of Graham's warriors who marked their path as they traveled along. The sentries had been struck from behind. Only someone from within the camp could have done that. Aila was right about one thing; someone amongst this group of men had turned traitor.

"She was stabbed in the back, and then her throat was cut," said Chaumont as they neared the body of the maid, which lay a few steps into the forest.

"Could she have been caught up in the fighting?" MacLaren asked doubtfully.

"The first strike in the back perhaps, but the slice across her throat was purposeful enough. Seems someone did not want any confessions from her."

"Aye," agreed MacLaren. The men before him were milling about, preparing to leave. One of them was not only a traitor but also a murderer. But who? And why? MacLaren had seen men turn allegiances for money or land, but surely Graham had more to give than McNab. MacLaren watched Graham's men with a wary eye. His soldiers seemed like good lads, many of them a bit young and eager to please.

"Ye, there," called Warwick to one of his soldiers. "I told ye to mount up. Why is yer horse no' saddled?"

"I-I'm sorry, I was…" The lad gestured toward a tree.

Warwick cuffed the lad on the back of his head. "Get moving," he growled in his rough voice. Warwick kept a tight rein on his men and expected immediate obedience. He was a gruff, sour sort of man, one who lived his life like he had never left the battlefield. MacLaren looked carefully at the Master of Arms; he could slit a girl's throat without thinking twice. Pitcairn the Steward, on the other hand, was fastidiously picking leaves off of his clothes while a young lad saddled his horse. He was efficient and clever, good qualities in a steward. MacLaren shook his head. Both Warwick and Pitcairn seemed loyal to Graham. And how could any of Graham's men benefit if McNab inherited Dundaff? It didn't make any sense.

On the other side of camp, Aila was sitting on a fallen tree branch. She had her arms wrapped around her and her head bowed. MacLaren regretted his harsh words. He felt an odd desire to comfort her, though he knew he was in the right. Her actions and words were a puzzle. Why had she delayed their union? Was she trying to get back to McNab and waiting for her lover to rescue her? MacLaren remembered Aila's scream with the knife to her throat. It had wrenched his insides. Clearly, she had not wanted to go with him. But could MacLaren really trust her?

MacLaren tore his gaze away from his wife and turned back to Chaumont. "Tend the wounded, pack the dead. Let's be away from this place."

Aila stared dully at the swirl of activity as the men broke camp around her. Someone retrieved her gown and brought it to her. It had been trampled in the fight and was now even filthier than before. She loathed putting it on, but she could hardly walk around in naught but a thin chemise. She pulled on the gown, trying not to think. Every subject was painful. Her maid had betrayed her and was killed for it. Somewhere among her father's soldiers was someone who wished her with McNab. Yet she could think of none of these soldiers as betraying her father. What possible reason could they have for doing so?

She sat back on the log, defeated. At one point last night her husband had shown some affection, but that was gone. He hated her now. She was tired, hungry, dirty, and discouraged. She wanted to retreat back into her tower and never leave it again.

A horse's frantic cry drew her attention away from self-pity. Shadow was upset. Two men were trying to prepare him for travel and had taken off his caparison, the large decorative horse blanket, and were attempting to saddle him

"Let him alone. That's no' how to handle him," she called as she ran toward the young men trying to place the saddle.

"Hold there, m'lady," called Rory, following along behind and catching her by the arm.

Aila turned on the older man. Barrel-chested, Rory reminded her a bit of her father. Frustration, fear, and doubt gave way to anger, and she stood tall, looking the warrior straight in the eye.

"Unhand me," she said coolly.

"Aye, m'lady," said Rory, taken aback and releasing her immediately.

"Am I to be my husband's prisoner?"

"Nay, m'lady."

"Then unless I'm about to fall off a cliff, ye'll ne'er grab me again."

Rory stood in stunned silence. His surprise matched her own. What had she just said to this man? Years of listening to her mother's rants, and now she was acting like her. She had always cringed at her mother's anger and sarcasm, yet now those words felt surprisingly good. Turning back to the men, she said with a strange sense of authority, "Stop that, immediately."

The men stopped. She grabbed the reins of the frightened horse and gentled him with soft words. As the horse calmed, she nodded to one of the soldiers, who was then able to saddle her mount.

"Now," she announced, "I am going home." She stood beside her horse, glaring severely at the men who looked blankly in return until they realized her intent. With a shrug, one man steadied her mount and another knelt beside her and assisted her into the saddle.

"Hold there!" called MacLaren's loud voice as he and Chaumont rode up to where Aila was now situated on Shadow. "What do ye ken ye're doing?"

At the sound of his voice, Aila's heart started to pound, yet she turned to him directly. She would not let this man control her or make her cower. She would give no man that power. In an instant, she understood her mother better than she ever had. If her mother could stand up for herself, so could she. "I am returning to Dundaff," she said defiantly.

"Aye, but ye'll no' be riding off again," said MacLaren. "Gilbert, take the reins," he commanded the soldier still standing beside her.

"Ye'll do no such thing," Aila told the man. Gilbert looked from MacLaren to Aila, confused.

"Come here, Gilby," called Rory, his arms folded across his massive chest and a hint of a smile on his face. "'Tis a domestic quarrel. Best no' get in the middle." Gilbert nodded and strode away to find his own mount. MacLaren glared at Rory before turning back to Aila.

"Get off that horse now. I'll no' have ye running away again."

"I'm no' running away. I've told ye where I go. Ye can go where e'er it suits ye, but I'll be taking myself home now." Aila turned her horse sharply and bolted into the thicket.

"Spurned by the ladies again, I see," Chaumont said with a droll smile. "Given your experience in France and here, I must say the marital state does not seem to agree with you."

MacLaren turned to give Chaumont the benefit of a ferocious glare. Chaumont was unimpressed. With a growl, MacLaren spurred his mount into the bush after Aila, leaving Chaumont's laughter behind. MacLaren loathed to be mocked, but somehow Chaumont had the ability to say things that would get another man killed. Most likely because Chaumont had saved his life more than once. Apparently, enduring his teasing was the price of friendship.

Lost in his own musings, MacLaren followed Aila's trail halfheartedly. He was riding Torrent, a black stallion known for strength and speed. MacLaren was confident he would catch his bride in short order, so he was surprised when he reached a clearing and caught only a glimpse of Aila as she entered the forest on the other side. She was fast! Somehow this all felt familiar. MacLaren kicked Torrent and gave chase to his errant bride.

Twenty-One

AILA RACED INTO THE FOREST, FREEDOM SURGING through her. She was well aware that by defying her husband in front of his men, this would probably be her last ride, though she doubted he would have let her ride free anyway. At least she would get one more ride, one more taste of independence before facing the reality of her life. She had rarely ridden during the day and never at top speed. To her delight, she found riding in daylight was a good deal easier, allowing her to race even faster. Reaching another clearing, she flew across the meadow, tingling with the sheer exhilaration of speed.

Upon reaching the other side, she slowed to glance behind her. She inhaled sharply when MacLaren entered the meadow, riding hard on his tall black horse. Her skin tingled with admiration. He was a fast rider, skilled and sure. His plaid flew behind him as he rode, and she caught her breath, remembering the night before. Perhaps being caught by this Highlander might not be so terrible. She had a sudden desire to run to him, to wrap her arms around him once more.

She shook her head to dispel romantic notions of her husband and turned to spur on her mount, remembering that MacLaren did not want to make love to her. He looked like he wanted to kill her.

Entering the forest, she urged Shadow forward. She was in familiar territory, heading back to Dundaff, and she was enjoying the ride and the chase. At one point, he seemed to be gaining on her, and she pushed the horse even harder than before, jumping fallen tree trunks and winding through the trees. At the heath, she let Shadow have full rein, since she knew the safe paths through the treacherous bogs and rode with confidence and speed. Despite her current situation, she laughed with sheer enjoyment. They pounded through another glen of trees until coming to a small loch. Shadow was beginning to labor, and she knew she had come to the end.

Aila pulled up by the shores of the loch and waited for MacLaren to arrive. Better to be punished here in private than at her father's gates for all to see. Before she could dismount, MacLaren charged to her, grabbing her reins and looking flushed with the exertion of the ride.

The sun sparkled on the clear blue water and bright green trees swayed gently in the soft breeze. She knew she was a sight, her mass of red curls flowing free, her clothes dirty and torn, but she didn't care. She was exhilarated and excited; she had never felt so wonderful. MacLaren looked stunningly handsome after their chase, and she beamed at him. MacLaren was breathing hard. He opened his mouth like he wanted to say something but continued to gaze at his bride, their eyes locked.

MacLaren scowled and shook his head. He dismounted and hauled Aila off her horse with ease. Aila reached for him willingly and slid down the length of his body. When she finally reached the ground, MacLaren still held her tight. Her arms were around his neck, holding him just as tightly. He leaned down toward her slowly. She stood on her toes, arching up to him.

"What am I going to do wi' ye?" he murmured.

She didn't know what he would do, and she couldn't wait to find out.

MacLaren touched his lips to hers, sending a shock wave through her. She wanted more, and he was moving much too slowly. She pressed into him, deepening the kiss. He made a growling, hungry sort of noise and responded with equal vigor. He pulled her down to the grassy bank of the loch until he was covering her body with his own. Her pulse raced, and she dug her fingers into his back, holding him closer to her. She had never wanted anything more in her life. She was not about to stop him this time.

"Damn it, no!" roared MacLaren and rolled off of her. He sat next to her, gasping for breath. Aila lay there, stunned. What had she done wrong? "I winna let ye use yer body against me. I winna be manipulated again, ye ken?" MacLaren glared at her.

Aila felt her bottom lip tremble and she sat up, looking away. She squeezed her eyes tight and concentrated on her breathing. The wind gently rustled the tall grass, the sound comforting and familiar. Gradually, the shock of his rejection dulled, and she wondered what he meant by being "manipulated again."

MacLaren stood and walked to the horses, which had ambled down to the loch for a drink, checking on them, busying himself with their care. When there was nothing left to do, he stood by the water, staring out across the loch. He bent and picked up a stone, flicking it over the water, the stone skipping five times before going under. He turned and trudged back to her.

"Honestly, Aila, I dinna ken where to start wi' ye. Where on earth did ye learn to ride like that?"

"My brother taught me."

"That woud'na happen to be his horse?"

"Aye," said Aila, busying her fingers with a blade of grass.

"Is it possible I've chased ye afore on St. John's Eve?" MacLaren's voice was rough, and Aila dared not look up at him, simply nodding in response. She had hoped to avoid this topic. She had made enough confessions lately without discussing her early morning equestrian habits.

"Damn it, Aila, ye would try the patience o' Job. Explain yerself, now."

Aila stood up, still concentrating on the blade of grass in her hand. "My brother and his friend Duncan used to go riding in the early dawn. Will used to love to ride." Aila glanced up at MacLaren, and he nodded. No one could best Will Graham on a horse; everyone knew that. "Well, when Duncan died of an unfortunate accident in the lists, I begged Will to let me go wi' him, and he taught me to ride… fast. After he left, I continued riding in the early morn on my own." There, that sounded reasonable.

"Yer father allowed ye to ride at night alone?" MacLaren was incredulous.

"I… well… I ne'er asked him."

"How did ye get out o' the castle?"

"Through the secret passage Will found in the stable," Aila said in a small voice, examining the muddy tips of MacLaren's boots. MacLaren started to pace up and down the bank.

"So ye dressed in men's clothing, snuck out at night wi'out yer father's knowledge, and went riding off on yer brother's horse. I dinna believe it. I seen it wi' my own eyes, but I still dinna believe it." He stopped and shook his head. "My men thought ye were the ghost of Robert the Bruce.

"The Bruce?"

"Aye. Now I ken why there are so many ghost sightings. People have been seeing you."

"Oh." Aila had never thought anyone had seen her, let alone mistaken her for a ghost.

"And ye were going to be a nun?"

Aila felt heat creep up her neck and burn her cheeks at the shame of his words. Looking at it from his perspective, she supposed she had been deceitful and sneaky. "I apologize for my faults."

MacLaren walked up to her. Despite her initial determination to stand her ground, Aila took a few steps back, but MacLaren closed the distance.

"I thought ye might be different. But nay, ye're like every other deceitful female, rotten to the core." Aila opened her mouth to protest but closed it again, realizing there was nothing she could say to this man. His words stung, and she felt the fatigue of the past few days. "Come now, let's get going."

Aila walked toward her mount on the bank of the

loch. The sun had gone behind a cloud, and the water lost its appeal. She started to try to mount Shadow but was picked up from behind instead. Startled, she found herself in MacLaren's arms atop his horse.

"What are ye doing?" she asked, shocked to be so close to him.

"Taking ye back to Dundaff."

"I can ride on my own."

"O' that I am well aware," MacLaren said grimly, tying Shadow's reins to his saddle and beginning the long walk back to Dundaff. Aila sat across MacLaren's lap, his right hand holding the reins, his left holding her close to his body. She tried to wriggle away, not wanting to be held against a man who thought so poorly of her, but there was nowhere to go. The more she wiggled, the tighter he pressed her against his body, until she was smashed against his chest, sitting between his legs, her own legs draped over one of his muscular thighs. She blushed fiercely and gave up the struggle. It was going to be a long ride home.

It did not take long for the silence between them to become unbearable to Aila. "I am sorry for riding off today. I dinna ken why I did it. I warrant I wanted one last ride before going to be yer wife."

Aila felt MacLaren stiffen. "I may no' have the stable's o' yer father, but I assure ye I have a few horses yer ladyship may deem acceptable."

"I dinna mean to suggest ye dinna have fine horses…" Aila stopped defending herself, as the implication of his words hit her. "Are ye saying ye'll let me ride when we go to Creag an Turic?"

"Aye," said MacLaren suspiciously, "but no' alone and ne'er at night, unless I'm wi' ye."

Aila threw her arms around him, surprising them both. "Thank ye. Thank ye so much. Ye dinna ken what this means to me. I thought when I was married I'd ne'er be able to ride again." Aila looked up at him with tears glistening in her eyes.

"Well there…" MacLaren cleared his throat and shifted a bit before trying again. "There are several places ye might like to see on MacLaren land. The overlook on the Braes of Balquidder is a nice vantage."

"Aye, 'tis lovely," she murmured.

"Ye've been there?" His voice regained some of its gruffness.

Aila swallowed. "Aye."

MacLaren stopped his horse and glared at her. "Now I want ye to tell me what ye were doing on my land. The truth this time and all o' it. Neglecting to reveal the whole of a matter is as much a lie as telling a falsehood."

Aila squirmed in his grasp and tried to look away, but he turned her face back toward him. Truth was, she had occasionally ridden to his land while he was gone but had visited there frequently since his return. She told herself she had wanted to see how he had rebuilt, but there were more personal reasons for her visits. The feelings she had felt for him as a child had never entirely left her. She had just denied them. But admitting to this man her girlish affection was not something she was prepared to do. Lying to her husband was not an unforgivable sin, was it? She would probably get some time in purgatory, but it might be worth it. Aila struggled with her conscience before resigning to her fate.

"I went there to see ye."

"Why? Who are ye working for?" MacLaren's voice was cold.

"No one. I wanted to see yer progress in restoring yer lands. I felt bad for ye returning to so little after ye had been so good to my family."

MacLaren shook his head in doubt. "Aila, I want the absolute truth. I will no' hurt ye, if ye tell me now. Are ye aligned wi' McNab or anyone else who is trying to help him?"

"Nay," she said emphatically.

"I wish I could believe that."

Aila pointed toward the bloody mark on her neck. The small knife wound was beginning to scab. "Does it look to ye like I be wanting to return to McNab?"

MacLaren grunted a reluctant concession to her argument. "So ye were spying on me because why, exactly?"

"No' spying. I… I always liked ye, even as a young girl. When ye came back, I wanted to see ye… to be close to where ye were."

"Are ye trying to say ye're sweet on me?"

Aila winced. She'd rather do anything but admit to a man who held her in such disregard that she had been attracted to him and, despite it all, still was. But she had promised to be honest, and she would hold to it. She nodded with reluctance.

MacLaren urged the horse forward, laughing sarcastically. "Ye expect me to believe that? After ye ran away to the convent to have our marriage annulled and refused me my marital rights last night? Yer so full o' deceit ye canna even keep yer lies straight."

Aila tried unsuccessfully to wriggle away from him again. Sitting on a man's lap on horseback left a lady very few options for a respectable retreat. Aila didn't know which was worse, admitting her childish romantic thoughts toward him or having them disbelieved and mocked. "Ye asked me for the whole truth, and I told ye. If ye dinna believe me, then please forget I said it."

Aila nursed her wounded pride and wondered about this man she had married. He had her emotions spinning round such that she didn't even know them herself. One moment she was desperately in love with him; the next she wanted nothing to do with him.

In love?

Oh no, not that. Anything but that.

Twenty-Two

MACLAREN RODE SLOWLY THROUGH THE BRUSH AND glanced down at the unhappy lass in his arms. Aila looked miserable, and he felt rotten. Gone was the beautiful lass who had raced through the forest and smiled at him like some sort of wild nymph. He had taken that smile away, and only a knave would have done that. He struggled to know whether or not to trust her. Despite his inner conflict, his words always came out harsh. It didn't seem likely she liked him, yet how could he know her feelings? Women baffled him in general, and this one was a complete mystery. He had been easily deceived by a beautiful woman before, and now he didn't trust his own judgment.

MacLaren sighed. He had bigger problems to deal with than discerning the emotions of this strange creature who happened to be his wife. Returning to Dundaff meant returning to the home not only of Graham, but a traitor, as well. Someone was after Aila and was ready to kill to get her. MacLaren shuddered at what would have happened had he not returned to camp in time to warn his men. They would have been slaughtered while they slept.

McNab had declared himself MacLaren's enemy and would need to be dealt with. MacLaren's own life, the lives of his men, and quite possibly Aila's, hung in the balance. He needed to think clearly and not be distracted by personal concerns. Rory was right. As long as Aila was not working for his enemy, this squabble was a domestic matter, one that could be handled later or, better yet, never.

"Aila, we will be returning to Dundaff soon, along wi' someone who wishes me and my men dead. I ask them to fight for yer clansmen to protect yer fields and to protect ye. But I canna fight both McNab and ye. 'Tis no' fair to me nor my men. If ye dinna wish to be married to me, tell me now."

If MacLaren expected a quick response, it was not what he got. They rode on in silence, Aila frowning as if in deep thought. It was as he expected; she wished to end this sham of a marriage. Her response, when it came, caught him off guard.

"Who hurt ye?" she asked softly.

"I am uninjured," responded MacLaren, a bit confused.

"Nay. Ye said ye woud'na be manipulated again. Who hurt ye?"

MacLaren turned cold, as if he had been plunged in ice water. This was not something he wished to discuss. Ever. He cursed himself—his own words had betrayed him. "'Tis none o' yer concern."

"If ye are comparing me to another, then it is. Ye've asked for my honesty, and I have given it. Now I ask for yers." Aila looked at him expectantly. Her eyes were two pools of water, brimming with anxiety.

MacLaren rode in silence, looking beyond her at the road. He never wanted to think of Marguerite. He never wanted to speak of her. He never wanted to be reminded of his greatest mistake, the one that had ripped his soul and killed his cousin. Yet, he had brought this on himself. Aila was too clever not to notice. He groaned inwardly. Best to make a quick confession and move on.

"I was betrothed when I was in France." MacLaren spoke without emotion, continuing to look at the road ahead. "She was verra beautiful, and she led me to believe her feelings of affection were similar to mine own. It was a lie. She used me to defend her land to gain better terms in submitting to the English crown. I wager my defense gave her quite a bit more coin. Afterwards, she had no more use for me, so I returned to my clan."

"'Tis horrible anyone could be so deceitful."

"Nay, dinna be too harsh on her." MacLaren could not keep the chill from his voice. "Like most females, she thought only to her own comfort. Words to her were just words, easily spoken, easily broken. Making love to me was part of the price she paid to get what she really wanted—gold."

"Ye ken all women to be like her?"

"Nothing in my experience o' this world has proved different."

Now it was Aila's turn to be quiet. MacLaren rode along, waiting for her answer. In the silence, he recognized his words again as harsh, but what else could he say? She had asked for the truth, and he had given it to her.

"I do wish to be married to ye," Aila said slowly, seeming to weigh every word. "I value yer alliance with my family and yer defense of our clan. But I would ask ye one thing."

"Ye've asked for much already, lass."

"Aye," said Aila, sitting straighter and looking him in the eye. "And I ask for this, too. I ask for ye to judge me by my own words and deeds, no' by those o' another."

MacLaren looked down at Aila. He had always believed in judging a man by his actions not by his family. He nodded. It was a fair request. "Aye, I will try to do so. If we have made peace, I propose a truce between us. At least until the danger has passed."

Aila nodded.

"It is clear McNab means to take ye by any mode possible," said MacLaren, getting back to their immediate situation. "I can easily see why he would want to claim yer inheritance, and it is also equally clear he has been given help from someone inside Dundaff. From what ye said, yer maid admitted to working for McNab and being afraid of someone at Dundaff. Considering the way she died, I expect the traitor is among those who accompanied us. Do ye ken anyone in the party ye might suspect as a traitor? Any disagreements between any of these men and yerself or yer father?

"Nay, none that I ken. But I would like to tell ye about the stable master. It happened in the early morn after my ride on St. John's Eve. I returned to the stables to find Fergus, our stable master, lying on the floor, his head bloodied." MacLaren felt Aila shiver and held her closer. "There was an iron bar next him, blood on one end. I heard someone coming toward me, and I almost called for help, but it felt wrong. I've been riding that early for many years, and I never have seen anyone in the stables at that time besides Fergus. So I ran back up to my tower. The man ran after me up the stairs, it was... I was verra much afraid."

"Did ye ken who it was?"

"Nay."

"Did he see who ye were?"

"Nay, well, I'm no' sure. I was wearing my riding clothes at the time."

MacLaren nodded. "I'm glad for that. I heard about the stable master when I returned, but I was told it was an accident."

"Aye, I heard that, too. My maid said he fell from a chair and hit his head, but there was no chair that I saw."

"So, 'tis possible someone tried to kill him and make it look like an accident. Who have ye told about this?"

"None but ye and Sister Enid. It was one of the reasons I was returning to Dundaff, to tell Father o' what I saw."

MacLaren rode in silence, thinking on this new bit of information. "Every time ye open yer mouth, I hear something unexpected. Do ye have any more surprises for me?"

"Nay, och, well, I should tell ye about the message."

"The message?"

Aila told him about the missive that had been sent by someone impersonating Sister Enid.

MacLaren considered her words. Her actions were starting to make a bit more sense. Someone was indeed playing with her loyalties. "So someone wanted ye to join the convent or at least leave the safety of Dundaff. Was it on the road from St. Margaret's that McNab seized ye?"

"Aye."

"Maybe McNab was afeared ye would marry another and forged the letter to get ye to leave the castle so he could capture ye."

Aila thought a moment. "Aye, 'twould be possible, I suppose."

"Any other confessions for me?"

"Nay," said Aila, frowning. "Well, there is another secret, but it belongs to my mother no' me."

"What is it?"

"'Tis no' important."

"I'll be the judge o' that."

Aila sighed. She had never told anyone about her mother before. "My mother's hands and feet are diseased, like Sister Enid's, ye ken? She wants no one to know. That's why she refuses to leave her tower. I have to feed her every day, because she canna do for herself."

MacLaren thought for a moment. "So that's why ye said yer mother needed ye." It was all beginning to make more sense.

"Aye. That is all I know. Do ye believe me?"

"I will consider yer words carefully. Some have the ring of truth. Others I ken to be false."

"When have I e'er spoke ye false? Ye have asked me for the truth, and I have given it. What is the point of telling ye the truth if ye winna believe it?"

"How can I believe ye when some things ye say make no sense? Last night ye refuse to honor my marital rights, yet this morn ye declare yer love for me. How can I believe that?"

"I ne'er said I loved ye." Aila's voice rose. "I said... well, ne'er ye mind what I said. As for last night, I wasna trying to avoid ye forever; I only wanted a little time and maybe a little respect. Since the moment ye knocked me from my horse, ye've treated me wi' contempt. Nay, e'en before that. I ken the only reason ye married me is for the money, but do ye have to remind me and my clan that my only value to ye is my inheritance?"

"Contempt? When have I disrespected ye?"

Aila's eyebrows shot up. "Ye've called me a traitor and a liar, rotten to the core, and—"

MacLaren kissed her. He had not realized he had been waiting, wanting to do that. She resisted for a moment then sank into him. He held her closer and slowly deepened the kiss.

"Why did ye do that?" Aila asked, breathless, when at last he let her go.

MacLaren shook his head. "Irksome lass, I dinna ken what I'm about when I'm wi' ye."

Aila slowly smiled. "I'm usually ne'er cross. I'm sorry if I've been irritating."

"Aye, ye have, lass. Verra aggravating." And he kissed her again. The horse slowed to a stop, and he let go of the reins to kiss her in earnest. "We were interrupted at a most inopportune time last night."

"Aye." Aila snuggled closer to him. "Perhaps tonight?"

"Assuredly. Though why wait? There's plenty of brush here." MacLaren was ready, more than ready. Riding along with her wiggling about in his lap, it was enough to drive a man daft. He wasn't made of stone, after all.

"Here?" asked Aila, her eyes wide.

"Here."

"Now?"

"Now."

"During the day?"

"It works the same, day or night. Would ye be willing?" MacLaren leaned closer and ran his hand slowly up her leg to her thigh. She shivered. He may have, too. Aila's eyes sparkled and she nodded.

"Truly? Ye would?" MacLaren winced internally. He sounded like an untried youth, not an experienced warrior. Aila gave him a shy smile and nodded again several times. Well, hell, he felt like an eager lad. MacLaren felt his face break into something he thought suspiciously might be a smile. This was getting out of control. Aila smiled too, looking warm and happy and beautiful and his. She shifted so she was facing him and put her arms around his neck to kiss him again. He ran his hands under her gown and cupped her backside, enjoying how her body responded to his touch. This was going to be sweet.

"Ho there! I'm glad to see the two of you have reconciled." MacLaren and Aila swirled around to see Chaumont trotting up behind them on the path. He smiled broadly as he came alongside them and pretended to become interested in a tree while they quickly shifted to a more modest position.

"Chaumont." MacLaren glared at him. "I love ye like a brother, but if ye dinna leave immediately, I'm going to have to kill ye."

Chaumont smiled broadly and gave Aila a bow of the head. "So it's like that, is it? Very well done, madam. My most humble apologies, but I am not alone." The unwanted thumping of hooves grew louder, and soon the rest of the warriors came into view.

"Perfect," MacLaren growled softly in Aila's ear. "This is going to make for a most uncomfortable ride back to Dundaff." MacLaren shifted a bit in his saddle. Situated as she was between his legs, she could not help but notice the point of his discomfort.

"I could go back to riding my own horse," Aila suggested.

"Ne'er. This may be torture, but it is sweet, and ye're mine," he whispered.

Aila smiled back and clung to him, resting her head on his chest. MacLaren turned so all the men could get a good view. *See this. I have caught her, I have tamed her, and she is mine.* MacLaren looked possessively down at his bride. *And she is happy.* For the first time, it was important to him to keep her so.

Twenty-Three

A CHEER WENT UP FROM MACLAREN'S MEN TO CELEBRATE their laird's capture of his wayward bride, and the entire group started back along the way to Dundaff. They had reached a well-traveled path through the forest and were able to ride two abreast through the trees. MacLaren and Chaumont took the lead, riding together. Aila's horse was still tied behind MacLaren's, providing a horse length between them and the next mount, which allowed some privacy of conversation if they spoke softly. Aila felt rather uncomfortable sitting on a man's lap in front of all these men, yet even she realized the act was a necessary one to restore MacLaren's pride after she defied him. So she tried to make the best of it, particularly since she had no other choice. Trying to appear as if nothing was amiss, she sought some topic for polite conversation.

"So what brings ye to Scotland, sir?" she asked Chaumont.

Chaumont's face lit up at her address. "I came following your husband. I got so accustomed to saving his arse in France, I found I couldn't rightly give up the job. Besides, we all were required to make a most hasty retreat after MacLaren killed Gerard de Marsan."

"Who?" Aila looked back and forth between them. This was not exactly the polite conversation she had hoped to elicit.

"A French nobleman."

"Why would ye do that?" Aila asked MacLaren.

"Probably because he was trying to kill me at the time," MacLaren answered coolly.

"Why was he trying to kill ye?" It was rude to ask so many questions, but really, how could they expect her not to?

"They had a small disagreement on which one of them was going to marry a certain lady," answered Chaumont. Aila gave the Frenchman her full attention, hoping for more of the story.

"I must thank ye, Aila, "said MacLaren without emotion. "This present conversation has most certainly cured my earlier discomfort." Aila waited for MacLaren to say more, but he seemed content to ride along in silence.

"I would be honored if ye would tell me the rest of the story," Aila said hopefully, looking first at MacLaren then at Chaumont. She had managed to get MacLaren to divulge a bit about his past experience with a woman in France, but she guessed there was more to the story. She felt sure it was something she needed to know if she was ever to understand her new husband.

"I would be happy to enlighten you," said Chaumont, pausing for a moment and glancing at MacLaren, who voiced no complaint. "We had just finished a bloody battle, defending the lands of Montois, when your husband rode off to see the countess."

"Countess?" asked Aila.

"Countess Marguerite de Montois." Chaumont spoke the name with flair. "A very lovely creature, but unfortunately without the character to match. She accepted MacLaren's proposal of marriage at a time when she was already betrothed to Gerard de Marsan. When MacLaren arrived at Castle Montois, there was apparently some disagreement as to which of the men she would actually wed. Marsan made his position clear enough." Chaumont pointed at the long scar down MacLaren's face. "But it was MacLaren who drove the point home." Chaumont paused, the irrepressible smile twitching at the corner of his lips.

"The countess was none too pleased with this turn of events and called for her men to arrest MacLaren. I do believe she wanted to use his skull for a chamber pot. I was alerted by one of Marguerite's ladies that she had submitted to the English. Unfortunately, I was unable to warn MacLaren before his audience with the countess. I stitched up his face, which was bleeding like a mother—"

"Chaumont," interrupted MacLaren.

"Begging your pardon, madam. What do you think of my handiwork?"

Aila ran her finger down the length of the angry scar. MacLaren froze at her touch, but stared at nothing but the road.

"I think ye make a verra good knight but a verra poor seamstress."

Chaumont roared in laughter.

"The only relevant bit of that story," said MacLaren, his own lips twitching, "is, when Chaumont learned the countess had betrayed us, he sent word to pull back the men off of Montois land. If they had stayed at camp, they surely would have been murdered as they slept, since the land then belonged to the English."

Aila frowned. "I'm confused. Ye say ye were protecting Montois from the English, and then ye say Montois had submitted to the English. Which was it?"

"Ah, that part confused us all," said Chaumont with his characteristic smile. "The Countess Marguerite of Montois convinced MacLaren to defend her against three English captains, which he did, but not without cost." Aila felt MacLaren stiffen, though he said nothing. "We were unaware the lady was in negotiations with the English for her submission to them. MacLaren's defense of her made her land more difficult to obtain by force, and thus she was able to exact a higher price for her switch of loyalties to the English Crown."

"So Countess Marguerite was the one who—"

"Dinna say her name," growled MacLaren. I dinna wish to hear that whore's name on yer lips."

Aila was silenced. Chaumont took the subtle cue and rode ahead, leaving MacLaren and Aila to ride along in awkward silence. Aila pondered his words, more clearly understanding his easy distrust of women. He would forever carry the visible reminder of the last woman who betrayed him. Other scars were not as visible but deeper and more painful. How could she ever gain his trust?

Aila did not have long to ponder this thought

since they were now approaching Dundaff, its seven towers rising high above them. They rode up the narrow path to the castle. Though the road was a main thoroughfare, it was kept narrow on purpose, to make a siege of the castle more difficult. Aila struggled to find the words to break through the icy shell around MacLaren. She did not wish to re-live her parent's marriage in her own life.

"Not all women are like that woman," she said to MacLaren, who had not looked at her since the talk had turned to his betrayal.

"But ye are a woman."

"Aye," declared Aila, sitting tall. "And I am a Scot and a Graham."

MacLaren looked down at her, the intensity in his eyes unnerving. "Ye are a MacLaren now."

"Aye," replied Aila with a soft smile, "that too."

MacLaren sat taller and drew her closer. Shouts rang out as they entered the portcullis and emerged into the lower bailey. Aila took a deep breath, and the tense muscles in her back eased. She was home and had made a fragile peace with her husband. All was well. Except, of course, she still needed to face her parents, who would be furious with her, and somewhere there was a traitor trying to kill her husband and send her to McNab. She sagged against MacLaren's chest. But other than that, all was well.

"Go get some rest," said MacLaren softly as the stable lads raced to take their reins and provide the required assistance.

Aila nodded. There was nothing she would rather do right now than remove the filthy gown. "I should present myself to my father first. He will be most displeased with me," she mumbled grimly.

"I shall speak to yer father. Yer discipline is my responsibility now."

Aila wondered if that was any sort of improvement.

"And the stable master?" she whispered.

"I will tell him. Is there anything else he should be told?"

"Nay, I've told ye all." Their eyes met, and she waited for him to express his disbelief. He said nothing and instead handed her down to a waiting page. After dismounting, MacLaren took her by the arm and walked her to Rory.

"Take her to her tower," he called to Rory. To Aila, he said, "Stay in yer room, and trust no one. Rest and refresh yerself. I'll send a lad for ye to come to supper. Dinna walk alone. And Aila, I expect ye to eat yer meals wi' me from this time forward."

Though weary, Aila gave MacLaren a weak smile. "I will be there, sir."

MacLaren watched her as she walked away. She was rather bedraggled, but still she managed to capture his attention.

"Well, what do you think of your errant bride now?" asked Chaumont.

MacLaren shrugged. "I want to trust her, but sometimes she says or does things that show I canna rely on her to speak true."

"She has the look of an honest mademoiselle to me. With what do you find fault?"

"She told me she has ne'er eaten in the Great Hall. That seems unlikely, does it no'?"

"Warwick, my good fellow," Chaumont called out to the Master of Arms as he dismounted. Warwick glanced around as if judging the possibility of escaping an audience with the French knight. But Chaumont walked up to him with a carefree smile, ignoring the older man's scowl. "I hear Lady Aila eats most often in her own chamber?"

"Aye, she eats wi' the Lady Graham in their tower."

"How often does she come for meals in the Great Hall?"

"Ne'er that I ken. Now I must attend to the men." Warwick moved away from Chaumont, barking orders to the stable lads and the soldiers.

"There now." Chaumont turned back to MacLaren. "Perhaps your *cherie* is more honest than you know. Fast, too. How did she come to ride so well?"

"Taught by the best. Her brother was the fastest rider I've e'er seen." MacLaren caught Chaumont's eye, adding, "She's faster."

Twenty-Four

AILA THANKED RORY FOR HIS ESCORT TO HER TOWER
entrance and dragged herself up the stairs. The siren
call of her waiting bed beckoned her. She debated
whether she wanted to bathe first or just go to sleep.
Before she made it up to her room, her mother called
for her.

"Aila? Aila, is that ye, darling? They told me
ye returned."

Aila cringed. She did not want to see her mother. She
did not have the energy to fight with her; she needed
rest. She looked with longing up the stairs to her room
but walked into her mother's quarters instead.

"I am well, Mother."

Lady Moira Graham sat in her usual chair, with
Maggie bustling about, caring for her many needs.
Both the maid and her mistress stared at Aila in shock.
Aila knew her gown was beyond repair. She tried to
smooth her hair and was dismayed to find leaves and
bits of twig. She must look a sight.

"What happened?" Lady Graham's face was white.

"I was kidnapped by McNab, I escaped the next

day, MacLaren found me, we were attacked by McNab at night, and then we rode home."

"Och, my poor darling. 'Tis a shame ye ne'er made it to the convent."

Aila held her tongue.

"I suppose we must now accept that MacLaren for yer husband, though he's hardly good enough for ye."

"He's a good man, Mother," Aila said in a low voice.

"He is what he is, and there's naught to be done about it now. How I wish ye could have joined the convent. 'Tis no' fair, but life ne'er is. If yer father had only consulted me, I would have made a better match for ye. A Campbell perhaps, or maybe a Douglas—now there would have been a good alliance."

"I am content wi' the match made for me."

"But no, he woud'na ask, and now ye're trapped in a loveless marriage wi' a grasping knave, concerned only wi' yer money— "

"And the land, Mother," shouted Aila. "Dinna forget about the land. I ken well enough why he married me, but I dinna care. I will have him for my husband, him and no other, ye ken? And I winna tolerate ye berating him e'er again."

Maggie gasped. Lady Graham's eyes went wide, and her face froze.

No one spoke.

Aila wondered what she had just said. She had never spoken to her mother like that.

"Well said, my love."

Behind her, MacLaren leaned against the door post. "Come now, ye must be tired after yer long ordeal. Time for rest. Maggie, can ye escort my wife upstairs and see that she gets a bath and some sleep? I wish to have an audience with Lady Graham."

Aila wandered past him and up the stairs. He followed her progress with warm eyes. She gave him a groggy smile and continued to her room. *Love? Had he called her love?* She was asleep before she could answer her own question.

MacLaren watched until his wife made it to her door, partly because he liked looking at her and partly because he wanted to make sure she didn't fall down the stairs. When she was safe in her room, he faced down the mother. MacLaren entered the room, shutting the door behind him. It wasn't quite proper, but he didn't care. It was time to have words with Lady Graham.

"I ken ye feel I am an inadequate marriage partner for yer daughter," MacLaren began, "but as ye said, there is naught we can do about that now. I would ask for yer blessing on this union."

Moira shifted in her chair and regarded MacLaren through shuttered eyes. "And what makes ye think I would e'er grant ye such a request?"

"The happiness o' yer only child?"

"I ken a bit more about caring for Aila than ye do," said Moira, her voice stinging with warning.

MacLaren tried a new tactic. "Ye are verra correct about the reasons I married yer daughter, but that does no' mean I winna take care o' her. I swear to ye on my honor, I will protect her wi' my verra life if need be."

Moira seemed to relax a bit and nodded for him to continue.

"I also am concerned for yer welfare, Lady Graham."

"And why would ye be concerning yerself wi' me?"

"As ye said, I am a grasping knave, Lady Graham. I want my children to inherit Dundaff. Therefore, I am determined ye shall be Graham's only wife." MacLaren paused to let the implications of his statement be understood. "I want peace between us. I ask that ye support this marriage, and in return, I will do all in my power to see to yer welfare."

Moira's eyes gleamed, and a slow smile spread on her face. MacLaren knew his proposal had been accepted and they were down to negotiations.

"I want Aila to remain at Dundaff," said Moira.

"Nay, she must live at Creag an Turic, but we can visit."

"Twice a week."

"Once a quarter."

"Once a week."

"Once a month."

"Done!" she said, smiling in a calculating sort of way. "And I want regular visits from any children ye may have."

"Done," said MacLaren.

"And I want ye to be faithful to her. If I hear ye have been sowing yer seed around, I will withdraw my support."

"That is none o' yer concern," said MacLaren, his eyes narrowing, "but done."

"Sir Padyn MacLaren," she said with a radiant smile, "ye have my blessing. Welcome to the family. Now go and bathe yerself before ye come into my presence again."

MacLaren bowed and quit the room. One dragon slayed. He wondered how many more this marriage would require of him.

Twenty-Five

AFTER HIS NEGOTIATIONS WITH LADY GRAHAM, MacLaren spent a long afternoon with Laird Graham, discussing all the new information he had discovered. MacLaren kept his meeting with Graham small, including only Chaumont. Graham had wished Warwick and Pitcairn present, but MacLaren respectfully requested they not come. All the men on the journey were suspect, even Graham's top men, as unlikely as that seemed.

At first Graham argued and raged at all MacLaren had to say, but he calmed down soon enough and got down to the business of planning their next move. For all his bluster, Graham was a practical and thoughtful man, one MacLaren found he could respect. His reasoning was sound, even if his body was broken. He reminded MacLaren of his own father, and MacLaren felt an odd twinge when speaking with him, feeling that beyond his material profit, he had gained other more intangible but no less valuable things through this alliance with the Graham clan.

Graham railed against the idea that there was a traitor

amongst his men or that any of them would have signaled the location of the camp to McNab, allowing a slaughter. Yet the truth was plain. They compiled a list of the men who had gone with MacLaren and examined each one as a potential traitor, but none appeared to be a likely candidate. MacLaren found Graham to be a fair but generous master, his soldiers were well treated and their needs tended, so he could find little cause for grievance.

Yet someone was trying to help McNab, but why? How could anyone amongst Graham's own clan benefit from having Aila and the substantial inheritance of Dundaff pass to another clan? There were more questions than answers. And yet, though he was loathe to admit it, Aila's little adventure had caused their enemies to reveal more than they intended. They now knew for sure McNab was their enemy and one of Graham's men was a traitor. As they ended their council to give the men time to prepare for supper, MacLaren felt a keen sense of apprehension.

"Be watchful," he said to the Graham laird before he left. "To inherit yer land, ye must first be dead. I fear for ye."

"And I for ye, my lad, since by marrying my daughter ye put yerself at the same risk." The men clasped hands and clapped each other on the back. "Take care o' her, my son, she's all I've got left."

"I will," replied MacLaren softly, feeling tears well up in his eyes at being called "son." He broke from Graham and marched to his quarters, trying to get hold of himself. Must be lack of sleep playing with his emotions. He would not let it get the better of him. Crying was such an unmanly thing to do.

MacLaren sat at the high table next to Graham, waiting impatiently for his bride to arrive. He had once more left room for Aila to sit next to him and hoped she would not embarrass him again. He had accepted her explanation with some distrust and was hoping to find her true. This time he had sent Rory to escort her to the table. He had been forced to send him twice, since the first time Rory returned with word that the maids insisted she was not quite ready. What was there to do? He bathed and dressed in ten minutes at most. He clenched his fists, fearing this may be the start of another very disappointing night.

Leaning over to talk to Chaumont, he heard Aila's arrival before he saw her. The collective gasps in the room silenced all conversation. He looked up and gasped too, his jaw dropping open. Lady Aila had entered the Great Hall. The assembly stood, and people bowed as she passed. Her gold gown shimmering in the candlelight, she indeed resembled royalty. Her auburn hair hung in long ringlets, and her face was framed with a gossamer chaplet veil. She was the most beautiful creature MacLaren had ever seen. He stood transfixed, watching her approach. All eyes were on her. Her eyes scanned the crowd until they found his. A small smile played on her lips. She approached, her eyes for MacLaren alone.

She walked up to the head table and first greeted her father, as was proper.

"I'm sorry, Father, for…"

"Enough, child, 'tis all forgiven." He gave her a warm embrace. "Ye look much like yer mother." It was quite a compliment. He smiled down proudly at his daughter and then motioned for her to take her seat by her husband. MacLaren had to fight the urge to grab her and steal her away, back to their chambers, or perhaps even a dimly lit passageway would do.

"A toast to the marriage of the Lady Aila and Sir Padyn MacLaren!" Chaumont was first to find his voice, and the rest of the assembly joined in the toast, cheering the happy couple.

Aila smiled at the crowd, looking around with delight. MacLaren glared back at the clamoring men, wishing they would all stop looking at his wife. After the initial shock of her beauty passed, he felt a pulsing mix of pride, possessiveness, and suspicion. He feared his lovely bride would use her beauty to manipulate him, as another lovely lady had done to him once before. But no, he remembered, he was not supposed to judge her using another woman's measure. MacLaren scowled. Aila was forever getting him to make promises that were wretchedly hard to keep.

"Ye look much improved," MacLaren told her and internally groaned. That hadn't come out quite right.

"A bath and a clean gown does help," said Aila, grinning as if he wasn't the biggest oaf in the world.

"What I meant is I've ne'er seen any woman as beautiful as ye are tonight." There, that sounded better. Aila's smile faded. What had he said wrong?

"I ken ye have little love for beautiful women."

"Ah, well," he stammered. She had a point there. "I find I may need to revise my opinion to say that perhaps I can tolerate beautiful women who are Scots." He leaned in closer. "Particularly, beautiful women I somehow had the good fortune to marry."

Aila's smile returned, and her eyes twinkled in the candlelight. "I find I may be able to tolerate a verra braw Highlander I happen to have married."

"Good to know you two have moved to the level of tolerance," said Chaumont, who was sitting on the other side of Aila and listening shamelessly to their private conversation. Both MacLaren and Aila glared at him, and he laughed with enthusiasm.

"Ignore him," said MacLaren. "Dinna ken why I tolerate the bastard." He pulled from his sporran an emerald necklace. "This is for ye. 'Twas my mother's." He awkwardly struggled with the clasp but managed to get it around her neck.

"'Tis beautiful," Aila murmured. "Thank ye. I will cherish it." She gazed at him happily. Oh, so happily.

He kissed her. Far in the distance, he could hear people cheering and knew he was becoming a spectacle. He didn't care. He kissed her again and would have gone on kissing her had not Aila realized people were watching and pulled away, embarrassed. He could hardly wait to have her alone.

The musicians struck up a lively tune, and the meal proceeded as normal, though MacLaren noted warily the addition of a taster for the food at the head table. Graham was indeed taking the threat to both their lives seriously. MacLaren also learned that Graham had "rewarded" the soldiers who participated on the recent mission by giving them some leave from their duties, thus reducing their opportunities for being in places where mischief may be done.

MacLaren was reassured by these security measures and that Graham was careful not to reveal their suspicions to the traitor amongst them. It was a dangerous game they were playing, but the potential rewards made it worth the effort. Aila grabbed his arm as jugglers started to perform, the light in her eyes dancing with childlike joy. Yes, the rewards would be great indeed.

After the meal was finished, Graham stood and addressed his clan. Voices hushed as the laird began to speak in a voice that rang strong and clear through the hall. "First, I begin by thanking my new son-in-law for his courageous actions in rescuing my daughter." A cheer rang forth from the crowd. "And I commend my daughter for defending her virtue from that bastard McNab." Another cheer brought heat to Aila's face.

"But I must tell ye the battle has just begun. Archibald McNab has declared himself our enemy. 'Tis he who has been deliberately, wi' malice o' forethought, set fire to our fields." Graham paused as there were gasps in the hall from those who did not yet know their enemy. "This dog, for I canna rightfully call him a man, wishes to steal the verra bread from yer table. He believes himself yer better. He would steal the Lady Aila and declare himself yer master. What do ye say to that?" Roars of protest ripped from the crowd.

"Remember, my clansmen, 'twas his clan what betrayed Wallace, was traitor to the alliance o' the clans, and denied the freedom o' all Scots." People were on their feet now, yelling their protests of McNab, banging their knives or goblets on the table. Aila was surprised at the racket and slid closer to MacLaren on the bench they shared. He put his arm around her protectively, amused by her response and by Graham, whom he determined was a master at eliciting the utmost loyalty of his clan.

"Remember, my brethren, that we are a free people. Though our king be imprisoned by the English and our land lies in ruin, still we remain true to our heritage, under the protection o' the blessed St. Andrew and the guidance o' the King o' Kings, we hold fast to the true inheritance o' the Scots—our freedom." More cheers erupted from the crowd as all were moved by Graham's words. He paused until the assembly grew absolutely silent, waiting in expectation for him to speak.

"I remember, though some have forgot, a day many years ago when we, the lairds o' Scotland came together at the monastery at Arbroath to write a treatise of our country and our people. It declared our freedom from foreign rule, the right o' the Scots to govern themselves and live in peace. The truth o' these words remains as true today as the day I signed it, for 'it is in truth not for glory, nor riches, nor honors that we are fighting, but for freedom—for that alone, which no honest man gives up but with life itself.'" More cheers again rang from the crowd, and more than one man wiped a tear from his eye.

Graham raised his glass to the crowd, and it was once again silent. "So I ask ye, my children, my true sons and daughters, to declare yer allegiance. I ask, no' demand, since ye are free to choose him whom ye will serve. If ye choose to serve me, declare it now. If ye choose to serve McNab, I will bid ye farewell wi' my sorrow."

MacLaren was first to jump to his feet. "Laird Graham, I drink to the alliance o' our clans through no' only our marriage vows but also a like-mindedness in devotion to freedom against the English and all who would subdue us. May our clans live in harmony forever. I pledge to ye my sword in defense of ye against that bastard McNab, along wi' the swords o' my men, as yer cause is our own." To a man, MacLaren's warriors stood and drank down their cups with Graham in a show of alliance.

Then Warwick stepped forward, pledging his fealty, obedience, and loyalty to Laird Graham. This was followed by Pitcairn and the rest of Graham's men, both soldiers and other clansmen.

As the men came forward one by one, Chaumont leaned to MacLaren, asking, "Would it be permissible for me to rise?"

MacLaren was surprised but said, "Ye are free to form allegiances where ye wish."

Chaumont nodded, and in his eyes was an earnest desire MacLaren had never seen before. He could not fault his friend for wanting to be part of this clan or wanting to form an alliance with this man. Yet he had thought Chaumont beyond the cares of fidelity and family, but perhaps that was only because he had none. MacLaren realized he had misjudged his friend's need to belong.

Chaumont stepped forward, and the crowd once again was hushed as they watched the tall French knight approach. Chaumont took a knee before Graham, saying, "I am but a landless knight, a bastard son, yet I offer you my sword, my allegiance, loyalty, and fidelity, if you would accept this unworthy vessel."

Graham glanced over at MacLaren, who nodded.

Graham raised his goblet to Chaumont, saying, "Rise, Sir Chaumont, and drink to our alliance. I accept wi' honor yer pledge o' loyalty." Both men drank deeply.

The traitor watched as, one by one, people rose to give allegiance to their laird. He had too, of course, swallowing the wine like gall. How he hated this man. Graham had taken everything from him. It was time for recompense. The traitor glanced at MacLaren. How many times did he have to kill this man? He should have been dead on McNab's sword last night. *No matter, the poisoned whiskey is still waiting for him. He'll no' avoid Aila this night, the rutting bastard.* The man sipped his wine, confident that this time his plan would not fail. By morn, MacLaren would be dead.

MacLaren walked back to the tower where Aila was waiting for him. He had sent her back with full escort so he, Chaumont, Graham, Pitcairn, and Warwick could make plans for war. They arranged a battle plan against McNab for two days hence. Unknown to Pitcairn or Warwick, however, it had been previously arranged with Graham that MacLaren's men alone would ride early that next morn and attack the McNab fortress. It was hoped that since Pitcairn and Warwick would spread the plans for battle to the men, the traitor would hear of it and send the news to McNab. In this way, McNab would be unprepared for battle.

Graham had argued to send some of his most trusted warriors, like Warwick and a few others whom he deemed beyond suspicion into battle with MacLaren, but MacLaren trusted none but his own men, and so the plan had been made. MacLaren hoped the ruse had been worth the effort, since it had kept him from his bed, and now he would have precious little sleep before rising again to ride back to the McNab stronghold. Tired or not, he was determined this evening to finish what he had started with his beautiful and most unexpected bride.

Pausing beside the guard he had posted by his wife's door, he dismissed the soldier to get some sleep and entered her chamber, locking the heavy wooden door behind him. His wife lay on the bed, dressed in a linen chemise ornately decorated with lace. She was beautiful and sound asleep. MacLaren breathed deep, enjoying the peace of the moment. She had been everything he could hope for tonight, vibrant and bonnie. More importantly, her words held more truth than he initially had given credence.

MacLaren watched her sleep, her hair splayed on the pillow, her mouth slightly ajar. She gave a soft snort and shifted position. He smiled. In sleep, at least, she seemed real enough and decidedly lacking in avarice or deceit. Sitting on the bed, he poured a glass of whiskey from a red jeweled carafe someone had thoughtfully left for him. He would drink a few sips then wake his bride and make her his wife.

Twenty-Six

AILA WOKE WITH A START TO THE SOUND OF POUNDING. She sat up, trying to get her bearings. She was in bed with MacLaren lying beside her. He was still fully clothed on top of the blankets, looking like he had rather collapsed in his current position. Someone pounded loudly on the door. She shook MacLaren tentatively, but he remained still.

"MacLaren, Lady Aila, are you well?" came the voice of Chaumont.

Still groggy, Aila opened the door to him. It was quite dark and must have been the middle of the night. She wondered why anyone would be trying to wake them.

"Good evening, sir. Is something amiss?"

"*Oui*, your husband didn't open the door when his squire knocked, and so he got me worried something had happened to you both." Another man appeared behind Chaumont, whom Aila believed to be MacLaren's squire. "Where's MacLaren?"

"Still sleeping. I'm sorry we didn't answer yer first knock. 'Tis the first sleep we've had in two days."

Chaumont gave her a knowing smile and walked

around to the collapsed form of MacLaren. "Come now, time to wake." But MacLaren didn't stir. "MacLaren." Chaumont gave him a shake, but again got no response. "Padyn?" He gave him a hard shove.

"What... what are ye about?" MacLaren sat straight up and looked around, bewildered. Aila regarded her half-asleep husband, his hair pointing in all directions, and stifled a giggle. He appeared uncharacteristically comical.

"Time to dress, sleepyhead. Remember, we have a date with McNab," said Chaumont.

"Och, aye." MacLaren turned so he was sitting on the side of the bed. He put his head in his hands.

"A drink to wake ye?" asked his squire, offering the cup of whiskey sitting next to him.

MacLaren grunted at the cup. "I dinna even drink it last night. Must have fallen asleep where I stood. Nay, I dinna want it now. Must have a clear head." As he spoke, MacLaren gestured, hitting the cup from the squire's hand, spilling it to the floor.

"Dinna worrit o'er it. I'll clean it later," said Aila, trying to be helpful. "Did ye say ye were going to face McNab?"

MacLaren gave a sidelong glance at Chaumont, who shrugged.

"Aye," said MacLaren, looking warily at Aila, "we ride to surprise McNab and finish this between us. But only my own lads are going. None else must ken it, or we will lose the advantage of surprise."

Aila nodded. "Thank ye for trusting me." Though still not fully awake, Aila knew it was significant for MacLaren to share with her his plans.

"Dinna make me regret it," MacLaren grumbled.

To Chaumont he said, "Go and ready the men. I'll meet ye in the lower bailey."

Aila wrapped herself in her plaid and sat on her bed, hugging her knees as she watched his squire prepare MacLaren for battle. She had seen men in full armor, but never had she been allowed to see the process of the dressing. It was an important time for the men who had earned the right to be called knight, steeped in tradition and superstition. She understood that by choosing to be armored in her presence, MacLaren was showing he trusted and accepted her.

MacLaren washed his face in a basin while his squire carefully laid out his armor. Aila bit her lip and watched wide-eyed as MacLaren stripped naked. Even in the dim light of a single candle, she was awed by his muscular body, emanating strength and power. Aila stared at his chiseled abdominal muscles, tight and firm, going down to... Her jaw dropped.

MacLaren caught her eye and gave her a wink. She hid her face in her plaid for having been caught gawking. When she looked up again, he was more decent in drawers and a linen shirt. Over this he put on an arming doublet that had waxed laces with which to attach the armor. Woolen hose were pulled on, and MacLaren tied them to the doublet while his squire wrapped his knees with cloth to provide padding under the armor. The two worked together quickly, and Aila sat silently, watching this practiced dance.

Chain mail chausses were slipped over the woolen stockings and tied to the doublet. The squire then began to attach the armor pieces, working from the feet up, starting with the spurs. Then steel greaves were added over the shins, and poleyn steel plates were strapped over the knees. Padded cuisses were attached to his thighs, dark green in color and studded with rivets holding small metal plates underneath.

A mail hauberk was placed over his head, which appeared to Aila like a mail shirt that hung down to just above the knee, reminding her of MacLaren's kilt. A green canvas cuirass was then placed across his chest. As the squire laced it in the back, Aila noted the studded riveting, indicating the steel plates that lined the inside of the cuirass, providing extra protection for his chest. Curved steel plates were laced to MacLaren's outer arms and elbows. Over his head, his squire pulled a surcoat of blue and green that hung down to his knees. The surcoat was belted, from which hung MacLaren's dirk. Finally, his squire strapped on his sword, the large claymore Aila had seen before. His helm and gauntlets he kept to the side, too hot to wear except in battle.

With shining eyes, Aila gazed at her fully-armed knight. Though she abhorred the thought of her husband riding into battle, still she could not help but admire the man before her.

"Anything more, sir?" asked the squire.

"Aye, pour some o' that whiskey into a flask for later and finish getting yerself armed. I'll be down shortly." The squire did as he was told and left quickly.

"Whiskey is no proper meal. Shall I fetch something else for ye?" asked Aila.

"Nay, my men will have collected the trenchers from last night. We'll eat as we can along the way."

Aila made a face at the mention of day-old trenchers, and MacLaren laughed softly, walking to her and taking her hands. "'Tis no' that bad. I've eaten much worse, I assure ye."

"I warrant 'tis pointless to tell ye to be careful."

"I am always careful wi' both my life and that o' my men. God willing, I shall return soon." He kissed one hand then the other, and Aila felt happy tingles at his touch. "Do ye have a crucifix?" he asked.

"Aye," said Aila, opening a drawer and handing MacLaren her rosary. MacLaren knelt, holding the cross, and prayed silently. She prayed as well, asking for his protection and safe return. MacLaren made the sign of the cross and stood, taking her hand in his.

"I must go. I wish I could leave a guard for ye, but I need every man."

"I'll be safe. Dinna worrit o'er me."

"Lock the door behind me and remain here. Yer father will come to bring ye food and drink. Trust none but him, ye ken?"

"Aye."

"If our task goes well, I'll be home by the morrow, or maybe even tonight." MacLaren took Aila in his arms, and she hugged him tight, feeling nothing but cold steel plates. He kissed her gently and looked at her as if he wanted to say something. Aila waited expectantly, but he only gave her another soft kiss and walked from the room. As promised, Aila bolted the door behind him and turned back to the window to watch his departure. She could see nothing in the moonless night.

MacLaren rode hard through the night and into the early dawn. He was tired of traveling the same path and was determined this would be the last time he rode to McNab's land. He hoped to catch the man by surprise, ending this feud quickly and easily. He gave the men instructions to leave McNab to him. He wanted to kill the man for what he had done to his wife.

Aila now encompassed many of his thoughts, and try as he might to focus on the task at hand, many times during his long night ride did he think upon her. He remembered her beauty last night at supper, yet even more attractive in his mind was how she had looked after their wild chase—dirty and unkempt but untamed and free. MacLaren fought against the images of his wife, telling himself all women were conniving and deceitful, but it didn't have the power it once had. Despite his best efforts, just as the hooves of his horse continued to trod down the hard-packed road, so did his mind return to Aila and their future together. He thought of giving her children, and more times than was comfortable did his thoughts turn to the process of making those wee bairns.

As they neared McNab's stronghold, they approached more cautiously, scouting for lookouts. They passed quietly through the fields of the crofters, and MacLaren witnessed their poverty, understanding the draw that marrying Aila must be for a young laird. This understanding changed none of MacLaren's plans; McNab had chosen to be his enemy, and MacLaren would see him dead.

Close to McNab's stronghold, they cut a large tree

as a battering ram. McNab's tower house had limited defenses, and MacLaren planned to ram through the front gate and into the house with speed and surprise. They had years of practice, and they made their makeshift battering ram quickly. It was carried in a series of slings, three men riding on each side.

McNab's square tower house loomed before them, an eerie black blight on the landscape in the grey dawn. MacLaren donned his helm and gauntlets, experiencing the tight, sick feeling in his stomach that plagued him before battle.

Shouting his warrior's cry, MacLaren charged the gate, followed by the thunderous sound of his knights. Shouts rang forth from the guards on the gate, but the battering ram was already in place before the defenses could be mounted. MacLaren's archers knelt and shot volleys at the heads of the men at the gate and toward anyone who approached the gate from the wall, providing cover for the men with the battering ram. They were through the main gate within five blows of the ram, and the fight was on.

MacLaren rode forward, slashing through the resistance, which remained light, as he had expected. After being carried across the yard, the ram soon battered down the main entrance to the square tower. MacLaren smiled when the door gave way with only two blows. His enjoyment was short-lived. Soldiers began pouring from the gaping hole, and a steady assault of arrows from the rooftop drove his men back. Where had McNab gotten all these soldiers and archers? MacLaren pulled his men back to form lines. Fighting together, they would have a better chance against the onslaught. He cursed for grossly underestimating McNab's forces, but it could not be possible. Confused, his men fought valiantly, but they were desperately outnumbered.

"MacLaren!" Chaumont's shout could barely be heard over the din, and MacLaren looked to where Chaumont was pointing. The world around him suddenly slowed to a stop. The noise of the battle faded into silence.

It was the Golden Knight.

MacLaren stared at the figure in disbelief. How could this be? He suddenly realized most of the soldiers emerging from the house were French, not Scot. He was fighting the most notorious knight in all of France. And he was going to lose.

"Mount, mount!" he called to his men, trying to give them some advantage over the sea of foot soldiers before them. Never had MacLaren ordered his troops to withdraw from battle. Never had he given his back to the enemy.

Until today.

"Retreat!"

Twenty-Seven

AILA SAT ON HER BED, ALONE IN HER TOWER ROOM, the light of a lone candle flickering on the walls. The room seemed much larger and empty now that her husband had gone. She drew her plaid closer around her shoulders and hugged her knees to her chest against the early morning chill. She could not help but smile, the image of her knight warming her deep inside.

MacLaren had not spoken words of love or even mild acceptance, but he had, she noted, stopped insulting her. Not much to be sure, but it was a start. More importantly, he had trusted her, trusted her with the plans of their surprise attack on McNab, trusted her by getting armed in her presence. She smiled and sighed with contentment. The realization of the depth of her feelings for him came without warning. She cherished his trust, but she wanted more. She wanted to be loved.

She stood from the bed and briskly shook out her plaid, shaking off those dangerous feelings as well. Best not to feel this way. MacLaren may have grown to accept her and trust her, but that was a far cry from loving her. He may eventually make a perfectly agreeable husband, polite and courteous, but she could expect nothing more. She must learn to keep her emotions under control, or she would live in disappointment and bitterness all her days. A vision of her mother crept to mind, and she shuddered at her potential future. She would not willingly travel down that path. She would protect herself from the pain of unrealistic expectations and false hope.

Aila stood barefoot on the cold stone floor, the warmth draining from her. Still, she was determined to be cheerful. MacLaren's treatment of her had much improved, and she was no longer in fear of being beaten or imprisoned. He was a good man, honorable and fair. It was pointless to wish for anything more from a husband.

It was time to get to work. Straightening her shoulders, she prepared for the day. She brushed and plaited her hair before remembering she was not allowed to leave her quarters, and even if she could, it would be hours before even the earliest riser in the castle awoke. She sat back down, feeling helpless to be waiting for the men to settle things while she hid in her room. She had never thought of herself as the courageous type, but somehow, waiting in isolation all day was maddening. Recalling the spilt whiskey, she hastened to clean it, grateful for something she could do.

When she leaned over to move the soaked rushes so she could mop the floor, a dead mouse lay in the puddle of whiskey. She recoiled instinctively from the sight. Why had the mouse had chosen that particular spot to die? It looked almost as though it had been poisoned.

Linguam autem nullus hominum domare potest inquietum malum plena veneno mortifero.

A chill crept up her spine. *It is a restless evil, full of deadly poison.* Senga had brought that red-jeweled bottle of whiskey from someone in the castle to celebrate Aila's nuptials. Aila had not drunk from the bottle, and it had remained on her nightstand ever since. But who sent it? She could not remember. Perhaps Senga had not said. But still, Senga had been working for the traitor, and if the bottle was from him…

With a sense of panic, Aila recalled MacLaren had asked his flask be filled with that whiskey. Aila flung off her chemise and dressed quickly in her men's clothes and cloak. She only hoped she could get to him in time before he drank from the poisoned flask. She paused at the door. He had specifically told her not to leave her room, and here she was sneaking down to the stables to ride off into the night. He was going to kill her. She did not even know for sure there was anything amiss with the whiskey. Yet if she was right and did not warn him, he would die. She was wide awake, her heart pounding. She unbolted the door. Her choice was clear.

Never before had she felt scared walking down the spiral steps to the lower bailey. The last time she had been on these stairs at night, she had been running for her life. Now the darkness frightened her, and she froze at every sound. She never realized how the sound of her steps echoed softly or how much like moaning was the sound of the wind along the castle wall.

Creeping on soft feet, she reached the side door to the stable and froze. There on the floor by the door was the slumped figure of a young lad. He was dead. She opened her mouth to scream, but no sound emerged. Visions of Fergus came to her unbidden. Once again, her feet were planted to the floor, and she was unable to move. The lad shifted a bit and began to snore. Not dead. She exhaled her held breath.

She snuck to the door of the stables and stood with her hand on the latch for a few minutes, gathering her courage. If she opened the door, would she find once again the man who had struck the stable master, who had betrayed her clan, and who had killed her poor maid? What was she doing? MacLaren, her father, everyone would be furious. She didn't even know if the flask was truly poisoned. She should turn around and go back to bed where it was safe.

Viriliter agite et confortamini nolite timere nec paveatis a conspectu eorum quia Dominus Deus tuus ipse est ductor tuus et non dimittet nec derelinquet te.

Aila closed her eyes and felt the comfort of the scripture. *Be strong and courageous. Do not be afraid or terrified because of them, for the Lord your God goes with you; he will never leave you nor forsake you.* Praying she would be filled with the courage she needed, she opened her eyes, breathing her prayer, her shoulders relaxing. She once again attempted to open the door, and this time her body complied. Pushing down on the latch, Aila jumped when the door creaked open. She glanced at the sleeping stable lad beside her. He snored louder.

Before her was the gaping darkness of the stable. No light from a lantern beckoned her; the stable master was gone. She started the move forward, her right hand trailing along the side of the stable. Reaching the main stables, she stopped and listened again. Hearing nothing, she gathered her courage and slowly began the walk into the gloom of the stable.

She counted down the stalls, her hand guiding her way. After the correct number of stalls, she stopped and opened the door to find Shadow. Even in the dark, she could tell it was him, from the feel of his silky coat to his nuzzled greeting. Saddling him in the pitch black was a challenge, but she had done it many times in dim light, and her fingers knew their way. She deftly finished her work, slipped out the false door into the cave, and locked the gate behind her.

Emerging from the tunnel, she breathed deep of the cold night air. It was a dark night with no moon to light her way, so she carefully picked her way down the slope and to the main path to McNab's holding. She trusted Shadow to guide her. They had traveled the path many times before and found their way by memory.

She rode as fast as she could safely travel, which unfortunately was not particularly swift. Worry knotted in her stomach. MacLaren could drink from that flask at any time, and she would be a widow before their marriage ever had a chance to begin. Since her anxiety could give her nothing but a stomach ache, she attempted to turn her thoughts back to the verse that had come to mind outside the stable door. She could trust in the Lord, for whatever the outcome, she would never be forsaken.

She rode along until the blackness turned to grey and dawn slowly brought color back to the landscape. Mist settled thick around her, filling her lungs with its cold, moist air. She could ride faster now and she urged her mount forward. She was well onto McNab's land and became wary, watching and listening for any signs of life. She kept the hood of her cloak over her head, obscuring her face, hoping if any chanced to see her, they would never guess her identity. If she rode back into McNab's possession, MacLaren would never forgive her, never believe her, and perhaps never come to rescue her. Of course that presumed he lived long enough to do or feel any of those things. She leaned forward and rode faster. MacLaren must be found before McNab found her.

Aila had never ridden this far into McNab's territory, though she had seen rough sketches of the area. She proceeded in the direction of McNab's tower house, using nothing but prayer and dead reckoning. The sun had risen above the horizon and fought its way through the thick mist, giving the dense fog a rosy hue. She picked her way through the trees up a slope to a ridgeline. From there, she hoped to gain her bearings.

From somewhere in the mist, horses approached, soft at first then rumbling closer. The sound echoed in the trees and the fog, making it impossible to ascertain from where the noise was coming, and she could not determine which way to flee. Suddenly, mounted knights sprang from the mist and raced down the hillside to her left without noticing her. She recognized MacLaren's colors. These were his men, but where were they going? Where was MacLaren? Had they finished their mission so soon? They raced past her only to be swallowed up in the fog again as they sped out of sight. Nay, something was wrong.

Without thinking, she raced up the hill to the crest

of the ridge just as the sun broke through the fog. In the valley was a veritable army, riding toward her at speed. She gasped at the image of their quarries— MacLaren and Chaumont, riding hard up the slope. Chasing them were hundreds of armored knights, the sun glinting off their helms. Thundering hooves beat the ground, shaking the very earth. Her mind swam. McNab could not possibly have raised such an army… could he? Wherever this army had come from, one thing was clear: MacLaren was going to die.

The thunderous approach was not lost on Shadow, who had memories of his own. He reared, kicking the air and swirling the fingers of mist around them. She was struck by a desperate idea. It was madness, but perhaps if MacLaren had taken her for the ghost of Bruce, others would too. Aila urged Shadow forward to the top of the ridge, in full view of the monstrous army. Shadow's shrill neigh pierced the dawn, and he reared again. The sound of the approaching army softened, and the air around her grew deathly still. The soldiers slowed to a stop. Shadow reared once again, his penetrating neigh cutting across the valley before she could calm him.

MacLaren and Chaumont reached the top, and MacLaren raced for her. She could not see his face behind his helm, but she tingled at his approach all the same. He was not dead. Och, but he was going to be angry.

"Aila, get down," he hissed as he rode toward her, and she complied. They rode down the other slope and stopped out of sight of the approaching soldiers. Chaumont dismounted and crawled back up to the ridge to determine what McNab's forces would do.

Grabbing the reins from Aila's hands, MacLaren snapped, "What are ye doing here?"

"Ye're alive!" she said happily.

"Have ye taken leave o' yer senses?"

Chaumont slid down to their location. "They are pulling back. Looks like they are going around the forest, though I cannot tell you why. Lady Aila, is that you?" Chaumont removed his helm and looked confused.

"Good morn to ye, Sir Chaumont."

"Mercy me, my lady. I thought you were some sort of apparition."

"They believe her to be the ghost o' Robert the Bruce," MacLaren snarled, also removing his helm. Aila thought for a moment he might throw it at her. Chaumont laughed, but MacLaren was finding no humor in the situation.

"Ah, so the superstitious Scots won't enter the haunted forest, and the French follow their lead. My lady, you are to be congratulated," said Chaumont, bowing low. "You have saved this morning from becoming a rout, and since it is my own life you have protected, I give you my utmost thanks."

Aila sat taller in her saddle and smiled back. "Thank ye kindly." She hoped MacLaren might also praise her valor. Her hopes fell the instant she saw his face. He was glaring at her, the veins on his temple bulging. "What the bloody hell are ye doing here?"

"The whiskey's poisoned. Dinna drink it," Aila's voice was timid in the face of such anger.

"What? How do ye ken that? And what are ye doing here!?"

"I… I'm trying to save ye from drinking the poison."
Aila's voice grew softer as MacLaren's grew louder.

"Did I or did I no' tell ye to remain in yer room?"

"Aye."

"When I give an order, I expect it to be obeyed. Ye could have been killed or taken prisoner by McNab, ye ken? Unless that was yer true motive for coming to his gate."

Aila gasped. She was beginning to wonder why she had bothered to come all this way to save him. "I was trying to save yer life."

"Just because ye take some scattered-brained notion into yer wee head 'tis no reason for disobedience. 'Tis time ye learnt that wi' disobedience comes punishment."

Aila leaned back, but he still held her reins.

"I'll take whatever punishment you had in mind." Chaumont said mildly, mounted once again and nudging in between their horses. "If the lady needs a champion, I will be he."

"This is no concern o' yers," MacLaren growled.

"Ah, but it is. The Lady Aila has saved your life and mine, though I'm thinking you hardly deserve the saving." He turned to Aila, asking, "What makes you think the whiskey was poisoned?"

"The whiskey was delivered for our wedding night by Senga. I dinna ken from whom. The mouse who tasted a drop is stone cold now." She glared at MacLaren. "If ye dinna believe me, why don't ye take a draft and see for yerself?"

MacLaren took the flask from where it was tied to his saddle. He removed the stopper, smelled it, and lifted the flask to his lips.

Twenty-Eight

"Nay, sir, dinna drink it!" exclaimed Aila.

MacLaren spat out the whiskey and poured the contents onto the ground.

"Poisoned?" asked Chaumont.

MacLaren nodded but kept his eyes on Aila. Neither noticed Chaumont slowly backing away, allowing MacLaren to come beside her again. MacLaren removed his gauntlets and returned her reins to her, placing his hands over hers. He opened his mouth to speak, but said nothing.

"I think the words you're searching for are, 'I'm sorry for being a horse's arse.'" Chaumont's words floated through the mist, making Aila smile. MacLaren glared in Chaumont's direction, the familiar scowl returning to his face.

"Let's ride. We need to reach Dundaff as soon as possible to warn them o' the impending siege." MacLaren released Aila's hands.

"Siege?" The very word struck fear in Aila's gut.

"Aye, 'tis likely. They have the soldiers now, though I canna begin to explain how."

"Can we survive it?" The mist suddenly felt more cold and foreboding.

"For a while, at least," MacLaren had been part of many a siege though generally on the offensive side. If you had a well-equipped, well-disciplined army and were willing to wait, the occupants, or what was left of them, nearly always surrendered. To be the object of a siege was not a thing he relished, knowing slow starvation would probably be his future. Yet he had made a promise to Graham to stand with him against his enemies, and he would do it.

"We've no' brought in the crops yet," said Aila, her eyes wide. "We'll starve."

"We have much to prepare afore they surround the castle. Let's ride."

"Wait! What if we could get more warriors to join the battle on our side?"

"Aye, that's the only way to defeat the army—meet them on the field. But we dinna have enough troops to face the army McNab has somehow raised, even with our forces combined."

"What if we sent a plea to the Campbells for help?"

"Aye, the Campbells have the warriors to do the job. But wi' all due respect, if they did naught to help yer father when McNab was burning his fields, what makes ye think they would help now?

"Because we are fostering Hamish, one o' the laird's sons. He would be caught up in the siege, too."

MacLaren raised an eyebrow. That was certainly interesting information. The lass had a point, a good one. They should certainly appeal to the Campbells for assistance. "'Tis a bonnie idea. We'll send a messenger as soon as we reach Dundaff."

"But we're half the way to the Campbells now. If we return all the way to Dundaff only to send a rider back here, it will waste an entire day. We should ride now to Laird Campbell."

"Nay, I must return wi' my men and make preparations. They take orders from none but me. I must return now."

"Then I will ride to the Campbells."

MacLaren replied instantly. "Nay, ye will return to Dundaff."

"Where it's safe? If Dundaff is to be sieged, I'd be safer riding the country requesting assistance than inside the castle walls fighting over the last scraps of food."

"Ye forget ye are what he wants. Ye canna ride around wi'out protection. Ye could be taken again or robbed and killed. Ye dinna understand the dangers."

"I will take the message," offered Chaumont.

"Do ye ken the way?" Aila asked.

"Not at all. Is it difficult to find from here?"

No one answered, leaving Chaumont to guess that indeed it was.

"I can do this. Please let me help me people," beseeched Aila.

"Nay, 'tis too dangerous for a woman alone," said MacLaren impatiently.

Chaumont spoke up again. "I will be her guard."

"Nay!" shouted MacLaren at Chaumont. "She'll no' be riding to the Campbells. I've lost all who are dear to me. I winna lose her, too."

"I'm dear to ye?" asked Aila.

"I'm not?" asked Chaumont.

MacLaren scowled at them, sputtering a few incoherent words. A small smile played on Aila's lips. Perhaps he cared for her after all. The thought warmed her, and despite the dire situation, she felt rather lighthearted. Somehow the revelation gave her courage, and she was even more determined to ride to the Campbells. She had thought she might be able to do it a moment ago, but if MacLaren felt something akin to affection for her, she knew she could.

"MacLaren… Padyn, I'm a fast rider. Ye ken it. None will catch me. Let me do this thing. Let me help save my clan."

MacLaren glared, but this time she interpreted the look as one of concern.

"Your wife makes a valid argument. I swear no harm will come to her," Chaumont said quietly. At least she had convinced him.

"After we secure the Campbells' assistance, we can return to the castle through the secret passage I told ye about," Aila continued.

"Nay." MacLaren shook his head, turning to Chaumont. "After ye return from the Campbells, take her to the convent where she will be safe from this. Then ye alone may return to the castle."

Aila's heart soared. "Thank ye. I will no' fail ye." MacLaren trusted her to do this mission, and it made her warm and tingly. She wanted to return to Dundaff after going to the Campbells, to stand with her people, but she knew better than to press her luck.

MacLaren looked from Aila to Chaumont. Aila sensed the struggle with his thoughts, or possibly his emotions. He looked decidedly unhappy. Aila waited, hoping for some declaration of love.

"We've tarried in this glen too long," said MacLaren. Aila nodded and turned to go. It was not exactly what she was hoping for. MacLaren called back to them, "Aila, take care. Ye are… well… ye are dear to me."

Aila smiled with delight. "As ye are to me."

"Ahem." Chaumont cleared his throat, looking at MacLaren expectantly.

"Chaumont, ye auld bastard, yer dear to me, too. Now look after my lady wife, or I'll run ye through."

"MacLaren," responded Chaumont with an easy smile, "oh lawful son of wedded parents, I love you, too."

Chaumont was a good rider, swift and sure. His mount was strong, his cause noble, and he had been saved from having to die bravely. It was his chivalric duty to be courageous in the face of impossible odds, in order to protect the life of MacLaren and his fellow knights. Had Aila not intervened, MacLaren and he surely would have been killed, hopefully allowing their fellow comrades in arms enough time to escape a rout and live to sing melancholy tales of their tragic last stand. Fortunately, Aila, or rather her impersonation of an apparition, had saved him from the honor of the type of heroism that generally proved fatal.

The sun rose in the sky, chasing away the damp and the mist. Chaumont was generally cheerful, but today was a sheer delight. All he had to do now was follow Aila's lead, guard her person, and secure an alliance with the Campbells. There was also the matter of the Golden Knight, far afield from his rightful place in France. But Chaumont wasn't about to let a few hundred well-trained knights come between him and his good humor.

Chaumont easily threaded through the trees down the slope, following Aila. When they reached the open heath, she nudged her mount into a gallop and raced away. He kicked his mount to follow, riding fast, then faster. Soon he was approaching dangerous speeds, but still the image of Aila kept getting smaller as she distanced him with every step. There was nothing he could do but urge his mount forward and hold on for dear life. She was as swift as the wind. No woman should be able to ride with such speed. It was maddening, humbling, and intriguing. He thought of MacLaren and couldn't help but smile. He had truly married a vixen despite her shy appearance. Chaumont raced after her, desperately trying to keep her in sight. It was unmanning to have a mere slip of a girl best him so easily, and as soon as he caught up with her, he would tell her so. It didn't appear they would be having words anytime soon.

Despite his wounded pride, Chaumont acknowledged she was leading them quickly off McNab's land. One could never accuse her of stalling to be retaken or joining up with McNab's forces. She rode like the very hounds of hell were nipping at her feet. It reminded him of how MacLaren rode at times. They were a perfect match. When at last they had entered onto MacLaren's land and the landscape started to look more familiar, Chaumont called for her to rest the horses. He could use a break from riding too, but he'd rather be tortured until death before admitting it. Well, maybe not death. He was not quite that proud.

Resting by a fresh spring, she explained they would travel to the Braes of Balquidder, bringing Creag an Turic into sight before heading northward to the Campbells. As they continued on their journey, Chaumont insisted he lead on familiar ground, so as to better protect her, he said, and to have more control of the pace and restore his injured pride, he thought.

So it was that Chaumont was the first to arrive at Balquidder. In the valley below him lay the smoldering remains of Lady Mary Patrick's farm. The barn had been burnt to the ground. The farmhouse still stood, but the thatched roof was gone. Chaumont's blood turned to ice.

"Mary!"

"Saints above, what has happened?" Aila's voice behind him reminded Chaumont of his duty to her. It was all that prevented him from bolting down the side of the cliff to check on Mary's well-being, though to remain still made his body shake with the effort. He must see if she lived, if she was injured, if she needed him.

"I must see to the Lady Patrick and her young son." Chaumont looked to her for permission to alter their course, twitching at the delay this was causing. Worry seized him so intensely he fought to take breath.

"Certainly, please go to her while I continue the road to the Campbells."

"Nay, m'lady, I cannot allow you to ride without a guard. I promised MacLaren I would see you safe."

"I would go down into the valley wi' ye, for I am

deeply distressed at the sight below, but if I do, I'll no' make it to the Campbells afore the castle gates are closed for the night."

The delay would cost them a full day before they could put their request before Laird Campbell. Chaumont knew his duty was to ride on and protect Aila and the lives of his comrades, and Graham, his newly acquired liege. Yet his duty was also to the Lady Patrick, and he could not, would not, leave her.

"Ye see to the welfare o' Lady Patrick. I'll continue on to the Campbells and meet ye here again when I am finished," said Aila.

"Nay, my lady, I cannot leave you. 'Tis not possible."

"MacLaren would want ye to check on the welfare of his clan."

"MacLaren would want me to protect you with my dying breath."

"I will be quite safe. I can ride faster wi'out ye."

Chaumont winced. That part was true enough, but it rankled to have it spoken aloud.

"There will be none who can catch me." That part was probably true too, but Chaumont could not let her ride alone. Yet the vision of Mary in need could not be banished from his mind.

"I must stay with you," said Chaumont, looking not at Aila but at the smoldering ruins below. Chaumont struggled with unfamiliar emotions. He had seen much in his few years. Keeping emotionally distant and finding humor in his circumstances were the only ways he knew how to survive. Getting involved led only to pain, something he took care to avoid. He had perfected the role of an agreeable outsider, distant from those around him. He lived life as if he were watching a play, laughing at the actors but always staying in the audience. He didn't feel removed or distant now. He wanted to be down in the valley but struggled with conflicting loyalties. When he turned back to Aila, she had already ridden off a fair amount, expertly guiding her mount over the rocky terrain.

"Aila!" he shouted.

She stopped and turned her horse. "Go! I'll be well. Ye'll no' catch me. No one will." She spun around and continued to rapidly traverse the treacherous terrain.

Chaumont indulged in an uncharacteristic curse. He had no doubt MacLaren would see him in hell if anything happened to her.

"Take care, Lady Aila. MacLaren did not jest when he said he'd see me at the end of his sword should any harm befall you," he shouted, but she was already beyond hearing.

Resigned and relieved to be given leave to see to Mary, Chaumont guided his horse down the narrow path to the valley. To his right, Creag an Turic loomed large and vacant. He cursed again, noting the wall he had so laboriously reconstructed was breached once again. He listened for any sound coming from the structure, but all was still. MacLaren had left twenty clansmen to guard the tower castle, and there would be more castle dwellers in addition to that. The silence was eerie. Despite the bright sun, a shiver ran down his back. He continued down the slope to Mary's house, an oppressive sense of foreboding growing with every step. What had happened here? Where was everyone? He feared what the answer would bring.

Chaumont approached the home of Mary Patrick. The door had been broken and lay in bits and slivers, leaving a gaping hole into the house. Dismounting with caution, he donned his helm and gauntlets, and drew his sword before entering. Just outside the doorway, he stopped, listening for any sound. He lingered longer than necessary. He was afraid to enter. Afraid of what he would find.

He forced himself to enter the farmhouse, his boots crunching on the splintered wood and crockery. He entered cautiously, sword poised, his eyes adjusting to the dim light. The room was very different from the last time he was here. The furniture had been smashed and thrown to the sides. A peat fire smoldered in the hearth, and a porridge pot hung above it. Chaumont wondered how long it had been there and where the attackers had taken the Lady Patrick. If she had been hurt in any way… He clenched the hilt of his sword.

A battle cry ripped through the silence, jerking Chaumont out of his reverie. Instantly his sword was up in defense against the figure who raced toward him with a pike.

With joy he recognized her and lowered his sword. "Mary!" he shouted with a surge of elation.

"Go to hell, ye French bastard!" screeched Mary and stabbed him in the chest with her pike.

Twenty-Nine

MARY THRUST HER PIKE MERCILESSLY INTO HIS CHEST.

"Ow!" cried Chaumont. His steel-plated cuirass prevented the spike from cutting into his flesh, but it would surely leave a good bruise. "Mary, 'tis me," said Chaumont, removing his helm.

"Chaumont?" said Mary, startled into stopping her second lunge. Unfortunately for Chaumont, Gavin continued his attack from behind. Chaumont received a painful thump on the back of his head, and the room started to spin. He turned with it to see the horrified face of Gavin and fell with a clank next to the frying pan Gavin had thrown at his head.

When Chaumont awoke, he was lying on the floor, his head cradled in Mary's lap. She was stroking his head and murmuring something in Gaelic. He looked up at her, gaining a clear view of the wondrous bounty of her womanly figure. He stared open-mouthed. He, a man not unfamiliar with the female bosom, was gawking like a fresh lad. He snapped his mouth shut and tried to turn away, but she gently turned his head, pressing his face into her breasts. The air grew thin.

A man could die this way, he thought, making no attempt to save himself.

"There now," she was saying in English and leaned over him to press a cool cloth on the back of his head. "I am so sorry ye was hurt."

Chaumont found his face pressed further into Mary's ample bosom. He let out a groan that had nothing to do with pain.

"Does it hurt overmuch?"

"No, not at all," Chaumont answered truthfully though muffled from between her breasts.

"Och, ye poor mon, I'm suffocating ye." Mary leaned back to give Chaumont some air.

Oh, what a way to die, mused Chaumont and pressed his lips together to keep from voicing his knave's thoughts.

"Ye poor dear, I can see how much ye are hurt. Come here, Gavin, and say how verra sorry ye are."

Gavin slumped forward, looking miserable. "I'm sorry. I dinna mean to hurt ye."

Chaumont was very content lying in Mary's lap and felt more like shaking the boy's hand than chastising him. If this would be the result, perhaps he could pay the boy to lob things at him on a regular basis.

"Do not trouble yourself, Gavin," Chaumont reassured the boy. "You did right to protect your mother. You're the man of the house now, and it is your right and responsibility to do so." Gavin's shoulders straightened at Chaumont's praise, and the smile returned to his face. "Especially when your mother is such a beauty." Chaumont turned back to Mary and smiled at her reddening face.

"Wheesht now. Ye dinna ken what ye're saying. Ye're concussed." Mary helped him to stand, Gavin giving him a hand. Chaumont sighed. It was too good to last forever.

"What happened here?" Chaumont asked.

Mary let out a long breath and shook her head. "I canna say, for I've ne'er seen the like. 'Twas yesterday a huge army o' knights came thundering into the valley. They was French, all dressed in armor, like ye, Sir Chaumont, though what they were doing in the Highlands, I dinna ken. They asked where the MacLaren was. I said naught. They became angered, and I ran into the house wi' Gavin. But they broke down the door, as ye can see. All they asked was that same question, o'er and o'er. Each time I answered I dinna ken, they would break something. Then they took to torching the place. There were so many o' them. They spread out to the village and up to Creag an Turic, too. But none would say where MacLaren was other than he had ridden east. Finally, when they was satisfied we could say no more, they all left. 'Twas the oddest day I e'er had."

Chaumont nodded slowly. It was strange they would just leave, but then the whole thing defied explanation.

"Was one of the French knights dressed all in golden armor?" Chaumont asked.

Mary's eyes went wide. "Aye, looked to be their leader."

"That was the Golden Knight of Gascony. The one I told you of earlier."

"But why would he be here?"

"That I cannot answer. 'Tis very odd."

"Aye."

They stood in silence, puzzling on this unanswerable question.

"But what of the men at Creag an Turic and the villagers? Was anyone hurt?" Chaumont asked. "Where are they?"

"None was hurt, as much as I can tell. They were threatened, and the property took a beating. Afterwards, folks decided to head up to the hills and live like they used to afore MacLaren returned."

Chaumont reached out and took her hand. "Did they hurt you, Mary?"

"Nay, I woud'na let them hurt my mother," said Gavin proudly. Chaumont turned to him. He had forgotten he was in the room.

"That's a good lad," said Chaumont with a smile, which faded at the troubled look in Gavin's eye. "How did you protect her, Gavin?"

Gavin gazed at the floor then looked at Chaumont with tears in his eyes. "No one would say where MacLaren went. They was going to do horrible things. I was powerful scared o' what they would do to my mother. So I... I told them where MacLaren went." Gavin stared once more at the ground.

"What did you tell them?" asked Chaumont softly. He doubted Gavin actually knew where MacLaren was heading. Last the lad had seen MacLaren was several days ago when they were riding to Dundaff.

"I told them they rode east, in the direction of McNab's land. I told them how to get to McNab's stronghold. Did I do wrong?"

Chaumont smiled. Gavin had seen their direction

and made a guess. "No, my boy. You did exactly the right thing, standing up and protecting your mother and the rest of the clan. MacLaren would be proud."

Gavin stood taller and gazed up at Chaumont in admiration and relief. Chaumont smiled. MacLaren would not have wanted his clan to be harassed in his defense. At least now he knew how the French knights had come to McNab. The French rode to McNab and found a willing ally against MacLaren. But why these knights were here, and why they were searching for MacLaren, was indeed a mystery.

"But why are you two here alone and not with the rest of your clan?"

"This is my home. My land. I winna run from it." Mary spoke with conviction, her determination shining in her eyes. She was beautiful, and he knew his admiration had nothing to do with being hit on the head.

"You are much to be admired, my lady, but I must ask you to come with me to the convent where you will be safe. Even now, those French knights are likely preparing an attack on Dundaff. MacLaren will make his stand with Graham. I need to return." Chaumont moved toward her until he stood directly in front of her. "I need to know you are safe."

Mary shook her head. "Dinna ask me to run."

"Not running, only a calculated retrenchment. For your son, if not for yourself."

"This house, this land, 'tis all I have left." Mary spoke softly, tears welling in her eyes.

Chaumont nodded. He understood. She was bound

to this land; she could not give it up without losing herself along with it. "Then I will stay with you."

"Nay. Ye must return to MacLaren."

"I will not leave you. I cannot leave you alone and unprotected."

"Nay, 'tis no' right."

Chaumont closed his hands around hers. "Come with me, Mary."

Mary looked up into his eyes. Chaumont gazed back into hers and was lost.

"Stay with me, Mary," he murmured.

She closed her eyes and nodded. Chaumont drew her into his arms and held her tight.

With a sense of relief, Aila approached the Campbell stronghold by mid-afternoon. She had made it. Now all she had to do was convince Laird Campbell to go to war against the French... their traditional allies. As she approached the castle, Aila was hailed several times by various guards to state her business. To each, she replied, "Message to the Campbell from the Graham." At the second gate, six mounted guards surrounded her and rode with her through the series of gates, drawbridges, and portcullises. Even though she was accustomed to castle life and formidable defenses, the Campbells were impressive, to say the least. The men around her watched her carefully, and she wondered if she was being escorted or captured. Probably a bit of both.

During her ride, she had focused solely on the road ahead, traveling as swiftly as possible. Now that she had arrived at the Campbells, she must devise a plan of what to say. But how could she explain the laird's own daughter coming alone, unguarded, to ask Campbell to go to war against the French? How could she even explain who was attacking Graham? A marauding hoard of French knights seemed unlikely to say the least. She stood in the entryway of the main keep, waiting with her ever-present guard, unsure of what to say. She had yet to lower her cowl, the hood obscuring her face, so she was treated as she appeared—a young messenger.

"Come here, lad," said a man Aila thought to be the steward. She followed him into a side room. "Give me yer message," he commanded, holding out his hand.

This was going to be a problem. "The message I have 'tis for the Campbell's ears only."

"Laird Campbell is no' here. Whate'er yer message, ye can give it to me, lad."

Aila inwardly groaned. The Campbells had more than one fortress on their extensive lands. She had ridden to the one closest to the border with MacLaren, hoping luck would be with her. It was not.

"My message regards the laird's own son. I must speak to him."

The steward frowned. "Ye refer to Hamish, Laird Campbell's seventh son, who is fostering with the Graham?"

"Aye"

"Is he well? Has he taken ill?"

"He is well enough for now, but he be in grave danger. I must speak to the Campbell. Please tell me where I can find him."

The steward looked thoughtful, then told Aila to wait, turned on his heel, and left. While Aila waited, a ghillie brought her food and drink. She had not realized how hungry she was until smell of food awakened her appetite. It was all she could do not to grab at it before it was even set on the small table. She ate ravenously, hoping for luck with whoever would come through the door next. Remembering herself, she paused her eating and turned her hopes into prayer. Feeling more at peace, she continued to eat her meal.

She did not have to wait long. She was completing her hasty meal when a large man, wrapped in the Campbell plaid, walked through the door. He was a young man, certainly not the old Laird Campbell, but he held a definite resemblance to the laird. His sandy brown hair was cropped to the level of his square jaw, and he stared at her intently with sharp green eyes. He planted his feet in a wide stance and folded his muscular arms across his chest. His mistrust for her was apparent.

"Give me yer message, lad," he commanded.

"David?" Aila gasped. She remembered him from childhood, the first son of Laird Campbell, and his heir. He had certainly grown up well.

David walked over and grabbed her shoulder, giving it a firm shake. "By what right do ye name me, boy? Who are ye?" Danger flashed in his eyes.

"'Tis I, Aila. Graham's daughter," said Aila meekly in the face of such a fearsome scowl and removed her hood.

David released her immediately. "Aila? What are ye doing here?"

"We are in need of the Campbell's assistance. We are under attack, and I am afeared it will be a siege."

David frowned, the action causing deep lines to spread across his forehead, surprising in such a young man, but the heir of the Campbell would never have been just another young man. "And why does the Graham send his only daughter thus, unguarded, to seek our support?"

"My father dinna send me. I came because I learned of the danger only early this morn and thought it would be better to come directly to request help than return to Dundaff."

David crossed his arms in front of him. "Ye were out riding alone?"

"Nay, I was wi' my husband, the MacLaren."

"MacLaren?" David's eyebrows shot up.

"Aye. He returned to Dundaff, and I came here. I did have a guard but lost him along the way. Please, we've no time for this. The McNab and his allies ride against us."

David frowned again. "McNab? What danger can he pose to ye? And what allies do ye speak of? I ken none who count themselves a friend to McNab."

Aila drew in a breath, hesitating. If she told him about the French soldiers, he might think her daft. The look he was giving her was already close to that.

Voluntas regum labia iusta qui recta loquitur diligetur.

Aila took a calming breath. *Kings take pleasure in honest lips; they value a man who speaks the truth.* The proverb reminded her to speak the truth, and that is what she would do.

"McNab has joined wi' hundreds o' French knights,

all armored and mounted. If I'd no' seen it wi' my own eyes, I'd no' believed it myself."

David slowly nodded. "I've had multiple reports of large numbers of French soldiers scouring the countryside, looking for yer MacLaren, if the reports are true."

"MacLaren? Why?" Aila asked, though she knew David Campbell would have no answer.

"Something is verra amiss, Lady Aila. We will come to the aid of Graham, for indeed I fear what would happen to Hamish if I do not. And I dinna like foreigners making war on the Highlands, even if they have been our allies. I winna take it from the English, and I winna take it from the French, either."

"Thank ye, David." Aila tingled with excitement. She had done it. She had really done it. "Now I must take my leave."

"Are ye daft? I'll no' have ye riding all the way back to Dundaff by yerself. My father, yer father, and yer new husband would have to cast lots to see who got the privilege of skinning me alive."

"I'm only returning to Creag an Turic. I have a guard there to take me to St. Margaret's."

"Well, now. That sounds a bit better. I'll have a room prepared, and ye can leave in the morn."

"Nay, my escort is waiting," Aila said, edging toward the door. "He'll be most distressed if I dinna return."

"I'll send ye wi' an escort to Balquidder, if ye wish it. Though I beg ye to reconsider. 'Tis near dark, and I fear ye may come to harm."

Aila smiled sweetly, saying, "Thank ye for yer kindness. I'll be riding hard back to Creag an Turic, but I welcome anyone who can keep pace." She curtseyed

and left the room. She was given access to the stables
and allowed to choose a fresh mount. She hated to
leave Shadow behind, but he had been ridden hard
and fast and needed to rest. He would be safe with the
Campbells until he could be returned. Aila allowed her
new escort to guide her out of the castle then broke for
home. She had chosen a fast horse and felt comfortable
riding in the dark. Behind her, the men called for her
to pull up. She smiled and gave her mount full rein.

Thirty

MACLAREN SAT IN GRAHAM'S STUDY, LISTENING TO him rage. Since the news of Aila's latest adventure from the castle was likely to cause this reaction, MacLaren had waited until after they had made preparations to meet the onslaught of knights before telling the laird his daughter was once again not where she ought to be. MacLaren calmly sipped his whiskey, paying little attention to Graham's tirade, first at Aila for sneaking away, then at MacLaren for not immediately bringing her back.

MacLaren's mind was focused on the enemy now surrounding their outer walls. They had been right to assume McNab and his French friends would attempt to besiege the castle. Fortunately, Aila's imitation of the Bruce had given the inhabitants of Dundaff a few precious hours to prepare, since McNab's men were forced to go the long way around the forest.

The burghers were brought into the castle along with every scrap of food available. The crops were not in, but there was nothing that could be done about that now. At least they had reasonable provisions

for the near future. Hoardings, the wooden frame-
work that encased the battlements, had been swiftly
built. MacLaren was impressed at how quickly and
efficiently Graham's men accomplished such a goal.
Graham may be full of bluster, but he was well
prepared. Warwick had suggested throwing nasty
little caltrops in the grounds around the castle, metal
spikes that hid in the grasses and hobbled a man if he
trod on them, but MacLaren advised against it. If the
Campbells were to come to their aid, he did not want
their feet skewered.

Thinking of the Campbells reminded him of Aila.
While he was glad she was not to be imprisoned in
the castle during a siege, still, he worried about her
safety. He hoped Chaumont would be able to keep
her safe and their mission to the Campbells would be
successful. He had every confidence Chaumont would
protect her with his life, but the thought of something
happening to his wife filled him with dread.

MacLaren said another silent prayer for her protection that joined the others as it floated aloft. He had
prayed more since letting Aila go this early morn than
the whole of the past year. He hoped he had made
the right decision. Nothing but her safety seemed
to matter. He smiled when thinking about her this
morning, beautiful even when dressed in an old grey
cloak, her face flushed, that wild look in her eyes. She
was the most attractive ghost he'd ever seen.

"Riders!" The call came from the tower. MacLaren
and Graham were on their feet and moving before
the ghillie could arrive and give them the official
news. MacLaren bounded up the circular stairs to the

watchtower, with Graham not much farther behind, cursing his injured leg. The sight before them was impressive, or it would have been if it had not been so dreadful. McNab and his little band of ruffians were in front, insignificant if it were not for what was behind them. The Golden Knight, gleaming in the midday sun, appeared undeniably formidable, with hundreds of knights, mounted and armored, behind him. McNab and the Golden Knight, with their seconds, rode forward to make their demands.

"Laird Graham of Dundaff," cried the appointed spokesman for the Golden Knight. "Surrender now, and you and your people will be treated fairly. We have no quarrel with you. We come for the knave, Padyn MacLaren. Throw him out, dead or alive, and we shall leave you in peace."

Graham turned to MacLaren. "What have ye done to incur the wrath o' this powerful knight?"

"I dinna ken," MacLaren answered truthfully. "I canna explain it. I fought for his cause for five years in France, but we ne'er met that I ken."

"Who is he?"

"I dinna ken that either. I've only heard o' him at the tourneys. It's assumed he is a great noble and dons this armor to remain anonymous against his foes. What he is doing here and what grievance he has against me I canna say."

"Are the vats of hot oil ready?" Graham asked Warwick.

"Not yet," was the grumbling reply.

"Pity," said Graham and then spoke in his booming voice to the army outside his walls. "Sir Padyn MacLaren fought for the defense o' France for five years, and this is how she repays her faithful servants? Get thee gone, ye bastards, or face the wrath o' Graham."

McNab and the French knight turned and rode back to their lines without further discussion. MacLaren and Graham watched as the well-trained French knights made camp and began their preparations to lay siege to the castle. Graham shook his head.

"I ne'er thought I'd see the like," said Graham with a sigh. "Soldiers at my walls. This castle has ne'er been besieged, and I ne'er thought it would. I've seen many a battle, but ne'er have I fought to defend my own keep."

"The Campbells will come," said MacLaren, speaking with more assurance than he felt.

"Good that Aila no' be here now," said Graham, as if it had been his clever planning that had removed her to the convent prior to being entrapped by the siege.

MacLaren nodded, his thoughts turning once again to his bride. Despite the danger, he missed her presence and wished she was here with him. MacLaren shook his head. What on earth was he thinking? Miss her? He needed to attend to their current troubles. A man did not pine for his own wife.

MacLaren followed Graham back to his solar. Within the inner ward was a churning sea of people, mostly burghers from the town, trying to figure out what to do. Men shouted, children cried, dogs barked, chickens squawked; it was quite a din. In the center of it all, Pitcairn stood, trying to organize the mob. MacLaren did not envy him his responsibilities. Pitcairn had been most distressed to learn Aila,

Dundaff's chatelaine, would not be here to help him sort out this mess.

It was a waiting game now. The French would decide how and when to attack the castle. If luck was on their side, tomorrow might bring word of the Campbells joining their cause. They did have one thing in their favor when it came to a siege—a way out.

"Laird Graham," said MacLaren when they were back alone in his solar. "About the passage we spoke of, the one Aila has used to get in and out o' the castle."

"Aye, I ken what yer thinking. I checked the passage myself. The entrance was concealed by a false door, and the iron gate in the passage was locked."

"We still dinna ken who has betrayed us, and now it seems we are locked in Dundaff along wi' the traitor. Is it possible anyone else knows o' that passage? If our enemy learns o' it…"

"I ken yer meaning—'twould be a massacre. As far as I ken, Aila is now the only one who knows about the passage. It has been a secret handed down from father to son for several generations. 'Twas built as a defense against siege and then blocked in my father's time when a siege seemed unlikely. I told my son o' it. I ne'er expected him to clear it and use it, though we may be indebted to him now."

"What o' this other lad, the one Aila said her brother used to ride wi'? Might he have told anyone?"

"Pitcairn's son? A rumor o' a secret passage would be hard to hold. If it was shared, I'd have heard o' it by now."

MacLaren nodded.

"Still, I've sent guards to the stables and told them

keep an eye on the horses and anything else that looks suspicious."

"Stables? Is that where the passage leads? Is that no' where someone tried to kill the stable master?"

"I still say Fergus's fall was an accident."

"But what if Aila was right and someone attempted to murder him? Maybe the stable master had seen too much."

"I'll send more guards," said Graham quietly.

It was dark, and Aila had lost her escort by the time she made it back to the Braes of Balquidder. Chaumont, Lady Patrick, and her son had built a fire and were waiting for Aila at the top of the peak. Hasty introductions were made, and Aila was grateful to take a rest from riding. Chaumont was overjoyed to see her and learn her news that the Campbells would be joining the fight. Part of his exuberance may have been due to his reprieve from having to face MacLaren's wrath.

After a brief rest, the group mounted again. Mary rode behind Chaumont, and Aila took up Gavin. Chaumont led them down the path by the light of the moon, arriving at the convent late at night. Aila was exhausted. All she wanted was to rest. A soft feather bed would be nice. A pallet would be acceptable. The hard ground would do.

An elderly nun bid them welcome and offered hospitality. The bedraggled little group stood in the courtyard to say goodbye to Chaumont, who would continue on to Dundaff. Assuming McNab's forces would have the castle surrounded, Aila explained to

Chaumont how to find the secret passage and gain entrance to the fortress. It was well hidden, so she tried to be careful in her description. A clear night and a bright moon would aid him in his task. She handed Chaumont the key to the iron gate and gave him the unnecessary reminder to make sure it was kept locked.

Though she was half asleep, Aila could not help but notice the looks Chaumont and Mary were giving each other. They hardly looked at anything else. Aila decided to take the very tired Gavin to find accommodations and give her two new friends a chance to talk.

"Thank you for leaving your land," Chaumont said quietly to Mary when they were alone with only the stars to bear witness. "I understand how difficult that must be for you. I promise, as soon as we deal with McNab and the Golden Knight, I will personally rebuild your barn and put a roof back on the house."

Mary looked up at him in the moonlight. "I've been stubborn about no' leaving. Ye were right to bring us here."

"A Scot stubborn? Never!" Chaumont smiled, and Mary laughed. Somehow they were drawing near to each other again. Chaumont reached out to take her hands.

"I must go," he said without moving.

"Aye."

"'Tis most urgent I return."

"Aye," Mary said again. Still, neither moved. Mary was bathed in the silvery moonlight. He could look upon that face forever. What he could not do was get his legs to move.

"Do be careful," Mary whispered.

Chaumont said nothing but leaned closer until his lips almost touched hers.

"I'll light a candle for ye," Mary said, turning her face away.

Chaumont straightened, rasping out a feeble, "Thank you."

Mary took a step toward the main building, then turned back, and, reaching up to hold his face with both hands, kissed him square on the mouth. "For luck," she explained breathlessly.

He gathered her close in his arms, kissing one cheek and then the other. "'Tis a dangerous task before me. I'm going to need a lot of luck." He kissed her gently. Then he kissed her thoroughly. When finally their lips broke, he felt a little dazed. He drew her close and stroked her hair, experiencing strange feelings for the first time. He had kissed many a pretty mademoiselle, but he had never felt anything like the way he felt when he was with her. She was special.

She *was* special. She was MacLaren's cousin by marriage. What did he think he was doing? The cold night air crept through the chinks in his armor and chilled him to the bone. He was naught but a landless knight, a bastard by birth. He had nothing to give her, not even a name. MacLaren would kill him for trifling with his kinswoman. Chaumont dropped his arms from her. Her smile faded, looking into his troubled face.

"I apologize. I forget myself, my lady."

Mary swallowed. Silence gripped them, and they stood awkwardly in the courtyard.

"I must away," Chaumont spoke. He felt something heavy in his chest.

Mary nodded. "*Bonne chance*," she whispered. She turned and walked into the convent without looking back.

Chaumont knew he had hurt her, but what else could he do? He would never be good enough for her. MacLaren would never allow their marriage.

Marriage?

He closed his eyes and ran his fingers through his hair. What was he thinking? He needed to get back to the siege. He had never tried to sneak *into* a besieged castle. With any luck, he would find an opportunity to die bravely and thus end this painful feeling that gripped him. With a flash of insight, he remembered MacLaren's heartbreak in France and regretted his mockery... well, some of it at least. Saints above, but this hurt.

Thirty-One

GRAHAM LAY ON HIS BED, FAR FROM SLEEP. HE wrestled with the question of who had betrayed him. He knew now his betrayer was one of the men who had accompanied MacLaren to retrieve Aila. But who? All seemed loyal. A few days ago, he would have bet his life all these men, his men, were true. Come to think of it, he had bet his life. Now he was trapped in this castle along with the traitor. Was this all part of the plan, or had events surprised the traitor as well? He had to stay one move ahead, but felt he was playing in the dark. They had tried to take McNab by stealth, but that had not gone according to plan. Why were all those Frenchies outside his gates, and why did they want MacLaren dead?

Many questions. No answers. He had hoped the traitor would make a mistake, revealing his identity, but so far, Graham knew no more than the day before, except now he was under siege. The situation was not heading in a good direction. Graham growled in the dark, going over all the pieces of information again. With soldiers camped at his doorstep, it was imperative the existence and location of the secret tunnel remain a secret. Graham remembered MacLaren's words. Was it possible the stable master was attacked because of what he saw?

Before he knew what he was doing, Graham was tugging on his trews, tunic, and boots. He had guards at the stables, but he could not shake the feeling something was amiss. He was the laird; he was responsible for the lives of everyone within his walls. He limped to the door, paused a moment, and returned for his sword, slinging the heavy claymore over his shoulder.

Graham frowned when he reached the main entrance to the stables. The two guards were not there. Graham looked around, but all was quiet. His men on the wall walk were double posted and keeping watch, their gaze mostly outside at the camping soldiers around them. Graham walked into the stables and was somewhat relieved to hear men's voices down the corridor. He could not hear exactly what was being said, but the sound was of amiable chatter. Graham relaxed. The soldiers were probably doing rounds, checking the inside of the stable. He followed the voices inside, limping in the direction of the faint glow of lamplight.

As he approached, the friendly banter suddenly stopped. There were several muffled sounds, a few thuds, and then silence. Graham drew his claymore and hurried forward as fast as his injured leg would allow. He was at the end of stable, before the stall holding the secret to the outside passage. Graham tripped over something. It was the body of one of the guards. Inside the false stall was the other. The back

.of the stall was open. A man stood within the cave silhouetted in the light of a lantern, attempting to open the lock. Graham's heart pounded. If that gate was opened, the castle would be taken, its occupants murdered in their sleep.

He tried to creep softly over the sandy floor of the cave, but he was a big man, and the days of being light on his feet were long past. The man suddenly turned from his work, sword in hand. With a battle cry loud enough to wake his ancestors, Graham ran forward. His blade clashed against the steel of his opponent— Pitcairn the steward.

"Pitcairn?" Graham gasped, drawing back a step but holding his sword at the ready. "Ye whoreson! Ye would betray yer own clan to the enemy?"

Pitcairn glared at Graham coolly. Though Pitcairn had never been renowned as a fighter, he had the advantage of being able-bodied and dressed in elegant armor. He held his sword at the ready, the blood of the guards still on the blade.

"I would do anything to get what I want," Pitcairn replied without emotion.

"And what is that?" Graham growled.

"Why to be Laird of Dundaff o' course."

"Ye? Laird o' Dundaff? Ye be nothing but a merchant's son. After all I've given to ye, ye would betray me?"

Pitcairn circled Graham, waiting for an opportunity to strike. The old laird struggled to keep his opponent in front of him. "Ye ne'er gave me a thing—I took it. Ye think the previous steward's death was truly an accident?" Pitcairn sneered in cold disdain.

Graham's eyes went wide with shock, and Pitcairn used the opportunity, swinging his blade low at Graham's uninjured leg. The slash caused another roar from Graham, who struck back, his mighty blade glancing off the mail at Pitcairn's shoulder. Pitcairn fell back but regained his feet with speed. The traitor smiled. Graham now, quite literally, had no good leg to stand on.

"Why?" asked Graham between heavy breaths of exertion and pain. "Why would ye do this to yer own clan? Think on the lives ye will destroy. Have ye no honor?"

"I am acting the way ye've taught me. Take what ye want. Is that no' how ye have always acted? Have ye e'er stopped to be concerned o' who ye hurt when ye found something ye wanted? Ye've taken from me, and now I'm going to take it back."

"When have I e'er taken anything that was yers? I've done naught but give."

"Selfish bastard, ye've done naught but take yer whole life." Pitcairn's face twisted into a sneer. "Moira should have been mine. She would have been mine. Do ye ken how hard I worked to gain enough coin to secure her betrothal? Do ye care?" Pitcairn screamed.

"It was ye who she was betrothed to?"

"Aye, 'til ye came down from on high to steal her from me. Just like ye took my boy."

"Duncan's death was an accident. He died at the lists."

"In service to ye. He died because o' ye."

"Ye're mad," said Graham, more an observation than an insult.

"Ye have taken everything from me," Pitcairn cried, attacking again, forcing Graham back. Both of his legs injured, Graham dropped to his knees.

Pitcairn panted with exertion. "This is how I've always dreamed it should be. Me the master whilst ye beg for mercy. Go on now, beg, if no' for yerself then for yer daughter." Pitcairn charged again, Graham deflecting the attack valiantly from his knees.

"What has Aila to do wi' this?" roared Graham.

"Ah, but she has everything to do wi' it," said Pitcairn, regaining his calm demeanor though Graham had glimpsed what lay beneath the surface. "'Twas sheer providence that made Aila sole heir and provided me wi' such a simpleton like McNab to use. Things have got a bit out o' hand, but I think it will still work out nicely. 'Tis really verra simple if ye think on it, but then ye've ne'er been a thinking man."

Pitcairn stopped his cool tirade to lunge again, attacking the injured man without mercy. It was only a matter of time now before the Dundaff laird would fall, and they both knew it.

"How did ye know o' this tunnel?" Graham asked as Pitcairn broke off the attack. He needed time to catch his breath and try to think of some escape from this trap. What he needed was a miracle.

"My son was no' as reticent to talk to me as yers was to ye, my laird," Pitcairn answered in a self-satisfied, mocking tone. "Now if ye will oblige me, I must kill ye, though I admit I canna recall when I've had more amusement. But I have much to do tonight—open the gate, loose the soldiers, take the castle, murder MacLaren and his men as they sleep. A steward's work is ne'er done."

Pitcairn approached again with malice, beating Graham back until he trapped Graham's blade under his own and stomped down on the flat of it, wrenching the sword from Graham's hands.

"And now good-bye, my laird. Have no fear. After I use McNab and his friends to take the castle, I'll rid these walls of the usurper McNab and take Aila for myself. Yer grandchildren will have my blood, my name. Think on that as ye die." Pitcairn sneered as he raised his sword for the death blow. Graham glared at him, not giving the traitor the satisfaction of seeing him cower.

"I'll see ye in hell!" Pitcairn screeched, the sound coming to a sudden and dramatic stop as a dagger caught him in a gap of armor at his throat. Wide-eyed, Pitcairn dropped his sword and reached for the blade stuck deep in his neck. The traitor dropped to the ground, dead.

"My lord, are you well?" Chaumont asked as he struggled to open the locked gate by reaching through the bars. Opening the lock, Chaumont rushed to Graham's side. The old laird looked at Chaumont as if he were a vision.

"My son," whispered Graham and reached for Chaumont.

"Nay, sir," said Chaumont with concern as the laird put a large hand on his shoulder. "I am Chaumont, your servant."

"Nay," said Graham with the growl of authority in his voice. "I say ye are my son. Help me to me feet, my lad."

Chaumont did what was asked, grimacing at the effort of raising Graham's large frame. Once on his feet, Graham put both hands on Chaumont's shoulders, both to steady himself and to emphasize the importance of what he was to say.

"I say ye are my foster son, Chaumont Graham. Do ye accept that name and the responsibilities that come wi' it?"

Chaumont stared at the Graham laird, saying nothing for a long time. He swallowed hard, but could not hide the tears in his eyes. "Father?" Chaumont's voice wavered.

"My son," Graham answered, his voice thick with emotion, and gave his new foster son a back-cracking embrace.

Thirty-Two

LADY AILA AWOKE LATE THE NEXT MORNING AND immediately wished she could go back to sleep. Several days of little or no sleep and hard riding had taken their toll. Everything ached, especially her backside. She had not been beaten for her misbehavior as she had feared, but she sorely felt like she had.

Dragging herself out of bed, she found a basin of water alongside a fresh linen chemise and tawny brown kirtle. They were homespun and plain but refreshingly clean. After an invigorating wash in the cool water, she felt revived in her fresh clothes. She found the good sisters with Lady Mary Patrick and her son, Gavin, at the midday meal. She was amazed at how long she had slept, and felt a little embarrassed lest someone think she was a sluggard.

"Good day to ye, m'lady," said Mary as Aila sat next to her.

"Good day to ye, Lady Patrick," replied Aila cordially. It had been a long time since she had the occasion to socialize with people her age, and she hoped in Mary she had found a friend. "Had ye a comfortable night?"

"Aye, verra well indeed. And ye, my lady?"

"I slept verra well and shamefully long. Please, would ye call me Aila?"

Mary smiled at Aila and nodded. "If ye will call me Mary. Thank ye for letting us come wi' ye to the convent. It was dreadful being set upon by those foreign devils. I fear my house may ne'er be the same."

"Ye were verra brave to stand up against them," Aila commented, truly impressed. "I'm sure there will be some who will help ye rebuild yer home."

"Aye, ye're right my... Aila. 'Tis sure MacLaren will help me rebuild, as he has done for so many this past year. Ye've married yerself a fine man, if ye dinna mind me saying."

"Thank ye," replied Aila, her heart warming to this new piece of praise for her husband. "But I was thinking of a certain Frenchman who seemed verra attentive last eve." Aila intended to touch on what she assumed would be a happy topic for Mary, but was confused by the sudden shadow of disappointment on Mary's face.

"He may help or no. I dinna ken. He has many interests that press his time."

"I'm sorry, Mary. I kenned ye and Chaumont were on friendly terms."

"We are." Mary focused on her trencher and poked aimlessly at the broiled meat with her knife. "But perhaps I mistook his friendship for something it is not. He set me to rights last night."

Aila now also poked at her food, feeling low for broaching what was clearly a sore subject. Searching for something to say, she pounced on the first thing that came to mind. "Tell me about MacLaren. I ken so little o' my husband."

Mary welcomed this change of subject with a smile. "He is a good mon, a strong leader, though he was gone far too long, fighting in France, and we suffered his absence. He was truly upset at our condition when he returned and has worked himself ragged to pull our clan back from the grave."

"He sounds a worthy laird."

"Och aye, there be naught he woud'na do for his clan."

"Including marry a wealthy heiress?" The words left Aila's lips before she could censor them. She looked down at her food. She had not meant to sound so sharp.

Mary turned a bit red, but it was the truth, and they both knew it. "Aye, even that. Though I'm sure he will treat ye kindly. And perhaps love may blossom between ye." Mary didn't sound particularly hopeful.

"I hardly know him, but I ken him to be an honorable man," said Aila softly.

"Aye, he is that. I married his cousin, James Patrick. They were good friends, like brothers they were."

Aila looked at Mary with eager eyes, not wanting to press her for more but hoping she would continue her story.

"MacLaren was a serious lad. He rode off to war a wee young, if ye ask me. He stood wi' the auld laird, his father, at the battle o' Halidon Hill. Poor lad, his father was killed, ye ken. He was naught but twelve summers, so the elders chose his father's brother to be laird. But poor Fin died a few years later. MacLaren was a mite young when the elders chose him as laird. He takes his responsibilities hard."

Aila soaked in every word Mary spoke. She couldn't get enough of hearing about her husband. She took a deep breath and decided to ask a question that had been nibbling on her consciousness, though she was not sure she wanted to know the answer. "Lady Patrick... Mary," Aila corrected as Mary began to protest the formality of address. "I have much respect for MacLaren and his defense o' his clan. But I need to ken if..." Aila tried to find the right words to ask what was burdening her heart. "Does MacLaren have another, er, woman to whom he shows affection?" It was the closest she could come to asking if MacLaren had a leman.

"Goodness, no." Mary's answer was immediate and reassuringly certain. Aila let go of her held breath, listening as Mary continued. "Though to be honest, many women, maidens or no, have tried to entice him to their beds, but he will have none of it. He seems distant and cold to everyone, though he has his reasons."

Aila nodded. She had heard enough of his betrayal in France to understand at least some of why he was distant.

The meal was finished, and Gavin asked if he could explore the convent. Mary admonished him not to get into mischief or bother the nuns, and got a wave in response before her son was out of sight. Aila and Mary walked arm in arm out of the hall.

"'Tis certainly no' my place to say," said Mary, "but do ye ken what happened to MacLaren in France?"

"MacLaren has told me a little, and Chaumont has told me more," said Aila, wondering if Mary knew any more of the story. They found a secluded place by the garden wall and sat on a bench to talk.

"Then ye heard o' the countess what betrayed him to the English?"

"Aye."

"Poor MacLaren, he blames himself for Jamie's death."

"Why is that?" Aila had come to understand Mary had lost her husband during MacLaren's campaign in France, but more than that she did not know.

"My husband, MacLaren's cousin, died in the battle he waged to protect the countess."

"Little wonder he is so distrusting," Aila said slowly, rethinking her interactions with her husband. Aila's mind drifted deep into thought about this, and she began to see MacLaren's actions from an entirely new perspective.

"Lady Aila." The deep voice in front of her made her jump. Father Barrick, the abbot, stood before her, his sword belted to his side. "A word with you, if you please."

It was not a request.

❧

Laird Graham stood on the wall walk of the upper bailey, grimly looking down on the scene below him. The castle was overflowing with people, burghers, and crofters alike, who had fled the approaching army of McNab and his unknown French conspirator. They were all looking at him, waiting for him to speak. Despite the crowd, it was eerily quiet, giving the morning a chilling air. They wanted to know Graham's plan to survive the siege. They also probably wanted to know why Pitcairn's severed head was on a stake in the middle of the lower bailey.

Beyond the castle walls, Graham counted his enemy as they surrounded his fortress, freely helping themselves to whatever bounty they could find among the houses and shops of Carron. At least the town still stood, which was another comfort, though probably due more to his enemies' own interest then any sign of restraint on their part. He was outnumbered, badly. Even with MacLaren's warriors, he had no hope of a frontal attack. To do so would be suicide, and he'd had enough of charging into battle against hopeless odds.

He needed to say something to his clan. He needed a plan. But what? He had the report that Aila had spoken to Campbell's son, but how could he rely on that? If Campbell did not come… How could he give his clan hope when he felt none? He motioned for MacLaren, Chaumont, and Warwick to join him on the battlements. Perhaps these warriors would lend him the strength and inspiration he needed at this moment. They looked grim. Even Chaumont looked uncharacteristically grave.

"Good morn to ye, my kin, my clan," Graham began his address to the silent, gray-faced sea of people surrounding him. "Today is a day of reckoning. It is a day when men's accounts are laid bare, and we are called to stand for judgment. It grieves me to say our clansman, my friend, Pitcairn our steward, was found in league with our enemies. In truth"—Graham raised his voice to a fierce roar—"I caught him trying to betray us to our enemies while we slept." Gasps were heard from more than one quarter. "This foul betrayer o' his own people turned on me, and I would be lying in my grave this morn if no' for the actions o' Sir Chaumont, who has saved all o' our lives."

Cheers erupted from the crowd, which seemed eager to grasp upon any strand of hope. Graham turned to Chaumont, who was looking somewhat embarrassed, and embraced him as well as the full armor they both wore would allow.

"Sir Chaumont," Graham said, his voice ringing through the silent crowd, "for yer honor and courage, and for yer defense o' our clan in her time o' need, I bestow upon ye our greatest thanks. Kneel, Sir Chaumont." Chaumont took one knee as Graham drew his long sword. "I wouldst knight thee, for surely ye exemplify the verra image o' a true knight, but others have claimed that privilege. Yet I wouldst show our thanks for yer courageous actions. So, Sir Chaumont, I bestow upon thee the name o' Graham and all the rights and responsibilities therein." Graham tapped Chaumont on both shoulders, the blade glinting in the morning sun. "Rise, my son."

Chaumont rose shakily to his feet, and the crowd cheered again. Pretending to shield his eyes from the sun, Chaumont tried to surreptitiously wipe the tears from his eyes, but then abandoned the effort and let the tears flow. MacLaren sniffed, nodding at Graham and clapping him on the back in a sure sign of approval.

"Though weeping may remain through the night," Graham said, speaking to the crowd, giving his rough paraphrase of Psalm 30, "in the morning there be rejoicing. The Lord has taken away but has given back again." Graham stood between Chaumont and MacLaren, taking their hands he raised them aloft. "Behold my sons!" The clan was moved to cheers once again, even louder than before. On the other side of the battlements, his enemies took note of the noise and scrambled into a defensive line. Graham smiled. *Good, let them worrit themselves, wondering what we're about.*

Gasps and stunned silence caught Graham's attention. On the other side of the wall walk the soldiers made way and stood at attention, revealing none other than his wife. Graham's jaw dropped. Two soldiers flanked her on either side, and as she drew closer, he could tell they were carrying her by her elbows so the clan would not see her limp. In truth, from afar it must look as if she floated to his side. Her blond hair was elaborately coiffed, and she wore a brilliant red silk gown, ornately embroidered with gold thread. She was carefully wrapped in fur, her hands hidden in long, flowing sleeves. She looked stunning.

With some effort, Graham shut his gaping mouth and gave her a bow, which she returned with a nod of her head. The crowd was silent once again. It was the first time most had seen their lady in ten years.

"My laird, my clan," Lady Graham said, her voice ringing out over the stunned crowd, loud and true. "It grieves me that we are now so beset. Yet together we will stand against our enemies. And together we will defeat them."

The crowd erupted once again. If their lady could

stand beside their laird, surely miracles could happen. Graham was so proud of his wife he could almost burst. In a few words, she had given them the confidence to fight. She looked so beautiful at that moment, regal, with her face glowing in the early morning sun, he could almost kiss her. The impulse seemed strange, but then, why not kiss his wife?

Graham moved his hand around her slim waist, pressing her to him and helping to take the weight off her feet, which he knew must be paining her. Slowly he bent down, brushing his lips against hers. He expected her to pull away, but she did not. In her eyes was naught but surprise. Encouraged, he bent down again and claimed her lips, remembering their sweetness and feeling surprised she could still command his full attention. The throng below was cheering even louder now, but John Graham heard none of it until the clarion sound of pipes pulled his mind back to the present.

Out across the heath, into the distance, troops were beginning their descent over the far hill. Squinting into the sun, he held his breath until he saw the familiar banner. It was the Campbells. Line by line, more soldiers came into view, and Graham felt like weeping in relief. Turning his gaze heavenward, he said a silent prayer of thanksgiving and noted with satisfaction that Chaumont and MacLaren appeared to be doing the same.

"The Campbells!" came the cry from the tower, and the cry was repeated up the battlements.

"We're saved," cried a woman's voice.

"To the armory," Graham shouted. "Prepare for battle. Tonight we drink to the defeat of our enemies!"

The people cheered with excitement, and Warwick strode off to see to the arming of the masses.

"Thank ye," Graham said quietly to his wife, whom he still held in his arms. "They needed ye... I needed ye. I've neglected ye too long, but no more. Tonight ye shall sleep in my bed." His wife trembled, though her eyes shone and a smile played on her lips.

"A command, my laird?"

Graham leaned closer, whispering for only her to hear. "Nay, only the pathetic begging o' a lonely auld goat who misses his beautiful wife."

Lady Graham did smile then and laid her head against his chest. "See to it ye dinna get yerself killed today."

"Wi' ye as my prize, there be little chance o' that."

Thirty-Three

FATHER BARRICK WORE THE PLAIN BLACK ROBES OF A priest, but the links of his chain mail were visible at his neck. From his belt, a rosary hung at his right side, a long sword from his left. Aila's stomach tensed in his presence, but she stood and curtseyed.

The abbot turned and walked away, Aila hustling to catch up. When they were alone, the abbot spoke without emotion and without bothering to turn to her.

"I understand you have been forced to marry. A serious matter, since you had already pledged yourself to the Church."

Aila swallowed hard. She had always intended to take orders, but she knew as well as he that she had never formally committed herself. The abbot spoke with such grave authority, however, that she began to feel the familiar pangs of guilt.

"Aye, Father. One canna ken the will o' God," Aila stammered weakly. The abbot turned on her a critical eye, and though he said nothing, she felt severely reprimanded. Clearly, this man knew the will of God. She, of course, did not.

"I am glad you have come to us. I shall grant you sanctuary for the next cycle of the moon to determine if you are with child. If you are, I'm afraid there may be little I can do to help you."

"Nay," Aila stammered. This conversation had taken a decidedly awkward turn. "There is no need. I... I am no' wi' child."

"But how can you be sure?" The abbot turned once again and scrutinized her carefully. "Have you had relations with him?"

Aila blushed from head to toe. These were matters she wished to speak of to no one, let alone the abbot. She stared at the ground and gave her head a barely perceivable shake. The abbot's eyes flashed, and the corner of the left side of his mouth curled upward in an opportunistic sneer that vanished as quickly as it came.

"Then fear not, for I will write to His Eminence the Pope, and your marriage will soon be annulled. You will be able to take your orders very soon."

Fear gripped her stomach and gave it a nasty turn. The irony that this had been exactly her plan not five days ago was not lost on her. But now... now she felt differently. Much differently.

"But MacLaren—" Aila began, not knowing quite what to say to the intimidating abbot.

"Do not concern yourself with him. In his current position, he cannot come for you, and if he does, he has no rights on this holy ground. Though I find it likely you will soon be a widow."

Aila gasped at Father Barrick's cold, emotionless evaluation of the situation. Could MacLaren really be in danger of losing his life? Blood thundered through her veins, and she felt her courage return. MacLaren stood and fought for her clan. She would stand by him.

"Nay, Father, ye mistake my intent. 'Twas no' my will to wed MacLaren, I grant ye, but now that I am his wife, I intend to honor my vows to him."

"And what does your will matter in this?" Father Barrick turned on her, his voice so fierce she took two steps back. "Come, I wish to show you something."

Father Barrick walked into one of the side buildings used to store food through the winter. Aila followed reluctantly. She sensed danger, and every instinct she had told her not to go into the building, but he was the abbot. How could she disobey?

He walked on a narrow path through the storeroom and then down a set of stairs cut into the earth, leading into the root cellar. At the bottom was a heavy oak door that was padlocked. It was here the sisters kept their more valuable food stores—tea, spices. The abbot unlocked the door and stepped inside.

"W-why are we here?" Aila wished her voice had not wavered.

"Come here. I wish to show you something."

Aila stepped into the room, her eyes gradually adjusting to the dim light. The abbot quickly slid past her, back outside, closing the door behind him.

"What are ye doing?" Aila cried as he locked the door.

"You are being tempted to deny your vows to the Church. As your abbot, I am responsible for your salvation, and I will ensure the sanctity of your soul.

Your marriage will be annulled, and you will remain in isolation until you are ready to take your vows."

"Nay!" Aila screamed, panic taking hold. "Ye canna do this. Ye canna force me to take orders"

The abbot only laughed. "Every wench has their breaking point. Do not doubt that very soon, you will do anything I ask. Do not underestimate your worth, Lady Aila. You will make a most valuable asset to the convent."

The abbot's words hit her cold and hard. She recoiled from them as if she had actually been struck. Aila slumped onto the floor, grim realization setting in. She was rich, very rich. Wealthy enough to make the Church authorities turn their heads to whatever tactics the abbot might use to make her consent to take her vows. She sat on the floor and put her head in her hands. She had known better than to follow him down here. She had sacrificed her freedom and her marriage because she had not wanted to seem rude. She was a fool.

MacLaren, Graham, and Chaumont rode forward slowly under a flag of peace to have speech with McNab and the French invaders. MacLaren still could not understand why the French would leave their homeland and come so far to attack him. It seemed these foreign knights held a grudge against him. But what had he done to the Golden Knight other than defend Gascony against the English? Nothing made sense.

They rode slowly out of the portcullis and down

the narrow, winding road to the base of the mountain to meet with McNab and his French allies. The horsemen waited for them on the flat plain between the castle and the town, their banners fighting with the breeze. Campbell rode forward with his second to join the conversation. All had their visors raised except the Golden Knight, who continued to conceal his face. McNab and his second looked decidedly shabby next to the Golden Knight and his second, a decorated knight named Forbier, whom MacLaren had fought beside in France. MacLaren tried to catch his eye, but Forbier stared only at Graham, ignoring his former comrades in arms with such determination, it could be meant only as a rebuff—or possibly embarrassment.

"Good morn to ye, my good sirs. To what do I owe the pleasure o' yer presence this early morn?" Graham's deep voice was deceptively mild as he adopted an attitude of disinterested courtesy in his discourse with the men who were intent on his demise.

"Greetings, Lord Graham. I regret we must meet under such trying circumstances."

"'Trying circumstances, ye say?" Graham exploded. So much for disinterested courtesy. After years of the diplomatic negotiations guided by rigid rules of engagement, MacLaren was amused by Graham's forthright manner, though he took care to betray no emotion. "Ye French are e'er quick to accept aid, but look how ye repay it. Was it no' enough ye called for our braw men to join in yer fight against the English king? But no, ye asked our King David to distract the English by marching against York. Did no' my clan answer that call? Is no' my only son lying cold in his grave for ye?"

Graham roared so loudly there was not a soul in Carron or Dundaff who could not hear his words. "Ye are naught but an ungrateful bastard, without honor, hiding behind yer bonnie helm like a bloody coward."

This time a faint smile passed over MacLaren's lips. He liked negotiations with Graham. Direct and to the point.

"You impinge my honor, sir!" replied the Golden Knight with feeling.

"That I do, and make no mistake about it," countered Graham, speaking French to ensure there was no misunderstanding. "Now make your vile demands, or get your sorry arse the hell off my land."

There was a moment's pause, and MacLaren imagined the Golden Knight was trying to regain his composure after being so abused. The French had much more false politeness in their negotiations than did John Graham.

"I regret my presence here. Let me state first that France appreciates all those who have fought on her behalf. But honor requires that I press my case, not against you or your family, Lord Graham, but against those you have given sanctuary. I challenge Sir Padyn MacLaren on the field of honor. Send him"—the French knight glanced at McNab—"and his wife forth, and we shall withdraw."

"I am Padyn MacLaren." MacLaren urged his mount forward a step, conversing in the familiar French he had spoken for so many years. "What claim do you have against me?"

"I accuse you of the murder of the nobleman, Gerard de Marsan. Do you deny it?"

Silence surrounded them. Even the wind seemed to hold its breath. Everyone looked at MacLaren.

"I do not deny de Marsan died at my hand."

"Then I challenge you to the field to avenge the death of de Marsan."

"I wouldst know my accuser."

The Golden Knight removed his helm and pushed back his mail, revealing sandy brown hair, blue eyes, and a long, thin nose. "I am the Duke of Argitaine and half-brother to Gerard de Marsan."

MacLaren nodded his head. He had been rightly challenged. It all made sense now. "Name your conditions, Your Grace."

"Joust of war."

MacLaren only nodded, a small smile playing on his lips. Neither he nor the duke had ever been defeated at the joust, but neither had they ever faced each other. It was time to determine who was best. MacLaren wished the stakes were not quite so high for this contest, but so be it. He would once again pay the consequence for his folly.

"And you will leave if MacLaren wins?" Graham asked.

The duke nodded. "My fight is not against you. This day, either Sir Padyn or I will meet our Maker, and my honor will be defended. Either way, my men will leave peaceably unless called on to defend themselves."

"But… Your Grace…" McNab stuttered.

"Ah, now ye must ken I'd ne'er give the likes o' ye my daughter," Graham mocked, giving McNab a penetrating glare. "But ye must no' come all this way for nothing. I'll see ye leave wi' a friend.

Pitcairn's head is on a stake in my bailey. I'll have it sent to ye."

McNab blanched, but his bad news was not over.

"This challenge doesna settle things between us, McNab," MacLaren said coldly to the man who had abducted his wife. "When I am finished wi' His Grace, I will come to settle my account wi' ye."

"I accept yer challenge," replied McNab gamely, "but ye will forgive me if I wish His Grace best fortune in the coming joust."

Thirty-Four

THE FIELD WAS PACED AND MARKED OFF IN SHORT order. It was a makeshift list at best, with no tilt as a barrier to keep the horses from colliding. Despite its deficiencies, it was the closest most of the Scots had come to a tournament, and the atmosphere was disturbingly festive. MacLaren could understand the people's enjoyment. They had learned there would be no siege, no battle, and no one was at risk except the two men who jousted. The people got not only a reprieve from war, but a show as well. What did they care if he ended up dead? People lined the field, baskets of food were brought, the French knights shamelessly chatted up the bonnie lasses, and the bets were laid. MacLaren was not favored to win.

"You look to me to have the advantage here," Chaumont said cheerfully to MacLaren as he helped him prepare for the first pass of the joust. "You'll look fine in that golden suit he wears."

MacLaren smiled at his friend's support, though he wished it had less bravado and more confidence. Slamming his visor down, he took up his lance and moved into position. He had jousted many times in tournaments with great success but never a joust of war. In the tourneys, the goal was to knock the opponent off his horse. Today, the goal was death. The lances, far from being blunted to avoid serious injury, were equipped with sharp metal tips. It would be a bloody day.

MacLaren studied his opponent. The Golden Knight was the brother of that weasel de Marsan. Bad luck that. It was the only kind of luck he seemed to have of late. The Golden Knight saluted him with his lance, and MacLaren returned the gesture. MacLaren took a breath, said a prayer, then spurred his mount to try to take the life of his opponent.

Racing at full speed, MacLaren stood up in his stirrups as he approached and leveled his aim to the duke's chest. With a blinding clash, the horsemen met. MacLaren's lance was deflected and shattered by the duke's shield. The duke's lance struck MacLaren's helm and glanced off. MacLaren swayed in his saddle as he struggled to retain his seat and his senses. The helm had held against the lance, but the force of impact addled MacLaren's brain for a moment, and he took his time walking his horse back to his position to give his fuzzy head time to clear.

"I thought you were supposed to hit him, not the other way round," commented Chaumont dryly as he handed MacLaren a new lance for another pass.

"Thanks for setting me to rights," MacLaren returned. "I shall attempt this new strategy."

MacLaren raced toward the approaching figure of the duke with resolve, this time aiming for the neck.

His Grace aimed for the same. Once again it was done in a flash, MacLaren's lance shattered and deflected. The duke had struck true, tearing a hole through MacLaren's shoulder armor. MacLaren turned and trotted back quickly, not wanting anyone to determine the extent of his injuries.

"I dinna like yer new strategy," muttered MacLaren upon his return.

"You're not doing it right," answered Chaumont grimly as he pulled mangled metal from the gash in MacLaren's shoulder and stuffed bundles of linen gauze through the hole in his mail shirt to staunch the flow of blood. MacLaren's left arm hung at a rather awkward angle. Chaumont took MacLaren's shield from the breathless squire, who had raced to retrieve it from the field, and wedged it into the saddle. The shield was now holding up MacLaren's left arm rather than the other way round, but there was naught to be done about it.

"I fear the question o' who is better at this sport will no' be answered in my favor," MacLaren said mildly, as if he was commenting on the weather.

"Then knock the bloody bastard off his horse and face him on the ground," commented Chaumont, looking away, but MacLaren had already seen the worry in his eyes.

"Aye," muttered MacLaren. He needed to do something drastic, or he would lose. And losing this time meant death. Feeling resigned, he moved back into position. Looking across at the man who was about to kill him, MacLaren's mind wandered to Aila. He wondered what she would do if he was to fall. Join the cloister? No, her father had already made it clear he did not want the Church to inherit Dundaff. No, most likely she would be given to another man in marriage. The thought rankled around in his brain. *Another man?* His blood began to pump again, and he could no longer feel the pain in his shoulder. *Another man?* Nay. He would not let that happen. He gripped his lance with determination and devised the hasty strategy of a desperate man.

He charged again at the Golden Knight, lowering his lance as before. The Golden Knight lowered his for what would surely be a death blow. Suddenly, MacLaren swerved his horse in front of the duke to the opposite side and held his lance sideways across his body, knocking the duke from his horse. The force of impact also knocked MacLaren to the ground, and he fell neatly, having expected this outcome. MacLaren avoided his damaged shoulder and regained his feet. His Grace landed harder and came up slower. It was a move that would have cost MacLaren points in a tourney joust, but a joust of war had no rules. Still, the move might be considered by some to be undignified for a knight, and MacLaren could feel the heat of the duke's glare even through his helm.

Both trudged back to re-dress and reequip. They would continue now on the ground. A duel to the death.

"That was inspired," said Chaumont with sincere admiration.

"Reset my shoulder. I canna feel my hand," returned MacLaren, focused on the next round. Chaumont and his squire eased him out of the armor he used for jousting, and Chaumont gave a quick tug on his shoulder, resetting his arm with a bone-grinding pop. MacLaren moved it gingerly. It felt exactly like a lance to the shoulder would feel—painful. But at least he could move his arm.

Back into field armor, MacLaren picked up his claymore and walked back to meet his opponent. MacLaren was good with a lance, better with a sword. He hoped the same would not be true for the duke. He saluted Argitaine, touching his sword to his forehead, and the duke returned the gesture. MacLaren was struck by the futility of this battle. He had nothing against the duke. He had spent years of his life defending this man's territory against the English. And now MacLaren was being forced to fight him because of Marguerite's treachery and Marsan's foolishness. What a waste.

Thoughts were soon silenced as the duke swung toward him, and MacLaren parried the blow. The duke was certainly capable of holding his own. And so it began, this fatal dance as they traded blows one with the other, attacking, fading, spinning jabbing, parrying. Each one testing the other, trying to find weaknesses, trying to find the opportunity to deliver the fatal blow.

The fight wore on, and MacLaren tired, succumbing to fatigue and pain. Visions of Aila came back to him, and he wondered if these would be his last thoughts. Aila dressed like a queen for the feast, Aila riding wild over the heath, Aila standing at his grave, Aila giving herself to another. The image was infuriating, and MacLaren charged Argitaine like the berserkers of old, striking him under the arm where the armor was weakest.

The Golden Knight slumped in pain, but regained

his footing. MacLaren circled round like a predator that had smelled blood. Striking again, he clashed against Argitaine's blade then sliced back and came down hard on the duke's right wrist. The sound of the bone breaking could be plainly heard, though the plate held and the hand remained attached to the body. The Golden Knight's sword fell from his useless hand.

Acknowledging defeat, the Duke of Argitaine removed his helm with his one good hand. His face was white, his mouth a thin line. Argitaine looked around him for a moment then took a breath and knelt before MacLaren to accept his death blow. MacLaren admired the man's courage. To kill such a man seemed pointless. Argitaine was desperately needed in France to counter the attacks of the English, who grew ever bolder in their determination to defeat all of France under their English king. MacLaren removed his helm.

"Yer people need ye, Argitaine. I have no wish to kill ye."

The duke looked up, and MacLaren could see the struggle in his eyes for a moment until His Grace claimed better control of his emotions.

"I am honor bound to defend the life of my brother. I have taken a blood oath to meet you on the field of honor. If you let me live, I will challenge you again."

"Ye have indeed met me on the field. The honor of yer brother has been answered. He died at my hand, yes, but it was he who challenged me first, in a manner."

"How do you mean?"

"Yer brother was engaged to marry the Countess

Marguerite, a woman I thought I had an under-standing with. As she was informing me of her choice of husbands, de Marsan snuck up behind me and tried to slit my throat. 'Twas him who gave me this." MacLaren pointed to the long scar that marred his face.

"That is not the tale Countess Marguerite tells."

"I'm sure it is not, but it remains the truth. I wonder, Your Grace, that ye would trust so implicitly the word of a woman who sold herself to the English."

"She said the choice was forced upon her by your lack of protection."

MacLaren gave a derisive laugh. "Protection was all I could give, and therein lies the rub. I could give only my sword and my heart. The English gave her gold. She was forced into her decision by naught but her own greed."

The Golden Knight sighed and shook his head. "You tell the same tale as one of her ladies-in-waiting."

"I'm surprised Marguerite dinna kill her maid."

"Indeed, the maid is dead. She died of fever, or so Marguerite claimed." The Duke of Argitaine sighed again. "By the saints, even I am beginning to disbelieve this woman's story. MacLaren, you have my submission. I acknowledge the challenge has been answered in your favor. Name your terms."

"I will not hold ye for ransom. France has become my second home, and I canna do anything to hurt her. Yer people need ye."

Argitaine stood and looked MacLaren in the eye for a long time. His features appeared familiar to MacLaren, and he stared back just as bluntly.

"You are an honorable man. I have rarely met the like," the duke said finally, handing over his helm and sword. "You are welcome to return to France whenever you desire. She will always welcome her sons with open arms."

"Thank ye. But this is my home. This is the place I intend to stay."

The Duke of Argitaine bowed and walked back to his soldiers. True to his word, his soldiers began to break camp.

From amidst the dust emerged McNab, wearing naught but some leather armor. MacLaren watched McNab's approach with disgust. MacLaren was exhausted, and his shoulder throbbed. He wanted to get off the field and hold Aila in his arms. He wondered how quickly he could kill McNab.

McNab knelt before him, taking the place of Argitaine, who had quit the field. "I acknowledge I have given you cause for this action against me. I canna look at my own actions wi' satisfaction. I ken I've done ye wrong, and I humbly ask yer forgiveness."

MacLaren regarded him warily. Unlike his compassion for the duke, MacLaren felt no hesitation in killing McNab for what he did to his wife, his Aila. Yet here the man offered him submission. He wondered if McNab submitted before him out of a guilty conscience or a drive for self-preservation. Did it matter? MacLaren was hardly in any condition to fight again against a fresh opponent. His shoulder was screaming for attention. He recalled from childhood that McNab was often challenged but had never lost. McNab had not the equipment, but he was fresh, unwounded, and had nothing to lose. MacLaren weighed his desire to kill McNab against his desire to claim his wife.

"Why?" asked MacLaren gruffly.

"Why did I try to claim Lady Aila for my own, or why do I submit to ye now?"

"Both, and ye dinna have my permission to call my wife by her Christian name."

"My mistake. I sought yer wife because my clan needs the sustenance her dowry would bring. I submit to ye now because my actions were dishonorable, and I wish to make amends."

"You will swear your fealty and loyalty to me and Laird Graham?"

McNab drew his dirk and held it before MacLaren. "I swear on my father's iron my fealty to Laird MacLaren and Laird Graham and that I will ne'er again raise my hand in war against them. If I speak ye false, may this iron pierce my heart."

MacLaren took the knife he was offered, saying, "Make no mistake. It will be my hand pushing this blade through yer chest if ye betray yer oath. Rise. I accept yer submission, but ken ye that I may call upon ye to prove yer loyalty, and I expect yer response to be immediate."

"Aye, it will. And MacLaren, please convey my apologies to yer wife. She is a worthy woman."

MacLaren smashed McNab's face with his gauntlet and grunted with satisfaction. McNab crumpled to the ground, blood spurting from his nose, looking up at MacLaren, confused.

"Ne'er speak o' her again," MacLaren growled. He

wearied of this conversation. He wanted to be with his wife. And he would happily kill anyone who stood in his way.

"Well done, my lad," said Graham gleefully as he clapped him on the shoulder. MacLaren winced in pain.

"You need some stitching," Chaumont observed.

"I need my wife," MacLaren returned. The ache for her was now even greater than his throbbing shoulder. MacLaren complained, but in the end he allowed himself to be bandaged and stitched as long as he did not have to return to the castle to do it. He refused to remove his full armor, saying it would take too long, so his squire merely removed the shoulder piece. Chaumont did the stitching, and the squire replaced the slightly mangled piece. When MacLaren was tended as well as he would allow, he mounted and rode with Chaumont to St. Margaret's, both men driven by an overpowering desire to be with the women who encamped in their hearts.

Thirty-Five

AILA SLUMPED IN THE CELLAR, SURROUNDED BY darkness. How could she have been so stupid? And how was she going to get out? Entombed in earth, she knew screaming would be pointless. Someone would have to come to the door before they could hear her, and how often would that be? She wrapped her arms around herself to try to press back the rising sense of panic.

She was buried alive.

Fighting despair, she remembered Sister Enid's teaching. Centering on her breathing, she meditated her prayer with every breath. Time seemed to drift away. When she opened her eyes again, she was not sure if she had been there for hours or minutes.

Pacem relinquo vobis pacem meam do vobis non quomodo mundus dat ego do vobis non turbetur cor vestrum neque formidet.

The verse was from the gospel of John. *Peace I leave with you; my peace I give you… Do not let your hearts be troubled, and do not be afraid.* God did indeed give peace, one that transcended the hopelessness of her current situation. Whatever her fate, God was with her, and it was enough. She eased back into the feeling, imagining God's loving arms around her. Taking a deep breath, she stood, focused and ready for action.

Now, how to get out? She felt around the door frame, searching for a way to escape. Dim light filtered into the room from gaps at the top and bottom of the cellar door, but no manner of escape seemed promising. The door had been securely locked. Yet the room had not been built as a prison. There must be a way out.

Aila's thoughts turned to MacLaren. What would he be doing now? Was he even still alive? Would the Campbells honor their promise to ride to the Grahams' aid? There was no way to know. It could be days, weeks, or months before MacLaren could manage to escape a siege. Aila shivered at what the abbot could accomplish in that time. She had been afraid of MacLaren, but she knew now he would never harm her. The abbot was another matter. She doubted she would be afforded mercy from that quarter until she relented to his demands.

For a moment, she considered giving in and joining the convent. In truth, all the abbot wanted was for her to comply with what she had planned to do her whole life. She was certainly more prepared to be a nun than a wife. Her few days as a married lady had revealed no lack of shortcomings in that regard. What would MacLaren think when he came for her and the abbot told him she had changed her mind? She winced, picturing MacLaren's face. He had been betrayed too many times; she could not add herself to that list.

In the darkness, it all seemed so terribly clear. MacLaren's brusque manner, his avoidance, it was all there to protect his wounded heart. She smiled, recognizing her own romantic attributions of his rude behavior. When had it been that she had fallen in love with him?

Love?

It was a startling thought. She could not possibly be in love. The darkness pressed her like a confessional, and her defenses slipped away. She did love him. She had loved him since childhood. She remembered the feel of his arms around her. If given a second chance, she would not deny his advances again. But would she be given that chance?

She must get out!

She felt around the door frame again. The door was securely locked on one side, but it opened inward, so surely there must be some kind of hinge. As her fingers felt along the cracks of the door frame, she thought of the man who had imprisoned her. The message she had received made more sense now. It had not been sent by McNab, as she had thought—why would he wish her to go to the convent? No. She wagered it had been written by the abbot. Privy to the confessions of the entire region, he must have heard a rumor of her impending marriage. He was a greedy, ruthless man, using guilt to manipulate her. Recognizing this released her from the last vestiges of guilt for marrying MacLaren. It was no sin. She could serve God married as well as cloistered. Her confidence soared, though her situation remained unchanged. She focused back on finding a means of escape.

Aila located the hinges, iron hooks on the side of the door, which nestled into sockets bolted to the wall. Aila's heart started to pound as an idea formed. If she could lift the door up a few inches, she could lift it off of the hinges. But could she do it? Crouching down, she grabbed the underside of the door and heaved. Nothing budged. Trying again, she pulled with all her might until her back and arms screamed in protest. The heavy oak door moved not a whit. This was not going to work.

Aila stretched her back and tried to think of what to do. With a flash of inspiration, an image of builders came to mind. She remembered as a child, when builders were adding onto Dundaff castle, they lifted huge stones using levers and pulleys. Pulleys might be difficult to contrive, but a lever might be possible. Excited once again, she searched the room for something she could use as a lever. She quickly found a heavy barrel by tripping over it. A long stick was more difficult to procure, but she finally found one hanging from the ceiling, holding up dried meats. Chomping on some dried venison for strength, she slid one end of the pole under the edge of the door and placed the barrel at the pole's center. Taking a deep breath, she pushed down on the top of the pole with all her strength.

She was rewarded by a grinding metal sound. It was working! She pushed harder, picturing freedom within seconds. When she let go of the lever, however, the door slid right back down in its hinges. She checked the hinges to be sure, but they were still stuck tight. Controlling her frustration, she tried again. Again she was able to lift up the door but she could not pull it toward her and off its hinges. Every time she let go of the pole, the door slid down into the hinges.

With mounting frustration and desperation, she tried a variety tactics, wiggling the pole farther under the door, pulling herself on top of the pole and bouncing up and down. Nothing worked. Exhaustion set in, and she sat down beside the barrel, utterly defeated. She put her head in her hands and bit back tears. There was no escape from her prison.

❧

MacLaren and Chaumont left Graham to ensure McNab and Argitaine left peaceably and immediately. This situation was resolved better than MacLaren expected, and he felt a growing anticipation to see Aila again. Their separation had not been long, but it had been illuminating. Perhaps it was the excitement of the day, but he was filled with uncharacteristic hope for the future. He had sworn he would never love again, but he feared that promise had been broken. Visions of Aila danced in his head and spurred him on toward St. Margaret's. Aila on the tower, wearing naught but her chemise. Aila as a wood nymph, flying through the forest on horseback. Aila's body pressed close to his. He wanted her more than he had ever wanted a woman. More than he had ever wanted anything.

A small voice inside him told him to be wary, told him to reserve his heart. He could be married to her, even enjoy her, but to love her was dangerous. *Do not give any woman your heart. Do not give any woman the power to hurt you.* The voice sounded reasonable, and he would have liked to oblige, but it was too late. His heart was gone; he was a man lost. Spurring his horse, he raced faster with Chaumont right behind.

As they entered the gated grounds of St. Margaret's, Chaumont nudged in front of MacLaren, blocking his path. MacLaren looked at him impatiently. He wanted his wife. Surely whatever Chaumont had to say could wait until after his reunion. Maybe tomorrow, or better yet, next week.

"I need to make a request of you." Chaumont looked uncharacteristically sober. MacLaren gave him his full attention. Chaumont was rarely serious.

"What would ye ask o' me?"

"Lady Mary Patrick. I believe you are her nearest kin and her laird." Chaumont paused, looking, of all things, rather nervous. MacLaren nodded, and Chaumont continued. "I would ask permission to court her."

MacLaren stared at him. He did not want to say he was surprised, but he was. He had noted Chaumont's interest in Mary, but he had noted Chaumont's interest in many a bonnie lass. Never had he known him to make a serious suit for anyone or apply for anyone's hand. He frowned, recalling Chaumont's history with the ladies of the French court. He was chivalrous to a fault, but he had never been troubled by monogamy.

Chaumont read his look and sighed, saying, "I know well I am unworthy of her, but I would like to make a new start with her and her son. Graham's acceptance of me and the gift of his name give me reason to hope I may be able to provide a future for her."

"I ne'er kenned ye to settle down wi' only one woman." MacLaren frowned. He would lay down his life for Chaumont, but he had a duty to protect Mary. "I dinna want Lady Patrick to be hurt when ye take a new lover."

"Indeed, I wish to have none but Lady Patrick. If we are wed, I give ye permission to deal with me most severely if I so much as look at another woman." Chaumont spoke with an ardent passion MacLaren had never heard before. He laughed at the thought of Chaumont falling for Mary.

"Dinna be so quick to condemn yerself, my friend. Ye've been true to me. Perhaps ye'll make a good husband for Mary. But only if she wishes to have ye. I'll give ye my permission to spend time wi' her and her son. After we mark the year of Patrick's passing, ye can court her openly."

Chaumont smiled a wide, honest smile. "Thank you, thank you." He laughed. "I'm gushing like the schoolboy I've never been, but thank you, my friend."

"Verra good. Let's proceed, shall we? I want to see my wife."

Chaumont smiled broadly, and they both rode into the main courtyard. Their presence attracted attention as the sisters emerged from their work to greet them. Mary Patrick was also quick to hail their return.

"Praise the Lord, ye're back!" she exclaimed. "And so soon, I woud'na believe it if I dinna see it wi' my own eyes. Saints be praised, but ye both look hale enough. What miracle has happened?"

The men dismounted, and after handing off their horses, Chaumont was quick by her side. Mary smiled and moved to put her arms around him but then flushed and turned back.

"MacLaren was challenged to a joust of war and won the day," said Chaumont, his eyes never leaving Mary. "The French are leaving, McNab is crawling back home with his tail betwixt his legs, and Dundaff is saved, thanks to your laird."

"Ye dinna speak the whole truth, Chaumont," said MacLaren beside him. "Mary, I ken introductions are in order." Mary frowned a little. She had been introduced to Chaumont many months ago. "Lady Patrick, may I present Sir Chaumont Graham. He killed a traitor trying to betray the castle and saved the life of Laird Graham. He single-handedly saved us all from getting our necks slashed in the night and was rewarded by being accepted as a son into the Graham clan."

Mary stared at Chaumont, her eyes bright. MacLaren noted how Mary looked at Chaumont and how he gazed at her steadfastly in return. Unbelievable as it seemed, they clearly had strong feelings for each other. "Lady Patrick," MacLaren continued, "I must also inform ye Chaumont has asked for permission to court ye. After yer year o' mourning, I will permit it, if ye wish it."

"Court me?" Mary asked Chaumont, her eyes wide.

"*Oui*. I love you, *cherie*. I would be forever honored if you would consent to be my wife."

Mary threw herself into Chaumont's arms. "Aye, yes, *oui*," she answered in every language she knew, accepting his proposal. Chaumont returned her embrace but glanced nervously at MacLaren when Mary started to kiss his neck.

"Oh, go on. Kiss her, and be done wi' it," said

MacLaren. So much for waiting another few months. MacLaren walked on to find Aila, anticipating her reaction to seeing him. Would she run to him? He had never been demonstrative with emotion, but just this once it would be nice. *Nay, great.* He needed her close to him. He was not ever going to let her go again.

"You are looking for Lady Aila?" came the low voice of Father Barrick, the abbot. MacLaren had never met the man before but was immediately wary, seeing his mail and sword. He had heard reports Barrick had been one of the few Knights Templar to escape persecution in France and flee to the relative safety of Scotland. If it was true, he certainly did nothing to hide it.

"Aye," responded MacLaren. "Do ye ken where she is?"

The abbot nodded his head. "She is in seclusion and does not wish to be disturbed."

"Pray tell her MacLaren, her husband, has arrived. I'm sure she will want to see me."

"Lady Aila is promised to the Church. Your marriage violated that promise and will be annulled. Returning to the convent made her realize her place is here. She wished me to express her regrets, but she has decided to take her rightful place among the Sisters of St. Margaret's."

Silence fell between the two men. MacLaren struggled to make sense of what the abbot had just said to him. Saints above, not again. It could not be possible he would fall in love with two women who would betray and reject him. No, it was not possible.

"I would speak to my wife," MacLaren replied,

emphasizing the word *wife*. If Aila was to reject him, let her do so to his face. He needed to hear her speak the words. He needed to try to convince her to change her mind, honor be damned. He was fully committed now, and he would see it through to the end.

"I think you should leave," replied the abbot, putting his right hand on his sword hilt.

"I winna leave 'till I speak to my wife," answered MacLaren. He still wore his battle harness, his giant claymore strapped to his back. He had never fought a priest before, but he had never loved anyone like he loved Aila.

He prepared for a fight.

Thirty-Six

AILA SAT DEFEATED, HER HEAD RESTING AGAINST THE barrel, when she heard soft noises, like the scratching of a mouse. At first, she doubted the noise was there at all, but then it came again.

"Hello? Is anybody there?" She sat still but heard nothing. The thought that the abbot had returned chilled her, but she persisted. "Please, is anyone there?"

"It's alright, Lady Aila, my mother said I could play as long as I dinna hurt anything, and I dinna hurt nothing."

Gavin! Aila had never been happier to hear a friendly voice. "Of course ye hav'na hurt anything," Aila said, trying to keep her voice calm, "but please come here. I'm locked in the cellar."

Aila heard the boy approach until he was standing outside the door. "How'd ye get yerself stuck in the cellar, Lady Aila?"

"I had some help wi' that, and now I need out. Will ye help me? I need someone who is verra strong."

"I'm verra braw, Lady Aila. Mama told me so, and Sir Chaumont, too!"

Aila smiled. She certainly hoped he would be able to help. "I'm going to lift up the door, and I want ye to push on the left side when I tell ye."

"But why?"

"We're going to move this door off its hinges. Do ye ken ye can help?"

"I can do it, Lady Aila. If I canna, I can get Chaumont. He's right strong."

Aila stopped. "Chaumont is here?"

"Aye, and MacLaren, too. All the Frenchies are running away. They winna bother us no more. That's what Mama said when she wasna kissing Sir Chaumont. They sure do like to kiss." Gavin's voice told her he was baffled by the interest in such sport. All Aila heard was that MacLaren was here.

"Where is MacLaren? Can ye bring him here?"

"He's busy having speech wi' Father Barrick. Is it a sin no' to like a priest? He says ye're in seclusion. What's seclusion?"

"Hurry, we must get me out," rasped Aila, putting the pole into position and thrusting it downward with all her might. Once again, the iron scraped as the door lifted out of its hinges.

"Now push!" she shouted. Nothing happened. "Push harder, Gavin!" She held the pole down as long as she could until the door burst open with a crash, dislodging the pole and throwing her to the ground.

"I ran into it, Lady Aila, is that alright? Och, I done broke the door. Mama will be powerful mad," said Gavin, looking dismayed.

"Nay, child, ye've done verra well," she said,

giving him a warm hug. "Now, quick, can ye take me to MacLaren?"

"Sure I can, Lady Aila," replied Gavin with clear pride at his accomplishment. "Follow me."

❧

Outside in the courtyard between the chapel and the main residence hall, MacLaren and the abbot faced each other, swords drawn. Father Barrick had demanded he leave. MacLaren had refused to go; he was on shaky ground, and he knew it. Chaumont and Mary stood nearby, and many of the nuns watched the scene, not sure what to do.

Chaumont came up to MacLaren and spoke softly. "Watch yourself, my friend. He's a Templar."

"How would ye ken?"

Chaumont looked away. "I know most of the old Templars out of France, those that survived the slaughter, that is."

MacLaren nodded, storing this information away for future questioning. There seemed to be much he did not know about his friend.

"Are you sure you want to pursue this?" Chaumont asked. "You are on holy ground. If you attack an abbot on Church grounds, you'll be excommunicated for sure." MacLaren weighed his options. He wanted desperately to talk to Aila. He distrusted this abbot, but he had to admit Aila had tried to run away to the convent before for just this purpose. It was possible she had changed her mind again. Would he fight the abbot and drag her back against her will? Silently, he prayed for wisdom.

He sighed and resheathed his blade. "I've no' come to fight ye, Father. I wish only to speak wi' my wife. If she wishes to stay, I winna press her." MacLaren was resolute. Aila was not Marguerite. He understood that now. If she chose God over him, how could he feel betrayed? Perhaps it would be the better choice for her. He realized he loved her enough to let her go, if it be her wish. Time would heal his heart. Eventually. Maybe. Not.

"Nay, wait!"

MacLaren turned with a jolt. It was Aila. His heart raced to see her, but then he frowned. Her dress was torn, her face smudged with dirt, her hair a mess. What had happened here?

"Father Abbot says ye wish to stay." MacLaren addressed Aila. "If that be so, I will leave at once. Tell me true for now and evermore. Do ye wish to take orders, or do ye wish to be my wife?" MacLaren spoke without emotion, preparing to walk away with at least a shred of his dignity intact.

Aila glanced between MacLaren and the abbot. Both men waited on her answer. "When my father said I was to marry ye, I was given no choice. Now, I do have the right to choose. But I would no' wish for bloodshed, especially no' in this holy place." Aila frowned, the concern clear in her eye.

"Go on, lass. 'Tis time to choose," MacLaren said gruffly.

Aila glanced nervously at Father Barrick then straightened her shoulders. "Sir Padyn MacLaren, I would be proud to be yer wife for the rest o' my days."

MacLaren closed the gap between them and seized

her in a kiss. She melted into his arms, and MacLaren wanted to hold onto her forever.

"Noooo!" shouted the abbot and rushed forth with his sword. MacLaren pivoted quickly, drawing his own blade and blocking the abbot's attack that would have cut Aila to shreds.

"I dinna want to fight ye, Barrick, but I will defend my wife to the death, whatever the consequences," MacLaren snarled.

"She was meant for the convent, until you poisoned her mind. I will not let her leave with you. Her inheritance belongs to the Church," seethed the abbot, striking again against MacLaren's sword.

"Her inheritance belongs where her father wishes. The Church has no right to interfere."

"Please, ye must no' fight o'er my inheritance," begged Aila as Chaumont dragged her away from the fight. No one was listening to her. She yelled louder, "My husband is a righteous, God-fearing man who intends to give my dower lands, the land the convent and abbey were built on, to the Church."

That got everyone's attention.

MacLaren and the abbot stopped and stared at her. MacLaren frowned.

"That is very generous of you, Sir Padyn," said Sister Enid as she limped in between the combatants. "We greatly appreciate your kind remembrance of our poor community."

The abbot scowled at MacLaren. "If this be your intent, give me your pledge now."

MacLaren had no intention of giving Aila's land to the Church. He needed her land for himself, yet he had not considered the holy community that had already been built on it. All eyes were on him now—the abbot, Sister Enid, Chaumont, Mary, Gavin, and Aila, who looked up at him beseechingly. Give up the land? That is why he had married her in the first place. Suddenly he felt the eyes of God on him as well, and felt ashamed at his own greed. It all belonged to the Lord anyway. He rolled his eyes heavenward. The land was gone.

"Aye, I pledge Aila's dower lands to the Church." MacLaren knew in that instant that he may have given away all of the land he had coveted, should Graham bear another legitimate heir. He didn't care. More than the land, he wanted Aila, not her inheritance, just Aila. Aila smiled up at him, the recognition of what he had given away not lost on her.

"I accept your pledge and will hold you to it," replied the abbot, looking most irritated as he resheathed his sword. "Thank you for your generosity to our community. You are welcome anytime. Now get thee gone." MacLaren smiled at Father Barrick's back as he stalked away, knowing only the last part of that statement had been the truth. It did not matter. He had all he had ever wanted.

Thirty-Seven

AILA SNUGGLED CLOSER INTO MACLAREN'S ARMS AS they rode back to Dundaff. She protested that she could certainly ride, but MacLaren smiled and said she would not be getting away from him that easily. Silly man; she had no intention of getting away. She closed her eyes, enjoying the feeling of his strong arms around her. She pressed her face into his neck to breathe in his scent and wrinkled her nose.

"Ye need a bath." But Aila must not have minded it overmuch, because soon she leaned into him again.

"It will have to wait." MacLaren urged his mount off the trail and into the dense forest.

"Where are we going?"

"Somewhere we can be alone."

Memories of the last time MacLaren had taken her into the forest to be alone flooded back to her. Heat flushed across her skin and she inhaled quickly. She tried to snuggle closer to the man who held her, but the steel-plated cuirass was a bit unsatisfying. They rode a little way until coming to a secluded spot. Trees surrounded the glen, and shafts of sunlight shone down through the leaf canopy.

MacLaren dismounted and helped Aila do the same, not releasing her once her feet were on the ground. Aila wrapped her arms around his chest and pressed into him. With all his armor, it was like hugging a tree trunk.

"I need to undress a wee bit," said MacLaren with a slow smile, removing the harness that held his claymore.

"Here?" asked Aila.

"Here," said MacLaren as he removed his surcoat.

"Now?" Aila's eyes gleamed.

"Now." MacLaren spoke with authority.

MacLaren deftly unlaced his shoulder armor. Aila had enjoyed watching him dress. She was enjoying this more. MacLaren had more difficulty unlacing the plates at his elbows, giving Aila time to ponder their encounter with the abbot.

"Why did ye agree to give away the land to the Church?" Aila asked in a small voice, wondering if he would be angered at her for speaking for him.

MacLaren shrugged without halting his work. "If I had not given it up, it would have been a fight 'tween me and the abbot. No' that I would mind dispatching that bastard, but the Church would no doubt take offense at his death. Giving up the land was the only way to leave wi' ye and no' be excommunicated for it."

"So it was right for me to speak so?"

MacLaren released the plates from one of his arms and began to work on the other. Aila chewed her lip and waited for his response.

"Aye, lass," he grumbled, "ye did well."

Aila hugged herself and smiled as the warmth of his words washed over her. For MacLaren, this was high praise indeed.

"But yer clan," she asked, "what will ye do for them if ye dinna have my dowry?"

"I pledged yer dower lands to the Church, no' the coin." With some fierce tugging, the plates on his arms gave way. "Yer father was most generous with yer fortune, and I warrant I can buy more land when I need it. And I plan on keeping yer mother hale and hearty so our bairns will inherit all o' Dundaff someday."

Aila smiled. It would all be well. Her smile broadened, thinking on his desire to keep her mother content. It would ne'er work, but it would please her mother immensely to have someone try. "I've ne'er felt so happy."

"Ah, but I hope I can amend that. I plan to make ye happier still," MacLaren said in a husky voice then cursed as he tried to remove his cuirass, which was strapped across his chest and tied in the back.

"Do ye... Can I help?"

MacLaren struggled a bit more before surrendering. "Aye, I've ne'er tried to undress wi'out the help o' my squire."

"I would be most honored to assist." Aila curtseyed and set about to help him undress. Unfortunately, she proved to be a very poor squire and struggled with the lacing.

"Hurry," MacLaren commanded. It did not sound as if his patience would hold much longer.

"What kind o' knot 'tis this? My word, but I've made it worse."

"Take my dirk to it."

"Nay, wait, I've got it." The cuirass fell to the ground. MacLaren heaved the mail hauberk over his head, and it fell with a clank. With determination, Aila set to work on the cuisses tied to his thighs. She knelt before him, head bowed, intent on her work. MacLaren took several deep breaths. He groaned, put his hand on the top of her head, and cursed violently in French.

Aila looked up at him reproachfully. "I do speak French, ye ken."

"My apologies." MacLaren ran his hands through his hair and looked up at the sky, taking several more deep breaths. Aila bent back at her work.

"Have ye got it yet?" His voice was harsh.

Aila started at his tone. "No' yet. I am trying my best."

"Have ye e'er seen a grown man cry?" MacLaren asked, his voice raw.

Aila looked up at him, unsure.

"Ye're about to if ye dinna unlace me quick."

Aila tried to hide a smile. "Maybe we should return to Dundaff for yer squire."

"I am in earnest. I will cry."

"Yer squire is quite the demon wi' a knot," commented Aila.

"Take a blade to it."

"I might hurt ye."

"No' any more than ye are right now. By the saints, lass, give me my knife." MacLaren grabbed a blade and proceeded to cut the laces of his Italian armor. Aila put up her hands to stifle a giggle. He was so dear, cursing himself blue, trying to contort around to release himself from his own gear. When he removed his arming doublet, she gasped. Bright red blood gleamed on a fresh white bandage.

"What happened?" She had seen injured men before, but the sight of MacLaren's blood made her a bit sick.

"Joust with the Duke of Argitaine. My tussle wi' the abbot must have ripped the stitches."

"Och, ye poor dear. We should return to Dundaff and get it tended."

Standing now in naught but linen drawers, MacLaren stopped his work and looked at her. "I swear to ye, if ye deny me now, my only recourse will be to throw myself on my own sword."

Aila smiled slowly. "I'd hate to be the death o' ye."

"No doubt ye will be, but no' today. Come here."

She went willingly into his arms and sank into his embrace. He smelled distinctly male, a musky scent of sweat, whiskey, and blood. MacLaren pulled back slightly and stared into her eyes.

"Why did ye choose me o'er life at the convent?" MacLaren asked, his gray eyes intense.

"I found I loved ye more." Aila bit her lip. Had she said that out loud? She looked away, unwilling to see distrust or mockery.

Slowly he pushed aside a stray lock of hair, his fingers gliding along her hairline. His touch tingled on her skin, sending ripples through her like a smooth stone thrown into calm waters. With his thumb, he lightly traced down the side of her face and brushed across her lower lip. Her heart quickened, beating with every ripple of sensation. She looked up, her lips parted.

"Ye love me." His eyes never left hers. It was more than a statement of truth; it was a command.

She twined her arms around his neck and closed her

eyes. His kiss was soft and warm. She wanted more. She slid her fingers up through his hair and pulled him down to her, deepening the kiss. He growled low and needy, lifting her off the ground and kissing her thoroughly. By the time her feet touched the ground again, the world swirled around her in patches of bright color, and she was glad he held her close, for she was not sure she could stand.

But still... but still, he had not said he loved her.

Aila's own clothes proved much easier to remove, and MacLaren had divested her of her gown before she quite knew what was happening. His linen drawers and her chemise took but a moment more to remove, and she shivered at the new sensation of standing naked as the trees surrounded them.

MacLaren said nothing, but spread her chemise on the grass and pulled her down onto it with him. He moved slowly, as if not wanting to spook a skittish filly, his eyes never leaving hers. She blushed at being so exposed, but soon she was completely covered with a warm male blanket. She gasped at the sensation, so much of her touching so much of him. Aila ran her hands over his bulging arms and down his back. Everything about him was muscular and hard.

MacLaren groaned. "Ah, but ye are beautiful." He nuzzled her neck and rocked his hips on hers. It was like nothing she had ever felt before, and she was suddenly very glad she had decided against the vow of chastity. His demanding kiss, hot and urgent, made her doubly sure of her choice. She returned his kiss and felt the world start to spin again. Good thing she was lying down.

Whatever he was doing, she wanted more of it.

She threaded her fingers through his hair. She ran her fingers down his back. She pulled him closer until…

"Ow!" Oh, but that hurt. She squeezed her eyes shut and turned her face to the side, determined to bear it silently. Padyn stopped, resting his head beside hers on the ground. Aila breathed deeply, feeling her senses heighten. The wind lightly rustled the leaves of the trees above them and the birds sang softly. Sunlight filtered down through the trees like golden ribbons from the heavens. She felt the broad shoulders of her husband begin to shake.

"Are ye… well?" she whispered, wondering if she had done something wrong.

"Aye." His voice was raw and anguished. "I love ye so much. I dinna wish to hurt ye, but I want ye something fierce."

Aila inhaled sharply at his revelation. "Ye love me?"

"Aye," growled Padyn slowly.

"Ye love me?" she said louder, a smile reaching to her toes.

MacLaren lifted his head, looking at her with a frown. "Aye, that's what I said."

Tension and fear and pain slid away, and she felt flushed with a joy she thought beyond her grasp. "Ye love me!"

"Hush, woman, ye're disturbing the trees."

Aila giggled and hugged him with arms and legs. "Ye," she whispered, planting a small kiss on one of his cheeks, "love"—she kissed the other cheek— "me." She kissed him softly on the lips.

MacLaren groaned and deepened the kiss, starting to move again. Aila surrendered to the sensation, feeling one with the creative force around and within her. Ripples of sight and sound coursed through her until the world around her faded away, and all that existed in the world was her and Padyn and the urgent tension that was building between them. She dug her fingers into his back, desperate for something, until all the colors and sounds smashed back into her. She arched and cried out, her own voice drowned by the primal roar of her husband.

Padyn collapsed on top of her, utterly still. Aila panted for breath, finding it hard to breathe with his weight on top of her. Had she killed him?

"Padyn?" She received no answer. "Do ye live?"

He moaned and rolled over, taking her with him. "I knew ye would be the death o' me."

She cuddled to him, laying her head on his chest. She was warm and happy. She smiled her first wicked smile. "Och, look, Padyn, the trees are gone. Ye scared them off wi' all your bellowing."

Padyn opened his eyes, confused. Aila started to giggle.

"Daft woman," he muttered, yet his lips twitched into a smile, and a rumbling sound came from his throat.

"Are ye laughing?"

"I ne'er laugh." But the low rumble continued, and soon her pillow started to convulse, he was laughing so hard. He held her closer, and they laughed until tears rolled down her cheeks and fell onto his chest. Spent and sated, she sighed contentedly.

"I love ye, Padyn."

"Aila," he said, speaking her name with a low contented purr that sent aftershocks shivering to her core, "saints preserve me, but I love ye, too."

Epilogue

Five years later

"HERE?"

"Here."

"Now?" asked Aila with a sly smile as Padyn slid against her.

"Now." Padyn closed his mouth over hers for a long, sensual kiss. Or at least that was his intent.

"Mama. Maaaamaaaaaa!" Four-year-old James burst into the room, and MacLaren rolled back with an unhappy grunt.

"Mama, where's my sword?" asked James as he crawled up onto his parents' bed. "Whatcha doing?"

"Nothing now," grumbled MacLaren.

"Have ye checked yer bed, Jamie? Ye went to sleep wi' it last night," said Aila, giving Padyn a playful nudge. Since Padyn had given the wooden toy sword to Jamie, he had refused to be parted from it.

"I'll go look," said Jamie and, after jumping several times on the bed, catapulted to the floor with a large thump and ran from the room.

"Hush," said Aila instinctively and lay back down. Instantly she was in Padyn's arms again, and she snuggled into his warmth.

"Noooooo!" came a mournful wail. "Gimme back. It's mine! Maaaamaaaa!"

"Oh for the love of…" muttered Padyn.

"Mama, Jamie took my blanky, and he winna give it back!" whined three-year-old Rose as she burst into the room, a mass of red baby curls bobbing around her shoulders. Jamie ran in, blanket around his shoulders, sword in hand, laughing hysterically. Rose screamed again and ran after him.

"Quiet both of ye, ye'll wake the"—a howl of complaint shattered their ears—"baby." Aila rolled out of bed with a sigh and picked up their six-month-old son, William, out of the cradle. Both children stood with their hands over their ears.

"How come he's so loud, Mama?" asked Jamie.

"Well, now, that's a wonder," commented MacLaren.

Aila crawled back into bed and put the baby to the breast, effectively silencing at least one of her children. Padyn gave her a smile, leaning over to give his youngest son a kiss on his head, and then slipped in a quick kiss on the breast before Aila shooed him away.

"This is no' what I wanted this morn," he whispered.

"'Tis yer own fault we've been blessed wi' all these bairns," she whispered back.

"So it is," he commented with a satisfied smile of masculine pride. The children climbed onto the bed, playing, if not quietly, at least more peaceably. Aila laughed as Padyn patiently allowed his children to crawl over him.

"Here's the happy family," said Chaumont with a droll smile as he strode through the open door, impeccably dressed and holding a sleeping infant draped over his arm like he was a born wet nurse. "My, but you people are loud."

"I'm sorry if we wakened ye," said Aila, but Chaumont waved off the comment.

"I hope you'll ready yourself soon. I promised Lady Graham no one would be late this morning. Heaven protect me if she is disappointed."

Aila smiled. There had been many changes in the last five years, none the least of which was Laird Graham quitting his own apartments and moving into his wife's tower, a move she complained about bitterly and most enthusiastically. She also had taken to attending meals in the Great Hall, which she complained was forced upon her by her unfeeling husband, always arriving being carried by two of the tallest and most handsome men-at-arms. However much she was suffering, it was clear she was enjoying herself immensely. Chaumont and Mary had moved into Dundaff while their large home was being built. Graham had rewarded Chaumont handsomely, but since Mary seemed to have inherited Aila's role as chatelaine, Aila felt they had more than earned their reward.

"Oh, there ye are," said Mary, swooping into the room, wearing an elaborate turquoise silk gown, her long hair down to her waist. "Could ye watch Johnnie?" she asked Chaumont, handing over their three-year-old son. "I've promised Lady Graham I'd let her personal maid do my hair. Please dinna be late," she said to Aila and Padyn, "or yer mother will skin me alive."

She gave Chaumont a quick kiss and then turned to run off, but Chaumont caught her hand and drew her back to give her a proper kiss. They smiled at each other for a long moment, until Gavin tried to sneak by unnoticed, wearing riding clothes.

"Where do ye ken ye're going?" asked Mary.

At fourteen, Gavin had grown into a strapping lad. "Fergus said he would let me ride Thunder today." Aila smiled at the stable master's name. His recovery had been slow but steady, and he was now back at his post.

"If ye're late, ye'll have to go to Lady Graham yerself and explain why," Mary warned.

Gavin blanched and returned back the way he had come, presumably to change clothes.

"Yer mother certainly knows how to strike fear in the hearts o' many," commented MacLaren dryly.

"Including my dearest husband?" asked Aila. They had responded to her mother's demand they visit with the family, since she claimed she had not seen her grandchildren for so long she would not be able to recognize them anymore, though in truth, it had been only one month since their last visit. MacLaren had grumbled about being manipulated but had made arrangements to go to Dundaff. Lady Graham had a full day planned for the family, and everyone was expected to participate.

The servants swooped in to take the children to dress, and Aila and Padyn found themselves alone for a few precious moments.

"We should dress," said Aila, but Padyn pulled her close.

"That would be counter to my desires."

Aila shrugged against him. "And mine, as well, but 'tis for family."

"Family? Are ye saying I am related to that she-devil?"

"Aye, 'tis true, and perhaps ye'll find one in yer own bed if ye dinna watch what ye say about my mother," exclaimed Aila.

She struggled against him briefly, but MacLaren held her tighter. "Aye, ye are my family," he said, looking down at her. "I have been blessed more than I e'er thought possible."

Aila sighed. "I do love ye, my husband."

"And I ye." Padyn started pulling up her chemise, and he kissed her gently from her temple down to her lips.

"But we'll be late." Aila broke away. "Mother will be furious."

"She'll be angry at us whate'er we do. At least this way we'll have a really good reason for her fury."

"What will we say to my mother?" Aila wrapped her arm around his neck.

"Tell her we were working on her fourth grandchild."

"I canna say that!"

Padyn covered her mouth with his, and Aila found she was not going to be saying anything for quite some time.

Author's Note

A great lover of history and kilt-wearing, sword-wielding men, I nestled this story into the intrigue of 14th century Scotland. In 1346, while England was theoretically busy fighting France in what would later be known as the Hundred Years' War, young King David of Scotland decided to invade northern England and took the town of Liddesdale. Unfortunately, King David underestimated the English response, aided by the superiority of the Welsh longbow, and he was captured in a bloody battle at Neville's Cross. According to legend, the leader of the Grahams urged King David to order a charge into the English archers, shouting, "Give me but a hundred horse, and I will scatter them all." Unfortunately, none followed Graham except his own clan, who were slaughtered by the longbow. This story picks up where history leaves off, imagining what happened next to the Grahams.

Aila Graham in this tale is destined for the convent and, as such, receives far more education than was standard for that time, particularly for a woman. Though not much survives, we still have some writings from women of that time (all nuns) proving at least a select few received extensive educations. Since one of the main fields of study would have been the Scriptures, Aila is familiar with the Latin Bible.

During the 14th century, no English translations of the Bible were available, since the Church had decreed anything other than the Latin was heretical. John Wycliff was the first to produce an English version of the Bible in the 1380s. This irritated the Pope so much that, even forty-four years after Wycliff's death, his bones were ordered to be dug up, crushed, and scattered in the river. One of Wycliff's followers, John Hus, was burnt at the stake in 1415, using copies of the English Bible as kindling. Lady Aila translates the Latin verses into English in her head, but never would be so bold as to put that translation down on paper. Thankfully, we live in more enlightened times, so I have listed the verses Aila pondered during her great adventure for the modern-day reader (including chapter and verse, which she also did not have in her day), just in case your Latin is a little rusty.

Aila's verses, translated using the *New International Version* of the *Holy Bible*:

Therefore, if anyone is in Christ, he is a new creation; the old has gone, the new has come! 2 Corinthians 5:17

The name of the Lord is a strong tower; the righteous run to it and are safe. Proverbs 18:10

For if you remain silent at this time, relief and deliverance for the Jews will arise from another place, but you and your father's family will perish. And who knows but that you have come to royal position for such a time as this? Esther 4:14

A noose is hidden for him on the ground; a trap lies in his path. Job 18:10

Proud men have hidden a snare for me; they have spread out the cords of their net and have set traps for me along my path. Psalm 140:5

Rachel said to her father, "Don't be angry, my lord, that I cannot stand up in your presence; I'm having my period." So he searched but could not find the household gods. Genesis 31:35

But small is the gate and narrow the road that leads to life, and only a few find it. Matthew 7:14

Let him kiss me with the kisses of his mouth—for your love is more delightful than wine. Song of Songs 1:2

But no man can tame the tongue. It is a restless evil, full of deadly poison. James 3:8

Be strong and courageous. Do not be afraid or terrified because of them, for the Lord your God goes with you; he will never leave you nor forsake you. Deuteronomy 31:6

Kings take pleasure in honest lips; they value a man who speaks the truth. Proverbs 16:13

Peace I leave with you; my peace I give you. I do not give to you as the world gives. Do not let your hearts be troubled and do not be afraid. John 14:27

About the Author

Amanda Forester holds a PhD in psychology and worked for many years in academia before discovering that writing historical romance novels was way more fun. She lives in Tacoma, Washington, with her husband, two energetic children, and one lazy dog. You can visit her at www.amandaforester.com.